Elizabeth Latimer
Pirate Hunter:

The Pirate Vortex

Deborah Cannon

Order this book online at www.trafford.com
or email orders@trafford.com

Most Trafford titles are also available at major online book retailers.

Note for Librarians: A cataloguing record for this book is available from Library and Archives Canada at www.collectionscanada.ca/amicus/index-e.html

Printed in Victoria, BC, Canada.

ISBN: 978-1-4269-0532-2 (Soft)
ISBN: 978-1-4269-2683-9 (Hard)
ISBN: 978-1-4269-0534-6 (e-book)

We at Trafford believe that it is the responsibility of us all, as both individuals and corporations, to make choices that are environmentally and socially sound. You, in turn, are supporting this responsible conduct each time you purchase a Trafford book, or make use of our publishing services. To find out how you are helping, please visit www.trafford.com/responsiblepublishing.html

Our mission is to efficiently provide the world's finest, most comprehensive book publishing service, enabling every author to experience success. To find out how to publish your book, your way, and have it available worldwide, visit us online at www.trafford.com

Trafford rev. 01/20/2010

 www.trafford.com

North America & international
toll-free: 1 888 232 4444 (USA & Canada)
phone: 250 383 6864 ♦ fax: 812 355 4082 ♦ email: info@trafford.com

For Jackie
The original "Rebel Goddess"

The Pirate Ghost

She had a red-painted thumb
With the Jolly Roger lined in black.
She wore a neon blue wet suit
And carried a neoprene sack.
What was in the sack?
Not Jack, not gin, nor rum.
She carried the ghost of her father
And the phantom of her adventuring mum.

Elizabeth was her name
And she sought no fortune nor fame;
Her journey had just begun
And again, she carried no rum.
The blasted pirates might get her,
The raging sea beset her.
She had to get to Nassau harbour
To find her meandering mum.

The time chute swallowed her whole;
Onto the ruffian's sloop she emerged,
Face to face she came with the captain
And his sword.
Where is my mother! she demanded.
To the brig with you! he commanded.
And Elizabeth found herself trapped
In his pigheaded world.

Now she needed the rum
If she was ever to find her mum,
And learn what happened to her pirate hunter dad.
It was so sad
The day he was lost
Was the day Elizabeth Latimer became
A pirate host,
And now she is forever haunted
Because of the pirate ghost.

CHAPTER ONE
Fight Like A Champion, Not Like A Wench!

Elizabeth Latimer was a pirate hunter. She wasn't always a pirate hunter. But even before she hunted pirates, she was a freakishly awesome fencer. She was also an expert scuba diver and a seasoned catboat sailor. She spoke four languages: English, French, Chinese and Spanish, and she had an uncanny telepathy with animals.

Her best friends were her fourteen-year-old sister, Lulu, who just happened to be a computer brainiac, and a talking parrot named CJ, which was short for Calico Jack. Her mom was the famous Tess Rackham, adventurer and treasure hunter bar none. Tess dug out pirate shipwrecks, salvaged cargoes and hocked the most valuable stuff to collectors. Four years ago, she was a prof at the University of Victoria where she researched sunken ships and taught a course called the Archaeology of Piracy. But then her husband, John Latimer, died. He was a fanatic of pirate history, a builder of model pirate ships and a sailing pro. He was also Elizabeth's dad. He drowned in a sailing accident and Elizabeth never went sailing again.

Elizabeth had no choice but to become a pirate hunter because Elizabeth, or Liz, as she preferred to be called, had the curse of pirates in her blood. But, in the twenty-first century, who, in their right mind, wanted to be a pirate hunter? Her supreme formula for life was to be an economics/commerce major and work in a bank when she finished school. She would then marry a lawyer and have a grand ordinary life, extraordinaire. It would be a life where parrots didn't cuss and fourteen-year-old sisters didn't hack into their school's computers, where moms didn't hunt treasure and dads didn't drown while sailing. And animals couldn't read her mind.

But the day her dad died—four years ago—Liz knew the pirate curse was there to stay. So, she had to do something to remind herself of *why* John Latimer died. She painted one nail, her lefthand thumb, and she painted it blood red. In the centre of her thumbnail, on the bloody background, she drew a skull and crossbones in black ink. Liz knew that what had consumed her parents might, one day, consume her, too. And crying great big cartoon tears wouldn't change a thing. It was only a matter of time . . . That time came, on a cool spring morning, around seven a.m., when Elizabeth Latimer entered the University of Victoria's gymnasium door.

On the fencing piste, Liz's opponent was waiting for her, strutting his stuff. He had a cool, cocky attitude, a lean, powerful build and the spin-worthiness of a dancer.

Liz drew on her protective glove with its white gauntlet and tested her sword hand's grip. She waltzed onto the fencing piste and rolled her eyes. In answer, her opponent flexed his foil as though it were a cutlass. She snorted. Who did he think he was? Captain Jack Sparrow? Unlike her, he already wore his face mask. He wasn't supposed to wear his mask until they were both in the start position. They hadn't yet begun the bout and already he was BTR.

Well, if he wanted to break the rules, she would teach him some. She fastened her mask to the protective bib at her throat. She plugged the body wires attached to her form-fitting lamé jacket into the spools connected to the electronic scoring box and indicated for him to do the same. He hesitated for a second. She waited, then raised her hands in a 'What gives?' gesture.

They had no referee. Laura Baeker, the fencing coach, wasn't due to arrive for another half-hour. He was required to hook himself up. Without a ref, it was the only way to keep score.

"What's the matter?" she said, irritably. "Plug yourself in."

He looked down at the complex set of wires attached to the special conducting cloth that made up his jacket, then turned his eyes to her. His expression was concealed behind the mask.

She rolled her eyes, reiterated, "You got a problem?"

He shook his head, mimed her act of plugging in the wires, then stood back.

Elizabeth tested the equipment against her lamé jacket which conducted the electronic signals. Lights flashed from 'the box' and she set the scoreboard to zero. She retreated to her en-guarde line and watched her opponent find his.

Okay, mystery boy. Let's see what you've got. She saluted him and he returned the gesture. She raised her foil and waited for the electronic voice to shout "Play!" She glared at him through her mask. He was tall and limber and deflected her blows with the sass of Captain Jack.

The floor of the narrow fencing piste pounded with the shuffling of their feet. He lunged and she parried, feeling the sting of his foil. His dizzying footwork was priceless. Where had he learned footwork like that? He had superior balance, speed and athleticism. The way he accelerated, decelerated and switched directions had her dancing at a cataclysmic pace.

They fenced for three minutes, then some lights flashed from the box and the electronic ref shouted "Halt." The points sprang onto the monitor. Liz ground her teeth, stamped her foot in disappointment and returned to her en-guarde line. "Play!" the electronic ref shouted.

The early morning sun shot through the gym windows, blinding her for a second. She blinked, lunged. Somewhere in the bleachers a voice shrieked as Liz was forced off-bounds. Her concentration smashed, Liz swung around. Her sister, the only spectator she could see, waved.

When had Lulu snuck in here? It was seven o'clock in the morning. She should be at home getting ready for school.

"You want to be a champion?" her opponent mocked. "Then fight like a champion, not like a wench!"

Wench? Liz spun away from glaring at her sister through her mask and focussed hard on her attack. She missed, and her opponent stabbed her in the ribs. Her protective chest shield took the crux of the blow, but before she could strike, he jabbed her again.

"No fair," Elizabeth shouted. "That's illegal. That was a double hit."

The boy laughed.

Elizabeth snapped off her mask, daring the boy to reveal his face. "Just who do you think you are screwing with the rules like that?"

The boy jerked up his mask and smiled at her. The first thing she noticed was an earring shaped like a flying dagger hanging from his left ear.

"Where I come from, lady," he said, "if you pay too much attention to rules, you die."

Elizabeth glared. "And just where do *you* come from? The *Black Pearl*? Do you even go to school here? If not, you should know that this gym is only open to UVic students and not to any old riffraff from off the street."

The strange boy unsnapped his kevlar bib and dangled it from his hand together with his mask. "May I proffer some advice, Ms. Latimer," he said. "If you don't want to die—and in the eighteenth century you would have died fighting like that—you must not allow yourself to be distracted so easily."

Elizabeth sucked in a breath. Her gloved sword hand pressed against the guard of her competition class weapon. She trembled.

The eighteenth century? Was he in her Archaeology of Piracy course? She scowled. She didn't remember ever seeing him in class. Either this boy was hopped up on goofballs or he was a psycho would-be pirate.

He smiled again as he noticed her effort to keep from shoving her foil into his chest. "Excellent," he said. "A polished swordsman never lets anger control a fight."

He was oddly good-looking. He was in his late teens like her. Or maybe even older. His hair was shoulder length and tied in a pony tail with a leather cord. His complexion was a sunny brown and his chin had a hint of stubble. His eyes were sea blue. They had a faraway look in them like his mind was elsewhere. Like on a schooner maybe. In a word, he seemed otherworldly. The earring made him seem other-oddly. And although that made absolutely no sense whatsoever, it was the only way she could describe him.

"This is *my* school and *my* gym. I am the reigning women's champ for this university and you're interfering with my practice." She planted her hands on her hips, still holding the foil by its grip. Was she pissed off at him because he was a better fencer than her or was she just plain pissed off?

"How do you know my name?" she demanded.

He pointed to the chalkboard. "It is listed on the roster."

Elizabeth had arrived at practice too late to see who Laura had teamed her up with. She squinted at the chalkboard and saw her name next to Andrea Hamilton. "Obviously, you are not Andrea. Who are you?" she asked.

He made a bow and swept the mask down cavalierly as though it were a stylish hat. "My name is Daniel Corker."

"I've never seen you here before," Elizabeth said.

"That is because I have never been here before," he answered.

"You talk funny," Elizabeth's sister said, walking up to where the two of them stood. "Are you from England?"

Liz had forgotten all about Lulu. She swung to face her sister. "Lu, what are you doing here? You should be in school."

"She is also in school?" Daniel said, sounding surprised.

Elizabeth felt like running an inch of steel into his gut just to wake him up. She couldn't even begin to interpret what he meant by that question. "Of course, she's in school. At least she should be." Liz turned and gave her younger sister an accusing stare. Lulu ignored Liz's scolding, fiddled with her camera phone and aimed it at Daniel Corker.

"What, pray tell, is that?" he asked.

"Fido. Smile." Lulu shot his picture and showed it to him.

He blinked and stepped backward.

"What's the matter, Daniel?" Liz asked, suddenly concerned.

Daniel looked like he was going to barf. He turned, ripped the wires from his ballistic lamé jacket, and quicker than one of the pet bunnies that overran the campus grounds, he bolted from the gym.

"Whoa, what was that all about?" Lulu asked.

Elizabeth scratched her head and undid the oversized clip that held her wave of sun-kissed brown hair in place. She unplugged herself from the scoring box. "Stay here," she told Lu. Liz ran outside just in time to see Daniel Corker cross the street and disappear behind a truck. Liz tightened her lips, turned back to the gym and saw Lulu outside the gymnasium doors.

"Come on," Liz said. She shoved Lu ahead of her. "I'll shower, then drive you to school."

"Wait, Lizabeth. This came for you." Lu always called Liz 'Lizabeth.' Lulu stopped just inside the gym. She showed Liz the text she had on her phone. It was sent to Pirate Hunter via Rebel Goddess from Cal Sorensen. Pirate Hunter was a screen name Liz used to annoy their mother, Tess.

Liz hesitated. Cal Sorensen was Tess's business partner. Their latest salvage project had taken them to Nassau on New

Providence in the Bahamas. Tess had been there for three months, leaving Liz at home to look after Lulu and Calico Jack.

A message from Cal couldn't be good. If Tess wanted to tell them something, she would get in touch with them herself. Liz wished Lulu wasn't here and that she had her own phone with her right now. Liz had switched off her phone before the fencing bout and had buried it in her pack in the women's locker room. She hadn't looked at any of her messages since yesterday.

Liz exhaled, read the text on Lu's phone. It said to check her e-mail.

She frowned. Should she wait until she got home before reading her e-mail? Lulu stared at her curiously. No, Liz decided. Lu could handle bad news.

Lulu passed Liz her camera phone. Liz accessed the e-mail on her home computer through Lulu's phone and almost had a heart attack when she read Cal's message.

"What's wrong?" Lulu asked.

"It's Tess. She's missing."

Lulu's eyes grew huge. "What do you mean she's missing, and why didn't Cal mention that to me in his text?"

"He couldn't mention it," Liz said. "He didn't know how you'd react."

Lu snorted. "I'd totally react exactly the same way you're reacting. What a WOMBAT."

Elizabeth didn't comment. She was inclined to agree. Cal Sorensen was a waste of money, brains and time. But if their mother wanted a partner who knew zilch about teenaged girls, no less how to text them, who were they to object?

Lulu sighed. "She's probably just jerking the poor goon around. You know how Tess is."

Elizabeth pursed her lips. But this sounded serious. She'd have to skip her classes this morning and get the rest of the story.

"You're going to school. I'll find out what's happened and come to get you at lunchtime," Liz said, returning Lu's phone to her.

"No," Lulu said. "She's *my* mother too."

"Fine. Just don't say anything when I talk to him. I'm going to call him on my iPhone. Then I'll go and see Stevie. She's good buds with Cal."

Stevie was Stephanie Rackham, their twenty-one-year-old cousin and Tess's niece.

Elizabeth started to strip off her white ballistic fencing jacket as she walked toward the women's locker room. Lulu followed, fiddling with her camera phone. Elizabeth swung open the doors to the smell of BO and steam. She went to her locker, where her backpack sat on the floor, and fished out her iPhone. She searched her contacts and tapped Cal's personal number. When no one answered, she tried the radio phone on board her mother's salvage boat, *Tess's Revenge*. She stared at the video display and frowned.

No one picked up. Where had Cal gone?

"This is so weird," Lulu said. She was still playing with her camera phone.

Liz clicked off her iPhone. "What's so weird?"

"The picture I took of Mister Yummy back there. It's gone."

"Did you delete it?"

"Why would I delete a totally awesome hunk like that?"

Liz turned back to look at the exit to the locker room.

"Who *was* that masked man?" Lu asked, sardonically.

Elizabeth laughed. "Well, he told us his name. Daniel Corker. He was probably just some guy off the street that snuck in. I should report him to Security."

She knew she wouldn't, of course.

Lulu smacked her lips. "Hope he comes back. I think he likes you. He was totally checking you out."

Liz rolled her eyes. Lu crushed on every boy she met. Liz

couldn't remember ever crushing on guys like that at fourteen. Even now at the ripe old age of eighteen, she hardly had time for boys. There was school and fencing and looking after the house, CJ and Lulu. Their dad died when Liz was Lu's age. An unexpected atom of resentment crept in and she glanced with mixed feelings at her sister. Elizabeth's worst fear was that she would die a virgin.

Liz fluffed out her wavy brown hair and stripped. She wrapped a short cotton robe around her shoulders and went to the showers.

"But don't you think it's strange?" Lulu asked, following her. "I mean, Daniel just bolting like that because I took his picture?"

"Maybe he was camera-shy."

"Nobody's camera-shy. Especially nobody that looks like him."

Liz shrugged. "He probably had a date. And for the record, Lu. Stick to guys your own age. That guy's legal. You aren't."

"Oh, totally," Lu said, and turned on the cold shower and shoved Liz, robe and all, into the spray, and giggled.

CHAPTER TWO
You've Heard Of The Bermuda Triangle?

It took Liz half an hour to shower and get dressed. She wiggled into a skinny black T-shirt, black stretch Capri pants and a shortie leather jacket.

She stared at her face in the mirror as she fluffed out her damp hair. Too pale, she thought and covered her light sprinkle of freckles with medium tan foundation. Her wide hazel eyes looked even bigger because she drew two black lines with liquid eyeliner. Could Lu be right? Did Daniel like her? She shined her lips with fresh strawberry lip balm.

Elizabeth and Lulu went outside the gym to be met by a pair of rabbits. The critters were all over the place. Liz squatted to pet one of them. The crazy rabbit sprang onto its hind legs with its nose quivering at a Honda in the parking lot. Liz rose, stared. She recognized the Honda. It belonged to her macro-economics prof, who was getting out of his car. He clicked his remote to lock the car door, then lifted his notebook computer from the pavement.

The bunnies scattered. Thanks for the warning, guys, Liz thought. Liz lowered her head. Time to split before her prof saw her. Lu took the helmet Liz handed to her while Liz twisted her hair into a knot and tucked it under her own. Her aviator Ray-Bans should finish the disguise. Hopefully, she wouldn't be missed in class.

At the far end of the lot, she hopped onto her electric scooter, a Suzuki Burgman 650. Lulu sat behind her. Their cousin Stevie worked, part-time, at the Centre for Oceanographic Studies on the Saanich coast, north of Victoria. Liz tried to call first, but Stevie wasn't answering her cell. Liz left her a voice mail, then texted her just in case, then Liz called the reception at the centre. Stephanie was busy with a computer simulation and couldn't come to the phone, the secretary told her. But she'd probably be finished by lunch.

It was a forty-minute drive on the highway. When they arrived, they were ten minutes early. Liz and Lulu went down to the beach in front of the Oceanographic Centre to sit on the rocks and watch the sea slap into the tide pools.

Lulu tried to retrieve the picture she'd snapped of Daniel Corker. Liz skimmed a stone over the water. Tess usually phoned every night. Liz should have known something was wrong when Tess failed to call after two days. If only she knew more about Tess's job. Marine Explorations Inc, her mom's salvage company, had found the wreck of the pirate ship *Curlew*.

She tried to call Cal again. Still no answer. If he was so concerned, why wasn't he picking up? Oh my God, what if something had happened to him, too?

Liz glanced up to see Lulu staring at her. Liz slid her Ray-Bans to the tip of her nose and smiled.

"What's up?" she asked.

Lulu pinched her lips together. It was not a good look for her. It made her look stern and too mature. "Let's go," Lu said. "I think Stevie's free to see us now."

Liz rose and shoved her Ray-Bans back into place. She dipped her head down to remove her helmet, then flung her head up feeling her brown waves catch highlights from the sun. She dropped the helmet next to Lu's by the bike and followed her sister into the building.

The secretary smiled at them as they walked into the large reception area. She knew them and asked them to wait. They kicked their feet on the tiled floor, wishing there was somewhere to sit. Their cousin, research assistant Stephanie Rackham, would see them in a minute.

The minute turned into five, then ten. Fifteen minutes later, Liz swept her Ray-Bans over her hair and whispered to Lu, "Let's blow this pop stand. We'll go and find Stevie ourselves."

They gave the secretary the slip while she was busy being mesmerized by her computer. They disappeared inside the elevator behind a lab-coated scientist like they knew where they were going. The scientist smiled at them, shoved his magnetic card into the key slot and asked them what floor. Elizabeth pressed 12 before the scientist could think.

Liz and Lu got out on the twelfth floor and searched for Stevie's office. This was not the first time they had been here. They found Stevie's office at the end of the corridor and surprise, surprise, the door was open. No one was inside. Liz glanced at her Swatch. It was past noon so everybody must be doing lunch. She stepped inside and dragged Lu with her.

The office was cluttered with tables, computers and filing cabinets. The blinds to the windows were up and Liz caught a view of Haro Strait. She went to Stevie's desk where the parrot pen Liz had given to Stevie last Christmas sat on a pad of graph paper. Beside the pen was a state-of-the-art computer. It was on, but the glare of sunlight washed out the screen. Liz went to the window blinds to lower them, then came back to the computer.

A simulation of some sort of oceanographic activity was displayed on the screen. So, Stevie must have just stepped out.

Liz studied the digital image. Islands. The Caribbean? And something that looked like a tornado in the sea.

Stevie stormed into the office, raging. "You guys weren't supposed to come up here without an official escort," she said.

Liz rolled her eyes. "We got tired of waiting."

"I was just downstairs to get you."

"Yeah, I figured."

Stevie was having a major hissy fit. Liz had disrespected her authority. Okay, enough of this, Liz thought, and spoke before her cousin could. "Tess is missing," she said bluntly.

"You know?" Stevie asked.

Liz scowled. "Of course, we know. Cal Sorensen texted us."

"What did he say?"

"I didn't talk to him so I couldn't ask for details. All I know is that she's missing."

"Yeah." Stevie swallowed. She returned to her computer with its wide screen and adjusted it to face them.

They hovered over the monitor, and Liz made a gesture of exasperated confusion. "What are we looking at?" she asked.

Her cousin clicked the mouse and expanded the image on the screen. "This is the area where Tess was working." Like Liz and Lulu, Stevie always called Tess by her first name. "You've heard of the Bermuda Triangle?" Stevie asked. "Well, this is an anomaly similar to that."

Elizabeth frowned. "I thought the Bermuda Triangle was a myth. Just because a few boats and planes have disappeared between those coordinates doesn't mean there's a space/time warp there." Stevie made crazy eyes at her. Liz turned her hands, palms up. "I was kidding."

Her cousin snorted. "Not a warp."

Elizabeth exhaled in exasperation. Even junior scientists were always spewing crap. No wonder Tess had resigned from her teaching job at UVic.

"What then?" Elizabeth asked, trying really hard not to roll her eyes. She drew over a five-wheeled computer chair to sit on.

"An anomaly," Stevie said.

"You said that."

Lulu pulled up another chair and sat down in front of the computer next to Liz. Lu squeezed in closer until she had access to the keyboard. She pressed a few buttons. Stevie started to object, then stood back. An image of the tornado-like thing expanded into a whirling multilayered mass.

"A vortex," Lulu said. "Awesome."

Stevie nodded. She punched a few keys and brought up the image of the remote sensing survey which revealed the shape of a shipwreck. "This is where the salvage operation was located. Tess was last seen northeast of this location."

Liz swept a hand over her hair, removing her Ray-Bans. "Nobody saw where she went?"

"From what Cal told me, No. She went alone."

"When did you last talk to Cal?" Liz asked.

"Early this morning. He called just as I got to the lab."

Liz was insulted. "Why did he call *you* first?"

Stevie pointed to the vortex. "He knew I was working on that."

"What else did he tell you?" Elizabeth asked.

"Only that the coast guard and the marine police are looking for her. They've sent divers. Cal and some volunteers are diving as well. Everyone is searching the area, but nothing has been found to tell us what happened to her."

"When did this happen?" Liz asked.

"Two days ago."

Liz rose from her seat, hands ready to throttle her cousin. "Two days ago? Tess disappeared two days ago, and you're just telling us now?"

Stevie straightened to her full height. "I didn't want to worry you and Lu unnecessarily."

"Screw that, Stevie. We *are* worried. Tess never goes more than a day without calling us."

Lulu clicked the mouse. "Look at this," she said, enlarging the image. "The vortex swirls northeast of the wreck. Look at the velocity. It spins just like a tornado. What does it do?"

Stevie glanced down at her hands, with their perfect French manicure, before looking at the screen. Liz knew she was worried, as worried as they were.

"Sit down," she said. Stevie was trying to sound calm, but there was something in her eyes.

"I am sitting," Lu said.

Elizabeth retrieved the five-wheeled computer chair and slumped down into it. "You know something, don't you?" she said.

Stevie inhaled. She stared at Liz and Lulu, her eyes sober and intense.

"You think she's dead," Lulu said, astounded.

Liz said nothing. That was exactly what Stevie thought. In fact, Liz would bet good money that Stevie was positive that Tess was dead. "Tess is not dead," Liz said.

"Look," Stevie said. "I know it's hard to believe that Tess is gone. I can hardly believe it myself. I didn't want to tell you like this. That's why I didn't say anything right away. I wanted to be sure, but . . . Oh shit . . ." Stevie never swore when Lu was around. That's why Liz knew Stevie was certain that she was right.

Neither she nor Lulu blinked a tear. They didn't believe it. And if Stevie thought they were going to have a major, twin meltdown, she could relax. Liz pointed to the computer monitor. "Tell me what all this high-tech cyberbabble means."

Lulu moved the cursor to the vortex. "You think she got sucked into that anomaly and was drowned."

Stevie nodded. She tried to explain the properties of the currents and tides, the interaction of the atmosphere with the sea and an unusual undertow. She was a marine physicist-in-training and it all made sense to her how the funnel had formed and then disappeared only to reform in another location. Liz scratched her head. Lulu seemed totally absorbed. This anomaly generated a subaquatic chute, a physical force beneath the sea, that sucked in solid matter and deposited it elsewhere.

Where?

"This chute," Liz said. "Is there a chance Tess was sucked into the vortex of that chute and dropped someplace else, somewhere the searchers haven't looked?"

"Anything is possible," Stevie said. "But the velocity of that vortex would have killed her. The search will only last a few more days. If Tess isn't found or if no clues to her whereabouts are discovered in the next forty-eight hours, they'll call off the search."

"You can't mean that," Liz said. "We have to go down there. We can all dive. Lulu and I will catch a flight to the Bahamas and look for her ourselves."

"No." Stevie slapped down her foot. "Absolutely not. Leave the search to the authorities."

Liz crossed her arms over her chest in supreme defiance. "You can't possibly believe that I'll wait around here while that idiot Cal Sorensen does nothing."

Stevie also crossed her arms. "Cal Sorensen is not an idiot."

"He's a WOMBAT," Lu said. "Waste of money, brains and time. I don't know what you see in that guy, Stevie."

Stevie blushed. "I don't see anything in him. He's just a nice . . . person. That's all."

"He's my mother's 'person,'" Lulu said, making air quotes with her fingers.

Stevie scowled. "Why don't you go e-mail one of your friends, Rebel Goddess." Rebel Goddess was Lulu's screen name. "Look . . ." Stevie turned back to Liz. "The authorities are doing everything they can to find Tess. You'll only get in the way."

CHAPTER THREE
I Just Don't Believe She's Dead

Elizabeth dropped Lulu off at school and went home. Her neighbourhood was in Gordon Head, part of the Greater Victoria municipality of Saanich. The house she shared with her sister was a converted farmhouse. All of the houses there were built on former farmland.

When she got inside, Liz went upstairs to the computer in her bedroom. She booked a flight to the Bahamas, but she only booked one ticket. She had been too impulsive, not thinking. She called Stevie, who agreed to stay with Lulu while Liz went to search for Tess. It was too dangerous to take Lulu diving. And besides, Lu would miss too much school. Lulu would be furious, but Liz refused to argue. Someone had to take care of CJ, her parrot.

Liz started to pack, but before she left for the Caribbean, there was one other thing she could try. She glanced at her Swatch. She had twenty minutes before classes were out. If she hurried, she could catch the last ten minutes of her Archaeology of Piracy class.

She snuck into the lecture hall through the back door and slipped into one of the seats nearby. The lights were dimmed. Like a movie theatre, the rows of seats sloped down to a podium below where Jerrit Wang, the student TA, was talking about the *Adventure Galley*, a ship belonging to the infamous Captain Kidd. The wreck was somewhere off the coast of Saint Mary's Island in Madagascar. In his PowerPoint presentation, he showed an old map of the site, a photo of some gold coins minted in the Ottoman Empire, and a scattering of blue and white Chinese export porcelain. The variety of artifacts found on the site, he said, indicated that the wreck was a pirate ship. But alas, it turned out that the ship did not belong to Captain Kidd after all, but was the ship of another notorious pirate, Captain Condent of the *Fiery Dragon*. The ship's timbers were constructed in the Dutch style, rather than the English style, indicating that the wreck could not be the ship of Captain Kidd.

"Next time, we'll look at the excavations of one of our former professors here at UVic, Tess Rackham, and her search for the wreck of the *Curlew*," Wang said.

Liz snapped wide awake at the mention of her mother. As soon as the class was out and the lecture hall empty, Liz swooped down the steps to the podium where Wang was gathering together his papers and computer equipment.

Jerrit Wang had worked for her mother a few years ago, before she left the department. Maybe he could give her a clue as to what Tess had been working on, which might have led to her disappearance.

"Jerrit," she said.

The teaching assistant was young, Chinese and extremely cool. Not the history nerd you would have expected. He reminded her of a young Bruce Lee, but more articulate. "Got a second?"

He placed the notebook computer that he had tucked under his arm onto the podium and nodded. He sighed. "I know you're a commerce major, Liz. And I know you're only taking this course as an elective because you need one. But you'll have to make it to class if you want anything more than a D+."

"You mentioned the *Curlew*," Liz said, "just before you let the class out."

"Ah, so you *are* interested in learning something about maritime archaeology."

Stop being such a stick-in-the-mud jerk, she thought. "Actually, I was interested in learning about Tess Rackham."

Jerrit Wang locked eyes with her. "Tess Rackham?"

She hesitated. "She's my mother."

He smiled. "Then I think you know more about her than I do."

"But you worked with her for years," Elizabeth insisted.

"I was her student. I did some research on pirate ships with her."

"Did you work on the *Curlew*?" she asked.

He shook his head.

He gathered together his things again and glanced up. "Anything else I can do for you? I've got a class to get to."

Elizabeth grabbed his arm to keep him from leaving. He stopped, surprised by her aggressiveness. "Tess has disappeared," she said.

Wang swallowed. His intelligent, dark brown eyes narrowed. "What do you mean disappeared?"

"Well, you obviously know that she was salvaging the *Curlew*. A few days ago, she went diving and she never came back."

Wang's jaw dropped. "A diving accident?"

Elizabeth shrugged. "No one knows. I just don't believe she's dead."

Wang replaced the computer and papers onto the podium and removed her hand from his arm. "How can I help?" he asked.

"Do you know if she found something? Something that someone might want?"

"Something valuable?" he asked.

She lowered her head, raised it. Yes. Professional jealousy was the name of the game in Tess's job. One of her rivals might have wanted her dead. No. Liz shook her head. Tess was not dead. But she might be in hiding.

"What do the marine cops say?" Wang asked.

"They say she's probably dead. Even my cousin believes that. She thinks there's some anomaly in the sea, near the wreck, and Tess got trapped in it and drowned."

Wang sighed. "Then it's probably true."

"But . . ." She refused to give up that easily. "Don't you know anything? Can't you suggest something, anything to explain why she might have wanted to disappear?"

"You think she disappeared on purpose?" Wang shook his head. "Why would she do that?"

"I don't know," Elizabeth said. "Maybe because of something she found."

Wang shrugged. "Stop being such a drama queen, Liz, and look at the facts." He paused. "Sorry, I didn't mean to be so harsh." He glanced down at his waterproof digital watch. "I can't talk about this now. I have to go."

He left before Elizabeth could get in another word. She wanted to curse or break something or hit somebody. Why wouldn't anyone believe her? Tess was not dead. Not until she actually saw her mother's body would Liz believe that.

Elizabeth walked through the exit, head down, discouraged. She had missed all of her classes today. And it had all started this morning at fencing practice with Daniel Corker.

She was still at the university, so she decided to find out just who the heck Daniel Corker was. She went back to the gym and found the assistant coach, Laura Baeker, training some newbies. The inexperienced fencers were not hooked up to the scoring box. They didn't even have foils in their hands. They were practising footwork. In a fencing bout, everything depended on being in the right place at the right time. Competitors were constantly manoeuvring in and out of each other's range. All had to be done with minimum effort and maximum grace, which meant that footwork could make or break a fencer.

Elizabeth waited until Laura saw her, then dragged her aside and asked about Daniel Corker.

"Everyone has to sign in before they can practice," Laura said.

"Are you sure that was the boy's name?"

"Positive," Liz said.

Laura ran through her computerized list again, then the paper version where students signed in. "Sorry, there's nobody by that name registered with us."

Liz nodded, thanked her, and just as she turned to go, something shiny on the floor caught her eye. She crouched down and scooped it up. It was Daniel's dagger earring. Liz hesitated, looked around. Laura had returned to training her newbies.

Liz dropped the dagger earring into her pocket and decided to go home to finish packing. When she got in, CJ her parrot was squawking. Lulu was home from school, sitting at her computer in her room, computing something and ignoring the poor bird's squawks. The house was a mess. Liz returned to the living room, picked up some clothes that were on the floor, tidied some magazines and CDs that were scattered over the sofa, and went to attend to Calico Jack.

"Crap," CJ warbled.

"Pretty bird," Liz said. "CJ wanna cracker?" Liz stuck an old Ritz cracker that was lying on the coffee table between the bars of the cage and went to get his food. She opened the cage door, filled the feeder, and removed the soiled newspapers at the bottom of the cage.

"CJ wanna fly," the bird said.

Elizabeth nodded, and let the bird out as she went to deposit the pooped-on newspapers into the kitchen garbage.

When she returned to the living room, CJ flew back to the cage and clung to the outside bars. He cocked his head at her and blinked. Liz blinked back. Water? Liz asked before she realized she hadn't spoken aloud.

"Water," CJ said.

Liz replenished CJ's bowl, watched him drink, then perched

him on her shoulder and climbed the staircase to her room. No one was going to keep her from trying to find her mother. It was hot in the Bahamas, wasn't it? She packed shorts, Capri pants, a couple of sundresses, her neon orange bikini and her diving gear into a suitcase on her bed.

The doorbell rang. Liz pounded down the stairs to answer it. She almost fell over flat when she saw Jerrit Wang on the doorstep.

"Hey," he said.

"Changed your mind?" she asked.

He smiled. "Let me in?"

Liz nodded. "Sorry the place is kind of a mess, but hey . . ." She shot a backward glance at the homey living room. It had two armchairs, a sofa, a coffee table, a fringed area rug, and the bird cage near the entrance. "Oh, who am I kidding," she said. "Tess never cared about a neat house and neither do I." She glanced down, "Except for the bird poop on the floor." She drew a Kleenex out of her pocket, wiped it up, and threw the tissue into the fireplace. CJ swooped in from her second floor bedroom and landed in a mass of red and blue feathers on her shoulder.

"Crap," he said and picked at an itch on his wing.

"Quiet," Elizabeth said.

"Screw you," CJ said and pecked her cheek.

Liz placed the parrot inside the cage and drew the cover over. Wang stared at her and laughed.

"It's just a thing we do," she said.

She waved Wang in but didn't ask him to sit. She wasn't used to having house guests, and the sofa needed vacuuming. "So, I'm not such a drama queen after all," she said with no more preamble than that. "I take it you have some info about Tess?"

Wang frowned, looked down his nose at her. "Why do you call your mother by her first name?"

Liz raised her chin and stared Wang straight in the eye. "Because that's her name."

He grinned. "Okay. None of my beez . . ." He paused.

"I'm leaving for the Bahamas tomorrow," Liz said. "So, I won't be in class. I don't know how long I'll be gone, Jerrit— "

He stopped her there. "Just call me Wang."

She stared at him. "Huh?"

He smiled. "I hate Jerrit. It sounds like something out of Star Trek."

It was her turn to grin.

"Nice teeth," he said.

Was this a come-on? Elizabeth pursed her lips.

"Ah. That's more like it. More like the Elizabeth Latimer we all know and love."

She shook her head. "Cut the crap, Wang. Why are you here?"

Wang nodded. "Straight to the point, I see. You'll never be a prof, Liz."

Elizabeth bit her lip. And you will, I suppose. He already was, sort of. "I have no intention of being a prof," she said. "I'm more banker material."

"Yousa," he said. His smile turned serious. "I wanted to talk to you. I'm worried about you. As a student and as the daughter of one of my most revered profs."

Revered? Okay, what was going on here?

Wang inhaled. "Okay. No more pissing around. I don't think you should look for your mom." His hand went out to stop her speaking before she could object. "But I know you won't do that, so I'm gonna tell you something that I think you should know." His hand went out again. "Don't talk till I'm finished. How much do you know about your mom's salvage work on the *Curlew*?"

Elizabeth shrugged.

Wang was silent for a moment. He ran his hands through his

brush cut. "She found something in the wreck. A letter in a glass bottle."

Liz was astounded. It survived? "How could it survive hundreds of years submerged in the sea?"

"Do you want a lecture on underwater preservation right now?" he asked.

Liz shook her head.

"Suffice it to say that it was so well sealed that no water got into the bottle."

Liz started to pace the living room. Wang didn't move from the spot that Liz had led him to when he first came to the door. He was on the threshold between the hallway and the living room, next to the bird cage.

"Your mother believed that this was a letter from the pirate captain, Jack Rackham, to his significant other, Anne Bonny," Wang said.

Elizabeth stopped pacing. "Okay. So what?"

Wang inhaled. "Okay, let me try this another way." It was his turn to pace the room. "Tess believed in time travel."

Liz almost tripped over the area rug. She looked up at Wang.

"Holy crap," CJ said from under his cage's cover.

Wang stared at the covered bird. "Who taught him to talk?"

"I did," Liz said. "Though where he picked up the potty mouth I don't know. I sure didn't teach him."

Wang laughed, then his face turned serious again.

Elizabeth exhaled. "You were saying? I believe it was something about my mother inventing a way-back machine?"

Wang's expression became stern. "I'm not kidding, Elizabeth. Do you know why your mom was fired from UVic?"

Liz crossed her arms over her chest, indignantly. "My mother was not fired. She resigned."

"All right. Do you know why she resigned?"

"She was sick of all the hoops the university wanted her to jump through."

Wang studied her thoughtfully. "When your father died, your mother lost it."

Liz glared. Angry tears were threatening to spill. "And I suppose if *your* dad died, you'd just go to McDonald's for dinner and then go back to school and give a seminar on Blackbeard's buried treasure the next day?"

Wang shook his head. "I don't have a dad. Or a mom for that matter. I live with my grandparents. But that's besides the point. I'm not saying that your mother was loopy. I'm just saying that everyone else thinks she was and that she couldn't do her job."

"Well, she's doing it just fine now."

Wang said nothing. Elizabeth reddened. That was a stupid thing to say. Tess was missing and nobody cared.

"I'm trying to help," Wang said. "I didn't come here to trash your mother. I want you to find her, dead or alive." He paused. "I know she wasn't crazy. That letter has something to do with her disappearance. I didn't tell you at first because . . . Well, because . . . what can *you* do?"

CHAPTER FOUR
Has Anyone Seen This Young Man?

Elizabeth didn't tell Wang what she could do or even what she was planning. He left her house a few moments later, and she returned to her bedroom. She decided that she wanted to bring the black Capri pants that she was currently wearing on her trip, and exchanged them for a pair of white shorts. She turned on her small, flat screen TV to watch the news while she finished packing.

She shook out the Capris to fold them up and something clinked onto the hardwood floor.

She had forgotten about Daniel's earring. She had forgotten to study the students in her Archaeology of Piracy class to see if Daniel was among them.

Liz looked up to find herself face to face with the sun-browned complexion and sea blue eyes of Daniel Corker on TV. "Has anyone seen this young man?" the newscaster asked. The picture had been snapped by a camera phone from a passerby after the mysterious boy had been accidentally hit by a truck. Liz gasped. He'd been hit?

But it wasn't his being hit by the truck that had her brow puckering. Daniel had disappeared before the ambulance even arrived, the newscaster said.

Wang had left twenty minutes ago. Why hadn't she asked Wang if he knew Daniel? Where did Wang live? Then Liz remembered that he had mentioned a gig at Pacific West Studios. To make extra money to pay tuition and other student expenses, on top of his TA job, Wang was a part-time stunt double. His specialty was free-running.

Liz clamped on her helmet and told Lu she'd be out for about an hour. When her sister heard where she was going, Lulu totally insisted on joining her. They hopped aboard Liz's Suzuki Burgman 650 and drove to Pacific West Studios on Shelbourne Street.

The studio was locked up. But a note was tacked onto the door for Wang, who was probably late because of her. It said to meet the film crew on Government Street, near the parliament buildings. Elizabeth pulled out her iPhone, then realized she didn't know Wang's number. She shoved the phone inside her back pocket and got on her scooter again.

Government Street was bustling with public servants leaving work. Up ahead she could see a movie set where the traffic was being diverted. Huge white trailers were parked at the curb, and trucks mounted with cameras were in position to shoot a scene. Liz scouted around for Wang.

There he was.

The director shouted "Action!" and Wang came racing down the street in a dirt-smudged, white, cropped T-shirt and kevlar pants. His young muscles bulged from his midriff and arms as his legs sent him flying over the tops of three cars toward the Empress Hotel. Up he went on a trellis that was reinforced with steel, repelling his feet against the walls of the building. He reached the roof, hammered his Nikes over the shingles until he hit the other side. Then he leaped down onto a trampoline that catapulted him onto the road again and headlong to the marina. He scissored onto a boat, shot around the corner of the deck onto another boat, then hurtled himself at a speeding outboard that was heading for open water. He missed the target and fell, legs splayed, into the sea.

The entire crew applauded. Spectators lining the street burst into raucous shrieks, thrilled out of their minds. Liz planted her scooter against a lamppost and raced, with Lulu ahead of her, down to the docks to join in the fanfare. Some assistants were hauling Wang out of the water, handing him towels and thumping him on the shoulder, congratulating him. The actor who was chasing Wang finally caught up, clapped him on the head and tousled his hair. Wang sank down into a folding sling chair and grinned.

"Oh my God," Lulu said. "That was awesome!"

"Winning is so pleasurable," Wang said, although he didn't know who he was talking to because the sun was in his eyes. Liz was still wearing her helmet. She stepped in front of him and released her long hair from the helmet and introduced him to Lulu. Wang sat upright, still breathing hard from the run. "Liz. What are you doing here?" he asked.

"First, I want to apologize for making you late," Liz said, fanning her helmet toward the cameras for emphasis.

Wang shrugged, grinned. "I'm a fast runner. I wasn't that late."

"I had no idea you could do that," she said.

"Do you free-run for lots of movies?" Lulu asked.

"Some," he said. "The pay's good. And it keeps me in shape."

I'll say, Liz thought. She dragged her eyeballs away from Wang's and jerked Lu's chin to stop her from ogling him. Lu scowled, then spotted a group of young actors to ogle instead.

"So, what's up? You two didn't follow me all the way down here to play groupie, did you?" he asked.

Liz bit her lip to keep from rolling over backwards and laughing out loud. "Um, no. I forgot to ask you about something when you were at our house."

He brought the towel to his face and mopped his forehead and eyes, then scrubbed at his hair. "Okay, go. What's up?"

Liz reached into the pockets of her shorts to search for the dagger earring. Oh, crap. Where was it? Had she left it at home? Wang rolled his eyeballs up at her curiously.

Lu turned from ogling the actors to watch Liz flip both of her pockets inside out and upside down. "I must've left it at home."

"Left what at home?" Wang asked.

"Yeah, what are you looking for?" Lu asked.

Liz took a deep breath, ignored Lulu and looked Wang straight in the eye. "I forgot to ask you if you know a student in our Archaeology of Piracy class named Daniel Corker."

Wang shook his head. "The name doesn't ding any bells."

"Are you sure?"

Wang nodded. "Why?"

Elizabeth didn't answer. This whole thing with Daniel Corker was so strange. Had she just dreamt him up? She didn't mention the hit-and-run because the runner had been the victim of the hit and then simply vanished.

Wang rose from his comfortable slouch in the sling chair and stood face to face with her. "Are you still planning to go to the Bahamas by yourself?" he asked.

"Yeah, why?"

"I don't think you should go by yourself."

"Yeah," Lu piped in. "I don't think you should go by yourself either."

Liz nudged Lulu away. "There isn't anyone else. My cousin can't go. She has a job. And Lu, here, has to go to school."

"Leave it to the authorities. They'll take care of it," Wang said.

"They're planning to wrap up the search. I can't let them do that. Tess is still alive. I know it." If Wang was going to be difficult, Liz intended to nix the conversation right now. She started to drag Lu off with her, but Wang grabbed her by the wrist. They both looked down at Liz's hand at the same time and saw the black skull on her red-polished, lefthand thumbnail.

Liz didn't feel like explaining the nail paint right now. If she did that, she would have to explain why she couldn't close on her mother's disappearance. Her father had also disappeared. Everyone said he was dead. He had to be dead. His sailboat had been caught in a freak squall. The sails were ripped to shreds and the boat capsized. Search and Rescue had dredged for days, but his body was never found.

Wang looked from Lulu to Liz. "What's this Corker guy got to do with your mother?" he asked.

Liz sucked in her cheeks, twisted her lips. Other than the fact that he was an awesome fencer, she knew nothing about Daniel Corker—except that he came and went like a ghost.

"He appeared at my fencing practice this morning. He wasn't supposed to be my partner."

Wang stared at her like she wasn't making any sense. So what if the guy was a stranger? She couldn't expect to know everybody on campus.

"Appeared? What do you mean, appeared?" he asked. "You mean like a ghost?"

Liz gave him a mean face for voicing her own thought. "Look, he was just really strange. He talked funny and—"

Lulu nodded vigorously. "Totally. He talked like he was British." She said it with a stupidly exaggerated accent.

Liz glowered at Lu. "I have something of his," Liz said.

Wang gave her a weird look. Wang may be her TA, but she knew he wasn't that much older than her. "I am not crushing on the guy," she said, annoyed. "So wipe that moronic look off your face."

"Oh yes you are," Lu said, with mock, world-weary disdain.

"Shut up," Liz said. "Go ogle those actors in the boat over there. Isn't that Hilary Duff?"

Lu spun on her heel to see, then waved a parting hand at Wang as she sauntered down the docks to introduce herself to the teen idol.

Wang smiled. "This Daniel Corker, was he a good fencer?"

Elizabeth nodded.

Wang grunted. "As good as a *pirate*?"

Now Wang was just poking fun at her expense.

"Did he wear an earring?" Wang asked.

Liz clamped her mouth shut to keep her jaw from dropping to her collarbones. The wind blew, washing Liz's hair away from her face. Wang pointed to her right ear. Liz clapped a hand to the side of her head. On her right earlobe, Daniel's dagger earring dangled freely, as light as dandelion fluff. She traced the sharp outline of the tiny flying blade with her fingers.

"How did you know?" she asked.

"I put four and four together," he said. "Fencing and pirates. That skull you painted on your thumbnail and a dagger for an earring."

"But how did you know it was his?"

"Fencing, and an interest in pirates, and that skull are what make you Elizabeth Latimer," Wang said. "But I've never seen Elizabeth Latimer wear only one earring."

Well, maybe she would now. Liz unhooked the dagger earring and stared at it. She didn't remember hooking it into her earlobe. She must have done that shortly after she found it and then, in a moment of absolute distraction, forgot about it.

"Can I see it?" he asked.

Elizabeth hesitated for a second, then she dropped the earring onto Wang's palm.

"Cool," he said. "I've never seen anything like this. I wonder what it's made of."

Liz sneered. Why didn't he bite down on it and find out? She didn't voice the sarcasm aloud and shot out an arm to take it back.

Wang hesitated, inspected it some more. He started to return it, then whipped it back. Liz made a decisive 'gimme or I'll strangle you' gesture with her fingers.

"It's not gold," Wang said, relinquishing the treasure.

"Silver?" Liz suggested.

"Too shiny," Wang said. "If it was silver, it would show some kind of wear from being worn against the skin."

"Platinum? Molybdenum? Cubic zirconia?"

"Now you're just funin' with me," he said.

Liz studied the earring closely. To be honest, she hadn't inspected it this way when she first found it. Now that Wang mentioned it, she had to admit it was LEET, meaning elite. She had never seen anything like this before. It positively glowed.

"You say the guy dropped it?" Wang asked.

"I didn't see him drop it. I just knew that he was wearing it before he bolted."

"Bolted?"

"Yeah, you know, left, departed, vamoosed, exited the gym."

"Sounds like he ran. What did you say to the poor guy to scare him off, Liz?"

Liz ran her free hand over her thick, brown hair, clutching it. Nothing. She had said absolutely nothing. And then, he'd been hit by a truck.

"What is it, Liz? Your face just drooped to your knees."

Liz shook off the thought. Daniel was alive somewhere and he didn't want to be found. Why?

"I thought I should return the earring since it doesn't belong to me," Liz said, releasing the death grip she had on her hair.

"Then, why don't you take it to the Lost & Found on campus? If the guy wants it back, he'll probably go there."

Liz nodded. "Good idea."

Something was jabbing into her hand. She realized that she'd been clutching the earring like it could somehow leap out of her fist on its own. She dropped the earring inside her pocket, making sure it was snug against her thigh, then turned back to Wang. The smirk on his face told her that he knew she had no intention of leaving it at the Lost & Found.

"Gotta go," she said, flippantly, to cover the wave of guilt. "And you'd better go and get some dry clothes. You're still dripping."

Wang plucked his damp T-shirt away from his chest, while Liz turned around and walked smack into Lulu.

"How long have you been standing there?" Liz asked.

Lulu smiled. "Long enough."

Liz scowled and Lu jutted her chin at her. Liz grabbed her by the wrist and dragged her up the walkway from the marina. "Later alligator," Lu shouted over her shoulder at Wang.

"Awhile, crocodile," Wang returned.

"So, did Wang know Daniel?" Lu asked as they hit the street.

Liz searched left and right for her Suzuki scooter. "No, you heard him. He hasn't a clue who Daniel is."

Lulu puckered her brow. "I think Wang knows something."

"About Tess or Daniel?"

"Both," Lu said.

"Why do you think that?" Liz asked.

"Because I was listening to you guys talking in the living room earlier."

"Good or bad?" Liz asked.

Lulu had an uncanny intuition. Although she could lie like the devil himself if she chose, she always knew when other people were hiding something.

They were standing on Government Street near the Empress Hotel. Lulu turned to face Liz, and Liz could see the resemblance to their father. Lu had feathery, light brown hair, huge amber eyes and eyelashes that a makeup artist would die for.

"Well?" Liz prompted.

"Did you notice the way Wang was ogling that earring?" Lu asked. "It was positively spectral."

Liz dug it out of her pocket. Yeah, she had noticed. It was like he wanted to keep it, which was why she had shoved it into her pocket PDQ.

Liz suddenly widened her eyes. No way. Wang couldn't think it was authentic. Did he think Daniel had swiped it from somewhere?

"I wonder where Daniel lives," Lu asked dreamily.

"I wonder where Wang lives," Liz said, frowning. Somehow, she felt like her conversation with Wang was not quite finished.

"Who do you like better?" Lu asked. "Kung Fu Boy or the Pirate Fencer?"

Liz sighed.

Both.

Neither.

Either way, they were both mystery men.

CHAPTER FIVE
My Sister Lost Her Hat

The next day, Elizabeth made sure that Lulu left for school before she headed for the airport. She paid the taxi and stepped onto the tarmac. Her bags were loaded and she climbed the steps to the small plane that would take her to Vancouver where she would catch her connecting flight to Nassau.

On either side of the single aisle there were two seats. Liz found hers and sat down. She took out her iPhone and tapped in Lu's number. She wanted to apologize for leaving Lu behind. Lulu didn't answer her cell. She was probably in class. Liz texted her a message:

Hi Rebel Goddess! SRY I had 2 leave u. Stevie will be home @ 4pm. TTYL 2nite. CYA. XOXOXO

Liz's screen answered almost immediately:

CYA sooner than u think

Liz frowned, tapped:

?

Lu's reply was:

TMWFI (take my word for it)

Liz tapped:

?

Lu replied:

Turn around. LOL

Liz turned her head. Lu grinned at her from the back seat. Next to her was Jerrit Wang, an evil grin spreading across his face.

"What are you two doing here?" Liz demanded.

"Laughing out loud," Lu said.

"Don't blame her," Wang said. "She *had* to come. Tess is her mom, too."

Liz exhaled in exasperation. "But what about school?"

"Yeah, what about it?" He tossed a sideways look at Lu who had returned to her cell phone and was busy accessing the Internet. "Both you and I are going to miss a lot of classes, Liz. We'll make it up. Your mom is more important."

Liz squinted at him. Why was Wang giving up his part-time jobs and school to look for Tess? The question must have been obvious because Wang answered before her lips ever opened.

"It's nothing perverted, Liz," Wang said. "If it wasn't for Tess, I wouldn't have been able to swing school. She got me the TA-ship and the free-run gigs. I want to help you guys find her."

Liz turned fully around until she was on her knees facing Lulu and Wang, bracing her hands on the back of the airplane seat.

"So you believe me? You don't think Tess is dead?"

Wang nodded. "Until everything that *can* be done *is* done, no, I won't believe that Tess is dead."

"Thanks for not blowing me off, Wang."

Liz's iPhone suddenly chimed with a rendition of Bob Marley's reggae hit "Jammin'."

Liz tapped the app for video on her iPhone and saw her cousin Stevie's worried face.

"Liz," Stevie said. "Lulu's school just called me. They say she didn't turn up for class."

"Chill, Stevie. It's okay. Lu had a morning dentist appointment. She'll be there later." Liz winked at Lulu who gave her a conspiratorial grin.

"Is there someone with you?" Stevie asked, sounding suspicious. Liz turned around and slumped down into her seat. She could see Stevie straining to see behind the seat to where Lulu sat smirking. Thank God, the video screen was too small to show more than Liz's face.

Liz vigorously shook her head. "Look, I gotta go. The plane's about to take off, and they want all cell phones and electronics off. I'll call you later. Don't worry."

Liz knew there would be hell to pay when Stevie learned that Liz had lied to her. But hey, like the man said, Tess was Lu's mom, too.

The flight was short with no food except for some lousy crackers that even CJ would have called crap. Elizabeth, Wang and Lulu caught the connecting flight without any problems and only one delay because some crazy was running amok in Security with a bag of fruit. The guy was an Asian immigrant and didn't know he wasn't supposed to take fruit—or anything else for that matter—aboard the plane now that terrorism had everybody paranoid. The whole security area had to be shut down for fifteen minutes while uniformed personnel relieved the poor bugger from his homegrown, genetically modified BC apples and pears.

Liz had Daniel's earring. She had taken to wearing it in her right earlobe. It seemed the safest place to keep it, except that now, for some reason, her earlobe itched. Was she reacting to the strange metal?

When they got through security, Liz, Lu and Wang went into the passenger lounge. Liz still didn't fully understand Wang's motive for accompanying them, but she didn't blow him off. He was keeping Lulu occupied so that Liz could think.

Liz wandered over to the window and stared at the airplanes on the tarmac. The itchy lobe was getting worse. She took the earring off and, immediately, the irritation stopped. She rubbed her ear. Bizarre, she thought, and decided to try the earring on the other lobe.

The earring dangled from her left ear. She could see her reflection in the window glass. She swung her hair to feel the weight of the miniature dagger against her jaw. How cool was that? She shot a brief glance behind her to make sure no one was watching her narcissistic display.

Daniel was majorly awesome. How was she going to nail him down? When she got back from finding her mother, she was going to do a flat-out search for him.

Her ear started to tingle. Liz pinched the earring over her earlobe. A flash of colour, outside the window, caught her eye. Was she seeing things? Out on the tarmac, she could swear she saw a young man with, *holy crap*, a sword in his hand.

Liz forgot all about her ear and leaped the two paces to the window so that she could flatten her face against it.

He was there, big as life, standing on the tarmac, next to a British Airways Boeing 747 jet.

He was leaning on his sword, dressed in a blousey white shirt, long-fitted vest, a red sash around his waist, and tight-cropped pants, with leather boots on his feet. His long, brown hair was tied in a ponytail and he wore a red kerchief knotted around his skull.

Daniel! Liz mouthed his name through the glass. Thank God, he wasn't hurt. The truck hadn't injured him. He cocked his head in a derogatory smile.

She flattened her hand against the window in reply. Why was he dressed like that? It wasn't Halloween. It wouldn't be Halloween for four months.

He raised the sword, gave her a two-fingered salute and disappeared as an Air Canada airbus taxied up alongside the jet.

"What's wrong?" Wang asked.

Liz was frantically clawing at the window, trying to see where Daniel had gone. Lulu touched her shoulder and she jumped.

"Did you see something?" her sister asked.

"Didn't you see that?" Liz pointed outside, hysterical. "It was Daniel!"

"On the tarmac?" Wang narrowed his brows, sceptically.

"Let me see," Lu said. She scoured the scene outside the airport passenger lounge, but there were only planes and airport personnel to be seen.

$ $ $

The flight from Vancouver to Nassau was a complete blur. Elizabeth couldn't remember if there was a meal or drinks or anything. She vaguely recalled buying a package of cashews and then choking. Eating, breathing and thinking wasn't the kind of multitasking she excelled at. Texting, surfing the net and chatting on the phone, now in that she was superlative.

Lulu had one more surprise for her when they landed in Nassau. When they went to pick up their meagre baggage, Lu went to the special luggage area and came back with—guess who?— Calico Jack, Liz's parrot.

"I couldn't leave him," Lu said, handing the cage over to Liz.

Liz raised the cover and CJ winked at her. Cry me great big cartoon tears, Liz thought.

Ditto, CJ said.

Behave yourself, Liz thought.

Ditto, CJ replied.

This was going to be tricky. Liz didn't want to have CJ quarantined, so they would have to slip past security unnoticed. Liz grabbed a baggage trolley, made an arch with their bags and tucked the covered bird cage under it. Lu and Wang walked on either side of the baggage trolley while Liz pushed. They arrived at Customs and Immigration.

Don't talk, Liz begged CJ.

CJ said, "Crap."

"I beg your pardon," the Customs officer said.

"Hat," Liz said quickly. "My sister lost her hat."

The officer frowned. Liz held her breath. The officer checked their passports and waved them on. Liz exhaled, and she and her accomplices rolled to the exit and outside to fetch a taxi.

Liz hadn't thought to book a hotel for them, so she asked the taxi to take them directly to the marina where *Tess's Revenge* had a slip.

The boat was berthed right where Liz had hoped it would be. No one was aboard. Cal and his volunteers must be on the Zodiac searching for Tess.

Liz gave the all-clear signal, and the three of them, plus parrot, clamoured aboard the ship. Liz stood on the deck and stared out at the Atlantic Ocean. She hadn't been on a boat since her dad's death. She felt a twinge. The slap of the sea against the boat's hull made her rocky and a little seasick. She tried to fix the barfy feeling by staring straight out to sea. The sun was getting low. It shimmered on the water. The air was soft and warm, so different from the cool, crisp air of the West Coast.

"I found the radio," Lu said, hanging by an arm from the stairway. "It's on the bridge. Wanna go up and try calling Cal?"

Liz turned to her sister. "He'll kill us if he knows we came on board without his permission."

"He mustn't be planning to be gone long," Wang said, pointing below. "Or why would he leave the hatch open?"

Good question. Liz loped down the hatchway into the galley. She searched the cupboards and lockers, then went down the companionway to where the cabins were. She found Tess's room and her computer. Liz placed CJ down on a small table and lifted the cover.

"Don't talk," she said aloud. "I need quiet to figure this out."

"Crap," CJ said.

Liz made a face at him and sat down at the terminal and logged on.

The answer to Tess's disappearance had to be somewhere. This was a good place to start.

But there were so many files. Mostly business files. Salvage operations listed by date. Some were listed by the names of the ships that Tess had salvaged. Maybe the one called *Curlew* would have some info on what Tess was doing before she disappeared.

No such luck. The file was another list of ship parts raised and the shipwreck's contents.

'CJ.' Now this was curious. Why would Tess have a file named after Liz's parrot? Liz tried to open it, but a message sprang up that said, 'Unauthorized User.' She needed the password.

Liz tried 'Parrot.' The computer said, 'Invalid.' Liz tried, 'Tess,' 'Elizabeth,' then 'Lulu,' one after the other. The passwords were invalid.

Maybe it wasn't the parrot the file name referred to. Liz tried something else. 'Pirate.' 'Calico Jack.' 'Jack Rackham.' She got nada.

Lulu came striding into the cabin and stood over Liz's shoulder.

"Where's Wang?" Liz asked.

"On deck," Lu said.

Liz tried a few more passwords, but the file refused to open.

Lu nudged Liz aside and sat down in her place at the terminal.

"How about 'Pirate Hunter?'" Liz suggested, hovering over Lu's shoulder.

Lu sucked in her cheeks, shook her head. "It wouldn't be anything that obvious," Lu said. "Or why have a password?"

"Crap," CJ said.

Lulu giggled. She typed in 'Crap,' CJ's favourite word.

The file opened, and Liz and Lu high-fived each other and would have high-fived CJ except that he kicked them with both of his feet instead. Liz eagerly turned back to the computer. Her heart stopped. She clasped her hands together in a mock prayer of thanks as the scan of an old letter appeared on the screen.

Liz exhaled, wet her lips and began to read.

July 17, 1719

Anne dearest,

You are trapped in the house of Governor Woodes Rogers, forced to return to yer husband. Ah, me pearl o' woman-ware, would that you was still mine, and we could face the open sea with the fresh mist in our hair and a fine wind on our tails. The ship's that is. I allow that ye do have a fine tail to be sure. But ain't that what got us into this fix in the first place?

The mansion is guarded by soldiers. Your chamber, I is told, be guarded too. Until you agrees to return to James Bonny, yer freedom is forfeit. What a load of malarky. I shall get you out of there if it's the last thing I do. And there's an end on it.

I do so hope this letter gets to ye. But fear not, I makes you my duty. There be better days ahead.

Jack

"Wang," Elizabeth shouted. "Get down here!"

Wang raced down the companionway to Tess's room.

"What's the matter?" Wang asked. "That was some high-pitched shriek you let loose. I thought you were being murdered."

Liz swung from deciphering the pirate script and faced Wang. "Look at this."

Wang stared, read the letter on the screen. "That's the letter I was telling you about."

"Then you've read it before?" Liz asked.

Wang shook his head. "No. I never actually got to read it. Tess sent it to me encrypted, but didn't tell me what the password was for opening it."

"But she told you what was in it?"

"She e-mailed me that she'd found an important letter from Jack Rackham to Anne Bonny. She said that this letter was the key."

"The key to what?" Liz asked.

Wang shrugged. "I don't know. I've already told you everything I know, Liz."

And everything that Wang knew pointed to Tess having lost her mind. Liz swung her chair back to the terminal and stared at the screen. What was so important about this letter?

"Where's Daniel's earring?" Lu asked suddenly.

"What?" Liz paused. "Why?"

"You were wearing it at the airport. Did you lose it?"

Liz fumbled at her hair and her ears. The earring was gone! She glared at Wang accusingly. "Hey, I didn't take it," he said defensively.

"Check your pockets," Lu said.

Liz checked the hip pocket of her low rider, cropped khaki's. It was there. She must have taken it off absentmindedly and stuffed it into her pocket unawares, sometime between the airport in Vancouver and their arrival in Nassau.

"Let me wear it," Lu said, jumping out of the computer chair. "You might lose it."

Elizabeth squeezed the earring in a death grip. No one was wearing this earring until she figured out what it had to do with Tess's disappearance. That's right. She was positively certain that Daniel's sudden appearance and Tess's equally sudden disappearance were related.

CHAPTER SIX
It's More Than A Coincidence

"Ahem." Someone was clearing his throat from behind them.

Mayday, Mayday, Mayday, CJ warned Liz.

You could have done that a bit sooner, Liz thought.

Liz, Lu and Wang simultaneously turned to see Cal Sorensen glaring at them from the gangway. "What are you girls doing here? And who the devil are you?" he said to Wang.

"Who wants to know?" Wang asked before Elizabeth could introduce him.

"This is Jerrit Wang. He's one of Tess's colleagues," Liz said.

"Colleague?" Cal raised his white/blonde eyebrows suspiciously. "You look more like a student."

"I used to be one of Tess Rackham's undergrads," Wang said. "I'm a grad student now. I've worked on a few projects with her."

Yeah, Liz wanted to add. Long before Tess met your sorry ass, Cal Sorensen.

Cal inflated his chest, trying to make himself look important. "Does Stevie know you're here?"

"Stevie is not our mother," Lulu said.

"I'm calling her," Cal said, fishing out his cell phone from his shirt pocket.

"She knows *I'm* here," Liz said.

"What about Rebel Goddess there."

Liz threw an arm around Lulu's shoulders. "She stays with me."

Lu thrust her chin out at Cal, then turned back to the computer and got busy with the keys, while Cal ignored her. Cal fondled his phone. "I could call the cops and have them take you home."

Liz frowned. "Why? What have we done?"

Cal glanced at Tess's computer where Lu was busy at the

keyboard. He jerked her away from the terminal and shut it down. "You're trespassing in more ways than one."

"I don't understand," Liz said. "You e-mailed me to tell me that Tess was missing. You didn't expect me to just stay home and wait, did you?"

He inhaled, stared at her. She widened her eyes in total disbelief. He *did* think that she would just stay home and wait. Who was he kidding? Then it dawned on her that Cal still thought of them as kids.

Cal looked oddly nervous. He kept glancing at the computer like he thought she wouldn't notice. What else was in that file that she hadn't had time to read?

"I want you girls to stay away from this room and that computer," he said, pointing deliberately at the wide, flat screen.

"Why?" Liz asked.

"I don't have to answer any of your questions," Cal said. "The business of Marine Explorations Inc is the business of Marine Explorations Inc, and none of yours. *Comprendez*?"

"We just want to find our mother," Lulu said.

"So do I," Cal replied.

But as far as Liz was concerned, he didn't sound like he wanted to find Tess at all. He stared at the parrot cage, shrugged like he couldn't believe they'd managed to smuggle the bird into the country, and handed CJ to Liz. He told them they had better be gone by the time he got back from sending some messages. He hustled them out of Tess's cabin and locked the door before heading to his own.

Elizabeth did not trust Cal Sorensen, but there were two reasons why she had to make him believe that she did. Number one, they had no place to stay in the Bahamas and she wanted to stay on Tess's boat. Number two, she wanted to get a closer look at that letter and anything else on that file.

Liz sent Wang and Lu off to rent diving equipment. She had brought her own gear, but Lu's and Wang's impromptu appearance on the airplane in Victoria hadn't allowed them enough time to pack properly. There probably wouldn't be time to go diving today, but at least they'd have the equipment first thing tomorrow.

"Cal," Liz said. She entered Cal Sorensen's cabin without being invited. "Can I talk to you a minute?"

Cal pressed SEND to a message he was e-mailing and turned around. "I thought I told you kids to go home."

Liz lowered CJ's cage to the floor. "We can't go home today. There are no flights."

Cal looked sceptical. He reached for his keyboard to access the airline schedules.

Liz hurried to change his mind. "Okay, I lied. There are flights. But please don't send us home. We don't have anywhere to stay tonight and we miss our mom."

Liz put on her best sad dog face. Cal bought the pathetic act and got up from his computer. He looked down on her paternally. "Well, I guess you kids can stay here until tomorrow. I'll call Stevie to let her know you're with me. But you're catching a flight out tomorrow, do you understand?" He glanced past her shoulder at the door. "Where's the Kung Fu Kid and the Rebel Goddess?"

"Don't worry, they're out of your hair. We can talk."

Cal raised his eyes. "Talk?"

"Sure. I know you didn't want to talk with a stranger and a kid around so I sent them on an errand. They won't be back for at least an hour. Unless they get lost. And that's quite likely. But I trust Wang. He'll find his way back."

Cal screwed up his lips. "Wang your boyfriend?"

Liz hesitated, sampled the idea, shook her head.

"Oh? Looks like he thinks he is."

Liz frowned. They were getting off topic here. "He knew Tess really well."

"Yeah, I'll bet he did," Cal said.

Liz wanted to slug him. What did he mean by that?

"Look, Cal," Liz said. She sat down on the edge of his bunk. The paternal manner vanished. He slanted his eyes toward the bed, making it pretty obvious what he was thinking.

She rose abruptly. "Did you and my mother have an other-than-business relationship?" she demanded.

He looked up at her, shocked. "Huh? What do you mean? Tess and I are salvage partners."

"I know that," Liz said, fuming. She wasn't sure why she was fuming. Was it because of her dad or because she knew Stevie had a thing for Cal Sorensen? "Okay, forget it," she said. "I want you to tell me the truth. I saw the letter from Jack Rackham to Anne Bonny, so don't even bother denying that it exists. What I want to know is this— What has it got to do with my mother's disappearance?"

Cal gave her a half-smile. "Why does it have to have anything to do with your mother's disappearance?"

"I know that the wreck you two were salvaging was the ship of the pirate captain, Calico Jack," Liz said.

He nodded. "Yeah. The pirate's real name was Jack Rackham."

"His last name is just like hers."

"Uh-huh," he said.

That 'uh-huh' sounded pretty suspicious. "If you don't tell me what you know," Liz said, "I won't go home."

Cal looked up. He narrowed his grey eyes suspiciously. "You mean you'll go home if I talk?"

Liz planted her hands firmly on her hips pirate-style. "I just said so, didn't I?"

He sighed, shook his head. "I don't know."

Elizabeth rolled her eyes. "What does this letter—this pirate,

Jack Rackham—have to do with my mother?"

Cal squinted at her, sizing her up. Maybe he was wondering how smart she was. Smarter than you, she thought.

He sucked in his cheeks, then exhaled. "It's more than a coincidence, Liz."

Elizabeth stared. "What do you mean?"

Cal was silent for a moment, obviously unsure of how much he should reveal. He ran his hands through his blonde hair. "Tess found out that she—and that means you, your sister and Stevie, and any other relatives you may have on that side—are direct descendants of Captain Jack Rackham."

Despite Liz's frustration, she had to laugh. Oh yeah, right, they were descended from pirates.

Cal nodded, smiling too. "I'm serious."

Liz squashed her laughter. "Okay, so what? What's that got to do with my mother's disappearance?"

"Did I say it had anything to do with your mother's disappearance? Now, get lost. I've got work to do. Tomorrow, you three musketeers had better be gone." He swung back to his computer, snapping over his shoulder, "And take that stinkin' parrot with you."

"Screw you," CJ said.

Ditto, Liz thought.

$$$

Liz didn't sleep a scrap that night. Cal had handed everyone sleeping bags and locked them out on the deck. He wasn't kidding when he said Tess's cabin was off-limits.

Fortunately, the night was warm. This was the Bahamas after all. The gentle slap of the sea on the hull seemed to rock Lu and Wang to sleep, but Liz was wide awake—and more than a little seasick. She got up and let CJ out of his cage. He perched on her shoulder, and they waddled over to the rail. She took a deep breath of the soft, salt air. It was almost fragrant, like shampoo. Liz combed her long hair away from her face with her fingers. She twisted her hair into a rope and tucked it down the back of her tank top. That was better. Liz stuck her hand into the pocket of her drawstring sweatpants and removed Daniel's earring. She touched her left ear, then felt the smooth, sharp shape of the tiny dagger. Why did she have this persistent urge to wear Daniel's earring?

"Avast there!" CJ said.

Liz swung around. "What's gotten into you? Since when do you talk like that?"

"Avast!" the parrot repeated.

"Who are you talking to?" Liz whispered.

All hands on deck, CJ said without speaking aloud another word.

Where did you learn that?

"Arrgh," CJ said.

Elizabeth laughed. He wasn't named after a pirate for nothing. She was feeling a whole lot better. CJ fluttered his wings and took off.

"CJ," Elizabeth shouted. She jerked around. No one woke up on the deck. She stepped over Lulu's outstretched hand and Wang's splayed legs, and stumbled on tiptoes toward the rear of the boat. Liz scowled as she tripped on the life preserver that she'd been using for a pillow. The blasted parrot could be such a pain. She sent him a telepathic query. Where are you?

Ho, Elizabeth. Aft here.

Liz made a beeline for the stern.

"Aft then, Elizabeth," the voice said out loud. It wasn't CJ's voice.

"Who's there?" Liz asked.

"Evenin' milady," Daniel Corker said.

Liz stood spellbound in the dark. The moon shone down on the young quartermaster, in his black britches, white shirt and red kerchief. He was no longer holding a sword. On his shoulder CJ perched, comically, as though he belonged there.

"Where did you come from?" she gasped.

"At your service, Elizabeth," he said.

She stared. She was suddenly acutely aware that her drawstring sweats hung below her navel and a midriff-length tank top was all that covered her above.

He swept his arm down in a formal bow. "You summoned me."

"I did?"

He drew a dagger out of his boot, and she stepped backwards and almost fell. CJ fluttered into the air and landed on the pirate's shoulder again. Liz's breath came to a verifiable halt as he swung the blade toward her throat. He touched the earring that hung from her left ear with the knife point. "You summoned me," he repeated and withdrew the blade.

She clapped her hand over the earring. "This?"

"Every time you wear it, I will come. But only if you place it in your left ear."

Elizabeth was positively speechless. She looked toward the bow of the boat where the sleeping figures of Wang and Lulu lay. She must be dreaming.

"I've come to take you to your mother."

Liz inched her way backward. CJ come here, she silently commanded.

Arrgh, CJ replied.

Liz swallowed. The accident with the truck must have addled Daniel's brains. He was knocked down, right? So he must have gotten a concussion and this was a wonky side effect.

"You should be in the hospital, Daniel," Liz said.

Daniel smiled. He gave her that same surly smile he had given her at the airport. How had he known she was going to be at the airport? How did he know about her mother? Liz had heard about stalkers, but she'd never had a personal stalker of her own. This was a first.

"I'm going to scream if you come any closer," Liz said. "I'm not alone on this boat."

"Aye, and it is a fine vessel, indeed."

"I mean it," Liz said.

"Come dawn," Daniel said, "you must hither to the beach and I will take you to your mother."

"How do you know my mother?"

Now, Liz was getting really scared. What if Daniel was a whacko and had kidnapped Tess and had her locked up in a ship's hold somewhere?

"You are the blood of Calico Jack Rackham, are ye not?" he asked.

"How do you know that?" Liz inquired.

"And if your foremother of three centuries, Anne Bonny, does not go back to the captain, your whole line will be doomed."

Now, Liz was intrigued. "This has something to do with the letter Tess found, doesn't it?"

"Aye, it does," Daniel answered.

"My mother has the letter."

"That she does. She took it with her."

"We only have a scan of it on her computer," Liz said.

Maybe they were getting somewhere. Liz stared at Daniel's handsome face in the moonlight. He was hatless and the red kerchief around his throat accentuated the blousey white shirt that was fluttering in the breeze. If she humoured him, maybe she'd get to the bottom of this charade.

"She took the letter with her . . . where?" she asked.

Daniel studied her in the dark. She knew the gleaming eyes that watched her were sea blue, although right now, they had no colour at all. "She took the letter to where she should not be," he answered.

Liz's fear had given way to frustration. It was clear Daniel had no intention of hurting her. She was even pretty sure that he wasn't a psycho. He was speaking half-truths. In riddles. And she was almost convinced that he was really a pirate.

"Your mother might alter the future," Daniel said bluntly. "If she doesn't return with the letter."

Liz's mouth dropped open. She was totally speechless. Time travel? Then Wang was right?

"Your mother knows the key," Daniel said with absolutely no accent at all.

"Key? What key? Who are you?" Liz demanded. "What happened to your accent?"

"Who I am doesn't matter," Daniel said. "At least, not immediately."

"Why should I believe anything you say?" Liz asked. "You've spent most of your time trying to convince me that you're the reincarnation of some absurdly surreal, eighteenth century gentleman pirate. And now . . . And now, you're talking about the future?"

"Listen to me, Elizabeth," he said. "I've discovered the same pathway that your mother found. We have to make things right. You have to find Jack Rackham and help him rescue Anne Bonny. Meet me tomorrow on the beach, at dawn."

"You're nuts," Liz said.

"Am I?"

She stepped back, tripped over a coil of rope, toppled onto her butt and shrieked. Daniel reached down to give her a hand up, but then a rumble of feet came down the deck.

"Lizabeth!" Lu shouted from the dark. "Where are you?"

"Liz?" Wang's voice followed.

Mayday, Mayday, Mayday, CJ warned her. All his efforts at playing pirate bird vanished. He was just plain old CJ, the obnoxious pet parrot, again.

WOMBAT at six o'clock, CJ warned.

Cal Sorensen was padding, in bare feet, close behind Lulu and Wang.

CHAPTER SEVEN
I Want To See The Wreck

"What happened?" Cal demanded.

Daniel had vanished. Liz glanced around her, feeling like she was drugged out or something. "I was sleepwalking," Liz said.

Lulu and Wang exchanged glances.

"Since when do you sleepwalk?" Cal asked. His eyes scouted around the rear deck. Nothing was out of place. "I swear you kids have aged me a whole year in one day. Go back to the bow and go to sleep."

There was nothing to do but obey. Lu stuck her tongue out at Cal's retreating back. Liz rolled her eyes to punctuate the sentiment. "Come on, guys. Do as the man says."

"Why should we?" Lu asked. "The deck's as hard as a board."

Wang laughed. "That's because it is boards."

They returned to their sleeping bags at the bow and sat down on the floor. CJ fluttered onto Liz's shoulder and promptly tucked in his wings.

"Okay, spill it," Wang said. "What happened? I don't buy that sleepwalking bit."

Liz squeezed her eyes shut for a long second, then opened them suddenly, startling Wang into flinching. Lulu laughed. "She does that all the time. Spooky, isn't it?"

"I saw Daniel again," Liz said.

Wang was incredulous. "Here, on the boat?"

"What did he say?" Lulu demanded.

"I think he's lost it," Liz said. "He gave me a bunch of mumbo jumbo about time travel and changing the future and junk. He wants me to meet him at the beach at dawn. He says he can take me to Tess."

$$$

There was no way Wang and Lu were being left out of this assignation with the mysterious vanishing pirate, so Liz let them come with her just around sunrise. Wang wore his sceptical 'I'll believe it when I see it' expression. Liz knew he was on the verge of writing her off. Not once had Wang seen the elusive Daniel Corker.

Well, if nothing else, this excursion would prove to Wang that the surly young pirate did exist. Whether he was kosher or not remained to be seen.

The three of them stood on the beach, not too far from the marina where *Tess's Revenge* lay berthed. Daniel had not specified exactly where on the beach to meet. Liz, Wang and Lu were ready in swimsuits and wetsuits, towing their scuba gear, because Liz had decided that, however this meeting turned out, they were going in search of the *Curlew*. Lu was busy surfing the Net on her waterproof, wireless, iPocket PC, while Liz paced the beach with CJ hopping behind her, kicking up sand.

"CJ can't swim, can he?" Wang asked.

"He-llooo, stud muffin," CJ said, turning to Wang and giving him a wink.

Liz shot a peeved look at Lu, who almost certainly taught him that. Lu smiled behind her hand. Shut it, Liz thought, and sent her most annoyed vibes to the parrot.

"Gotcha," CJ said.

Wang laughed. "You know, I wouldn't be surprised if he *could* swim."

Liz shook her head. "No, he can't swim. But he *can* waterski."

"What?"

"He can, really," Liz said. "I'll show you one day, but not today."

Wang smiled at the bird, then frowned. "Don't you think he'd be safer in his cage on the boat?"

Liz shook her head. "I don't trust Cal. He's pretty anxious to get rid of us. I think he's hiding something."

"Speak of the devil." Wang pointed to the bridge of the salvage ship. Something flashed in the morning sun, and Liz could see that Cal was up and had his binoculars turned on them.

This was a public beach, wasn't it? This was a free country. Three young people were entitled to loiter on the shore, waiting for a pirate, if they wanted to, weren't they?

"Oh, crap," CJ said. He had leaped to Liz's shoulder and was perched precariously.

Amen to that, Liz thought. WOMBAT at two o'clock.

Cal was on the warpath, making his way from the marina toward them. Would Daniel show up with Cal here? Liz wondered. She tucked her hair behind one ear, Hawaiian girl style, and realized she'd forgotten to place the earring into her left ear. Now, it was too late.

"You kids going diving?" Cal asked as he swaggered up.

"Looks that way, don't it?" Lu said.

Liz nudged Lu back to her Web surfing.

"You promised me you'd go home," Cal said to Liz, puffing up his chest and crossing his arms solidly over the biggest part of his overinflated anatomy. "Stevie's expecting you. And, man oh man, is she mad."

"She's not my mother," Lu said, jutting her chin at him.

Liz nudged Lu again, this time harder. "Look, Cal," Liz said. "Our flight doesn't leave until tonight. I want to see the site where Tess disappeared."

Cal shook his head. "No one knows the exact spot where she disappeared."

"Stevie says there was a subaquatic chute, an anomaly."

He narrowed his eyes like knife blades. "You kids go poking in there, and you'll get sucked into Kingdom Come and disappear—just like her."

Liz raised her eyes. Cal had said they would disappear. Not that they would be *killed* by the chute, but that they would *disappear*. Disappear into where? Did Cal know something about this anomaly that he hadn't told anyone? Did Stevie?

"Okay," Liz said. "In that case, I want to see the wreck site."

"No," Cal said. "That's off-limits until the search for Tess is over and the case is closed."

Right, Liz thought, sardonically. And I suppose there's yellow police tape strung around the shipwreck. "Fine," Liz said, crossing her arms, mimicking Cal.

Wang suddenly stepped up beside Liz and puffed out his chest just like Cal. "You can't stop us from diving," Wang said. "It's a free country after all."

Cal scowled. "Stay away from the wreck site."

"Cal, Cal. He's nobody's pal," CJ said in a singsong voice.

Lulu giggled.

Cal glared at the parrot, nostrils flaring. "I have a good mind to pluck you and fry you for dinner," he said.

"Fry *you*," CJ said.

Cal went for the parrot, but CJ fluttered onto Lulu's head. Cal threw his arms up in disgust, stormed off, flaring nostrils and all, and Liz watched him return to *Tess's Revenge*.

Wang exhaled, deflating his chest. "Oh, man, that guy is a jerk. Do you even know where the wreck site is?"

Liz sighed. "No." She hadn't had time to dig up the coordinates on Tess's computer.

Lu poked CJ off her head and waved her iPocket PC. "I know where the wreck site is," she piped in. She pressed some buttons on the handheld device, and several survey designations appeared on the miniature screen. Tess had done the remote sensing survey with a Geometric 881 Cesium Vapor magnetometer and a Trimble GPS receiver. A differential GPS shore beacon and a single point-positioning algorithm fixed the coordinates to which Lu had locked down the site. "I downloaded the location while you were busy justifying our existence with that WOMBAT yesterday. I got all the coordinates before he cut me off."

Liz grinned. Lulu raised her hand for a high five. CJ, who now hogged Liz's shoulder, obliged her with a firm kick.

"Well, what are we waiting for?" Wang asked.

"We're waiting for Daniel," Lu said. She glanced around. "Where is he?"

"Oh, that again," Wang said, snorting.

Liz removed Daniel's earring from a zippered pocket in her neon blue wetsuit and hooked the shiny dagger into her left ear.

She ran her eyes along the shoreline and then behind her. Nothing happened.

"Let's go diving," Wang said, getting impatient.

Elizabeth jammed a hand onto his chest, then thought better of it. He might mistake that gesture for a come-on. "Wait," she said. "Give him a few minutes."

Wang exhaled. Lu said, "Maybe Daniel found a new girlfriend."

Liz scowled. "I told you, I don't like him that way."

"Yeah, don't I know it," Lu said, shooting a sneaky glance at Wang. "You like *him*."

Swiftly, Wang looked away and busied himself by strapping on his scuba tank and flippers.

Lulu smiled. "Gee, Liz. I think he feels the same way."

Liz punched Lulu in the arm. Liz twisted her hair into a rope and tucked it down into the back of her wetsuit.

"Just shut up," she hissed under her breath. She strapped on her gear, picked up a small rectangular float and led Wang, Lulu and CJ down to the water. They strode into the sea, then belly flopped onto the turquoise waves. With an attached nylon cord, Liz dragged the float for CJ to perch on while he waited for them above the water. The lazy bird flew for a short minute, then landed on the float. He preferred a free ride to exerting himself.

Liz dived into the sea and felt cool water surge up and over her body. The deeper they went, the cooler the water became. Lu checked the coordinates on her waterproof iPocket and nodded toward a dark patch on the ocean floor.

Liz adjusted her mask, followed an orange clownfish to the reef. She made a backwards wave, motioning for Wang and Lu to hurry. This was an artificial reef. There were exposed coral-covered planks peaking like a ship's keel, and mounds of rusted metal, the remains of cannons.

Liz looked at Wang. Was this the *Curlew*? His eyes indicated 'Yes.' Liz nodded and shot down toward the careened hull of the ship. Tess had excavated and exposed much of the wreck. But if these wooden planks and beams weren't salvaged soon, they would rot and perish.

The clownfish darted into Liz's mask, right between her eyes. It was like the fish wanted her to follow it. All right, Nemo, she thought. Lead on.

The orange clownfish flipped its tail and shot through a hole in the hull. Liz released the cord to CJ's float and followed. It was dark, but she knew she was in the bilge of the ship. Light arrowed through several holes and slots in the planking. In the shadows, something moved.

Liz's heart stopped. Was it a shark?

No. It wasn't a shark. Daniel swam up to her and pointed to an exit hole on the other side of the bilge. Liz powered through the water, petrified that she might lose him. He catapulted through the sea into a sunlit area. She shot after him. She darted a backward glance to see if the neon pink and purple of Lu's and Wang's wetsuits were visible. She hoped they were following, but she couldn't see them because the hull of the *Curlew* blocked her view.

She turned her head back in the direction where she'd last seen Daniel. *Daniel!* she shouted the name in her head. The pirate was gone. Liz floundered for a second, then got her bearings. Daniel wasn't wearing scuba gear like they were. No matter how good a free diver he was, he couldn't hold his breath forever. He must have gone to the surface.

Liz headed upward, then felt a tug on her leg. Wang and Lu, in their purple and pink gear, were right behind her. She jabbed her finger to topside.

Liz broke the water into fresh air, ripped up her mask to see Daniel Corker smiling at her. CJ was sunning on his float just in front of him. On either side of them, Wang's, then Lu's head popped up.

Daniel was naked from the waist up. He wore black britches and no boots, but she remembered seeing a dagger slung into the sash tied at his hips as she surfaced. No intros were needed. Lu immediately recognized the pony-tailed young man with the sea blue eyes. She lifted her mask to ogle him better.

Wang narrowed his eyes, squinted, then slowly drew off his mask. For some odd reason, he unzipped his wetsuit to expose the top of his smooth, tanned chest, which was now wet.

Liz rolled her eyes. No time for this.

"Where's my mother?" she demanded.

"Yeah," Wang said, voice suspicious. "I'm assuming you're the mysterious vanishing pirate. What have you done with Tess Rackham?"

Daniel looked from Wang to Lu, water dripping down his bronzed face. He wore a red headband around his forehead that made him look totally cool.

He glanced back at Liz and asked, "Are they up to it?"

Liz frowned. Up to what? What was it that he expected her to do that Wang and Lulu couldn't do?

When Liz didn't answer, Daniel said, "You are the pirate hunter."

Liz almost laughed out loud. And CJ, Wang and Lu were her gang of merry men? She frowned. How did Daniel know her screen name?

Wang spat out water as a wave splashed him in the face. "What sort of a sick game are you playing?" he demanded.

Daniel gave Wang a surly look. He turned from Wang back to Liz. "We are running out of time," he informed her. "Are they or are they not up to it?"

"Up to what?" Liz asked, annoyed.

Daniel sized Wang up like he was some sort of enemy or rival. He glanced at Lu, at the waterproof handheld device she had looped on a synthetic cord around her neck.

"Your mother is in eighteenth-century Port Royal," Daniel said. "Come with me if you want to save yourselves."

What was he babbling about? "Save ourselves from what?" Liz asked.

"Yeah," Wang said. "What kind of a nut bar are you?"

They were treading water and their air tanks were heavy, although the salt content of the Caribbean waters made them extraordinarily buoyant.

"We've got to go to shore," Liz said. "I can't tread water much longer with this torpedo on my back."

"No time," Daniel said.

He looked east at the rising sun and dived into the sea.

"Liz, wait! The guy's a nutcase!" Wang yelled as Liz yanked her mask over her eyes and followed.

Lulu didn't waste time shouting. Liz knew she would come.

Liz surfaced as Daniel surfaced. He was an awesomely strong swimmer. She glanced back to see where the others were and saw Lu in her pink gear, just behind her, with Wang in purple, trailing and dragging CJ on his float by the long nylon cord. CJ fluttered into the air, did a show-off circle, then landed back on his float.

Thanks, Wang, she thought.

Liz turned back to find Daniel. She didn't want to lose sight of him. What she saw before her eyes stopped her breath.

A swirling mass of water broke the surface and looked like it was going to swallow Daniel into its depths.

CHAPTER EIGHT
I Don't Know If This Gizmo Will Work There, But If It Does, Text Me

Daniel was pointing to something fastened to his headband, a videocam. Liz stared. Wang grabbed her by one arm and Lu clutched the other. The sun on the sea was blinding. The saltwater made their bodies so buoyant they barely had to move to stay afloat. The water behind Daniel swirled with the velocity of a tornado.

"Your device," Daniel shouted to Lulu. "Switch it on!"

Lulu obeyed, and the iPocket showed video of every direction Daniel's head turned. The sky, the sea, CJ. Three stunned faces. Liz looked up from watching the miniature screen. Daniel intended to enter the spinning mouth of the vortex and he wanted them to follow.

Daniel dived. The vortex swallowed him. Liz was so shocked she forgot to view Lulu's iPocket until Lu yanked at her hair to make her look.

At first, there was only swirling motion and bubbles, then an incredible scene of a port harbour that was clearly eighteenth century. There was a long stretch of shimmering blue water, like the water they were currently floundering in. Between multiple wharves, lining a town's waterfront, were tall masted ships, brigs, schooners, frigates and Spanish galleons. Men clustered on the piers dressed like Daniel, only uglier and dirtier. And women, with their hair piled like cotton candy on top of their heads, strolled in long flowing dresses on the arms of gentlemen.

Now they were seeing a stretch of long sandy beach and palm trees and a small canoe. The canoe moved out onto the water and glided stealthily toward a single-masted, twelve-ton sloop. The ship had four guns on her wide, sun-whitened decks, and two swivel guns attached to her rails.

Liz stared at Lu, then at Wang.

"It's a trick," Wang said. "There is no way you are going in there."

Liz took the cord that was attached to CJ's float. "I don't want you to come," she said. "CJ will keep me company. Take Lulu back to Cal's boat, but don't tell him where I am."

"Are you nuts, Liz?" Wang asked. "You'll be killed."

"No, I don't think so. Cal said Tess disappeared. He didn't say she was *killed*. He thinks she's still alive. I know it. I just don't know why he won't admit it."

Wang gulped, spat water out of his mouth. "If it was safe, if he thought the vortex, the subaquatic chute, was some kind of time machine, wouldn't he have gone after Tess himself?"

Liz shook her head, gulping water that was splashing into her face. "You saw him. He's too much of a coward."

"I'm going with you," Lulu said, swimming closer to Liz.

"Not this time," Liz said.

"You can't stop me."

"Lu," Liz begged, treading water. "If I don't make it back, then you're the only one left."

"I don't want to be left," Lu said.

"You have to be the one to tell Stevie what happened. You and Wang."

Wang stared, his eyes melting her. "Liz, I can't let you go. It's suicide."

"Please, Wang. I have to find out. I think Daniel was telling me the truth."

Lu nodded, started to tread water slower. "Yeah. I think so, too. Because otherwise, where did he go?"

"But, where *did* he go?" Wang asked, his voice rising hysterically.

"He went into the past," Liz said, firmly. "He told me Tess is there as well. I have to find out why she won't or can't come home. And how her being there can possibly affect the future."

"I can't believe I'm hearing this," Wang said.

"You were the one who told me Tess believed in time travel."

"I know, but—"

"And you told me you didn't think she was crazy. Now prove it, Wang. Prove it to me."

Wang went silent. They were still treading water. Seagulls were swirling around the vortex. The chute was shrinking.

"Take care of Lu," Liz said.

"Lizabeth." Lu stopped her. She lifted the iPocket from around her neck and looped its cord over Liz's head. "I don't know if this gizmo will work there," she said. "But if it does, text me."

"I will." Liz swallowed and kissed Lulu on the cheek.

Liz shut her eyes and dived into the swirling hole in the ocean. CJ squawked, "Man overboard!" before he went tumbling, too.

When Liz opened her eyes, she couldn't believe what she was seeing.

$$$

She was still in the water, only now the colour of the sea was a dark sapphire blue. It was almost sundown. In front of her was a single-masted sloop. The last rays of the sun made shadows of three figures on the main deck. Two of them fenced unsteadily with swords. It was the same sloop they had seen on Lulu's iPocket.

The *Curlew*, Liz thought. But where was Daniel?

Near the rail, a one-eyed gorilla of a man, the ship's first mate, sucked on a bottle of rum, while he egged the duellers on. Were they crazy? They were all obviously loaded, plastered on rum.

Playing with sharp instruments while under the influence was asking for certain death. Or at the very least, a severed arm.

Calico Jack, Liz recognized, and—she almost choked—the man the pirate captain was fencing with was Daniel.

"Holy crap," CJ said.

I'll say, Liz thought. She placed the parrot on her shoulder and swam up to the port side of the ship. The sloop was not large and she could hear every word.

"What kind o' pirate be you, Daniel, lad?" Rackham mocked.

Daniel swung, Rackham ducked. His tricorn hat went flying, and Daniel's blade nearly sliced off the head of the *Curlew*'s first mate.

God almighty, Liz thought. She had witnessed Daniel's awesome swordplay before, but this was something else.

The first mate chucked his empty rum flask at the young quartermaster, his rolling muscles glistening in the dying light. Rackham jerked his head back in a spooky laugh, then stooped to lift his hat from the deck. He looked down into the water as he rose and stumbled to the rail. Liz cowered. In her most stupendous shock, she hadn't even thought to hide herself.

"Anne!"

Liz frowned. Oh my God, the pirate thought she was Anne Bonny. She stayed where she was treading water. If he saw her dressed in her neon blue wetsuit, how was she going to explain that?

Jack Rackham reeled out of the furled mainsail's shadows. His voice slurred as he leaned over the rail. "My God, Anne? Is that you? Sharp now boys, look lively. Me girl needs yer help!"

Daniel ran to the side and looked down. He grinned. Liz threw him a nasty look. How was she supposed to explain what she was doing in the water in a rubber suit?

Daniel stripped off his shirt. "Ho, there. Come aboard, lass, and get ye dry." He nodded to Calico Jack and his first mate who were both too drunk to help hoist her up. Daniel hauled her aboard, wrapped her in his shirt and told his captain he'd fetch her dry clothes. He dragged her aft to the officer's quarters and into the quartermaster's berth. CJ stayed with the pirates.

Daniel handed her an armful of smelly clothes. "Here, strip. And look lively. I'll hide your things under my bunk."

"I am not undressing in front of you," Liz said flatly. "And you can can the pirate talk. We're alone."

Daniel glanced up toward the deck and let fly a gust of exasperation. "All right then. Do you want to strip in front of *him*?"

Daniel held a blanket in front of her while she stripped. She put on the pirate clothes he handed to her which apparently belonged to one of the cabin boys, AKA Anne Bonny or Mary Read.

"What now?" Liz said, tightening a purple sash over her black britches. "Listen up, Daniel. I think you'd better start explaining. That drunken oaf thinks I'm his woman."

Daniel nodded and tossed the blanket onto his bunk. He tucked her gear beneath it, then demanded she take off Lu's iPocket PC.

"No," Liz said. "It's my only link to reality."

"Your reality is this for now," Daniel said. "That is, if you don't want to be at the business end of a cutlass."

Liz wet her lips, swallowed. OK, she was convinced. She removed the small handheld device that hung on a cord around her neck and passed it to Daniel.

"As I was saying," Liz continued. "You've got some explaining to do. Where's Tess?"

"She's in Port Royal," he said, tucking the pocket-sized computer under his bunk with her wetsuit.

"And where are we?"

"Nassau harbour, New Providence."

"I want to see my mother," Liz demanded, planting hands on hips, pirate fashion.

"In time," Daniel said. "But first we've got some business to do."

Liz grabbed his arm. He seemed real enough. She wasn't dreaming. She was in some kind of time warp or else she was on drugs. "I am not going anywhere with you until you tell me what's going on."

"All right. Sit. But we've got to make this fast. Calico Jack is waiting for you, and by that, I don't mean your parrot."

Liz sat down on the edge of his bunk. Daniel clasped his hands behind his back and paced.

"There's a complication. I can't take you to your mother because she's the cause of all of this. You know that letter she found? Well, she's brought it here, to the past, and changed the course of events. If the letter isn't returned to your time—"

Here Liz stopped him. Her time? What about *his* time? Weren't they one and the same?

"Elizabeth," Daniel insisted, when she remained frozen with her mouth open. "We are running out of time."

She clamped her mouth shut. Too much exposure to these pirate rogues was turning her into a mouth breather. "Okay, sorry. Continue."

"Your mother refuses to give up the letter because it's her key to this time zone. But if the letter is not returned to the present as part of the salvage of the *Curlew*, then you and your mother and your sister will cease to exist."

"What?"

"Jack Rackham and Anne Bonny have been separated by the governor, Woodes Rogers. If they don't get back together—and it's this letter that gets them back together—then the future of your family will not exist."

"You mean because we're their descendants?"

"Exactly," Daniel said.

Liz puckered her brow. She narrowed her eyes at him. "And this matters to you . . . why?"

"I can't tell you that," Daniel said.

"Why not?"

"Because it will change another part of the future."

Liz exhaled. She was getting frustrated and confused and pretty much fed up with Daniel Corker. Who was he?

A sound came from outside and the door to the quartermaster's berth was opened. A gruff voice called in. "Lassie, me Anne, where are you?" It was Rackham, drunk as a skunk.

"Come on, let's go," Daniel said. "Or he'll think I'm up to some hanky-panky with you, and I would like to keep my head."

Liz followed Daniel through the door and onto the main deck behind Rackham.

The pirate captain grinned like an idiot. "Ah, Anne, me sweet soul. For a second there, I thought I was seein' a phantom. You escaped! I knew ye couldn't be held, me feisty little wildcat. A gal who'd stab a serving wench for the misfortune of trampling her dress couldn't be held by mere mortal men."

Rackham hoisted a half-drunk bottle of rum from his leather baldric, where a pistol should have been, and blinked stupidly at the bright orange bikini top that showed beneath the white pirate shirt Liz was wearing. He quaffed a slug of rum and wiped his lips with his knuckles.

If he was drunk enough to think she was Anne Bonny, was he drunk enough to buy it if she told him she'd come from the future? That would be the fastest way to reunite them.

"Well, never you mind," Rackham said, rubbing his grubby hand on his calico shirt. He threw his arms out to hug her and Liz dodged him. "What's this here, now? I ain't so foul, am I, love?

Me and my shipmates here, we was only nippin' a bit into the rum. Isn't that right, Black Patch, me lad?"

The first mate grinned wickedly and Rackham thumped him on the shoulder. Rackham turned back to Liz and tried to grope her again. She ducked.

He frowned, took a swig of the rum, corked it, then slowly replaced the bottle in his baldric. He stared boldly at her pirate costume and suddenly became sober.

He signalled the first mate to hand over his own cutlass. When he did, Rackham tossed Black Patch's cutlass to Liz.

"Spar," he said.

Fortunately, Liz's best sport was fencing. But drunk or not, she was no match for a genuine pirate. He advanced with his cutlass and swung. She parried and jabbed. He blocked her. She glared at Daniel. Why wasn't he helping her?

"What plagues thee, luv?" Rackham teased. "Too much o' the primping in the governor's house? You're losing yer touch."

"Not enough practice," Liz said through clenched teeth.

Rackham backed off and allowed Liz to collect her footing. He lunged forward, crossed blades with her and repelled her strike. Then in a masterful move, he swung his blade out from under hers, raising it high, and stopped just short of her throat.

He swung down, nicking her below the left jaw. Then, with a violent strike, he knocked the cutlass out of her hand. It crashed to the deck in a metallic clatter. Liz clamped her stinging hand to her neck and felt the cut under her jaw smart. When she removed her hand, she saw a trace of blood on her fingers.

"Anne would ne'er have lost to me," Rackham said, retrieving the sword. "Not with me full o' the drink." He shoved his blade into his baldric and tossed the other to his first mate. "Avast, then, who be you?"

Liz glanced at the first mate and Daniel.

"Who be you, lass? You look exactly like my Anne. But ye neither speaks like her nor fights like her."

"But if I look like her, I must be her," Liz said, innocently.

"Drunk as all that, I is not," Rackham answered, hotly.

He took Liz by the arm and pulled her to him, turning her face to the dying light. The sun cast a haunting shadow over his face. Past his shoulder, Liz noticed for the first time that the ship was anchored in a narrow bay. On the horizon was a large bean-shaped island, stark against the orange sky.

"Enough o' yer dilly-dallying about. Where d'ye come from, wench?"

"It's not the first time you've had female crewmates on your ship," she said defiantly.

Rackham's face purpled. Daniel stiffened. And the first mate gave his captain an uneasy stare.

Pirate code strictly banned the presence of women aboard ship. Only Calico Jack dared defy that code. He had carefully protected his lover Anne Bonny's disguise as one of the ship's boys.

Daniel moved a hand to his sword grip. Rackham noticed. "To yer quarters," he ordered, waving a dagger at Daniel and the first mate. "The both of ye."

When Liz and Rackham were alone, he turned back to her, his dagger's blade catching the last rays of the sun. He thrust the knife into his baldric and went to light a lantern that hung from the main boom over their heads. He picked up his rum and offered it to her. Okay, why not? If she drank with him, it would keep him drinking. And if he was drunk, he wouldn't question who she was.

She rubbed the lip of the bottle with the sleeve of her shirt before taking a sip. She gagged. His deep blue eyes twinkled under his tricorn hat.

She decided to go for bust. "I come from the future," she said. "My name is Elizabeth Latimer."

He laughed. "I told ye, I is not that drunk. But if yer passes me that rum, I could get drunker."

Liz looked at the brand name blown into the glass. Rum bound for England. This was probably booty from the last merchant ship the pirates had looted. She remembered seeing something like this in one of her mother's salvage collections.

"Wait here," she said. "I've got something to show you."

She went aft to Daniel's quarters. He was pacing his cabin. When he learned her plan, he told her she was nuts.

"He'll keel haul you," Daniel said. "He'll think you're a bloomin' witch."

Liz shook her head. "I don't think so. I think he likes me. I remind him of Anne."

She reached under Daniel's bunk and grabbed Lulu's handheld computer before Daniel could stop her, and raced outside to the deck. Daniel followed.

Rackham was swaying, waiting for her, muttering some oaths to CJ to which the parrot responded with some cuss words of his own.

"Quiet," Liz said to CJ.

"Arrgh," CJ said.

Daniel grabbed Liz's arm from behind, but she shook him off. She showed the drunken pirate the wireless electronic iPocket. He stared at it, eyes threatening to fall out of his skull. He made the sign of the cross. Liz laughed. She had been expecting some pagan sign against the evil eye, not the Catholic gesture to ward off demons.

"Look," she said. She displayed a picture of the surviving pieces of the *Curlew* that Lu had downloaded while they were diving. A view of the upturned keel, some beams and planks. A rusty cannon and anchor. "That's your ship—or what's left of your ship in the twenty-first century. "

Rackham almost dropped his rum, glanced at Daniel. "What devilry is this?" he howled. "The *Curlew*, she be scuttled?"

Daniel opened his mouth to protest, then shut it. He made a gesture of frustrated and total exasperation. Liz ignored him.

"This is the future," Liz said. "What remains of your sloop in the twenty-first century. My mother and her partner dredged the sea bottom and found your ship under a layer of mud. They raised what was left of the ship."

"Hogwash and devilry," Rackham spewed.

The pirate captain swilled a good portion of his rum before he handed the bottle to Daniel. He seized the minicomputer to glare at the excavated *Curlew*.

"By the bones of Davy Jones's locker, I must be drunker than I thinks," Rackham said. "And the only cure for drunken apparitions is to get drunker."

"Aye." Daniel agreed. He returned Rackham his bottle of rum and retrieved the iPocket from the staggering captain. Daniel would have tossed it overboard, but Liz snatched it out of his hand. Daniel gave her a nasty face. She sneered.

Rackham tipped the bottle again. It was three-quarters empty now. He swayed unsteadily on his feet as he sized her up. "Let's say, my pretty poppet, that I believes you and that you are not some spectre of the drink. Why would a wench from the future seek the ship of Calico Jack?"

Liz paused. She decided to tell him the truth. "I came here to find my mother."

Rackham reached out to touch a long lock of hair that had blown across her eyes. He tugged at her hair. "If you be real, and ye seems to be solid enough, then ye speaks of witchery."

"I'm a descendent of yours and Anne's," she said, without moving a muscle.

That stopped Rackham in his tracks.

Liz pulled her head away as Rackham dropped his hand from her hair. "By the bones, that's why you're the spittin' likeness o' her! Except for the colour o' yer hair. Hers is not so cacao-like. But why do ye sport your hair so indecently, like a lad? Though I must say, I like it."

Rackham took another slug of rum, his eyes fixed onto hers. Suddenly, he laughed out loud. "Tis a bonny dream I must say. And now it is time for me to wake up."

"It's no dream," Liz said. "I know it sounds incredible. But pictures don't lie."

"Pictures," Rackham repeated. "That is another thing. These pictures. How are they made?"

Liz hesitated.

"Aye, so the phantom has no answer for that. Then answer me this. If yer comes from the future, then yer must know how I die."

Liz was absolutely quiet now. Everything she'd ever learned about paradoxes and time travel came rushing at her. In *Star Trek*, Captain Kirk would never tell someone in the past how they were going to die. Knowledge of their own death would make a person try to prevent it.

Jack Rackham's shadow bounced, long and sharp. He turned his face aside to show a thin, slightly hooked nose. In the dim light, he looked like something out of a movie.

Grimy calico covered him from neck to shin. He wore a yellow calico shirt, bright red cravat, tan britches, a matching red sash of silk around his waist, and a dark blue calico jacket. They didn't call him Calico Jack for nothing. Over all hung a leather baldric that crossed his shoulders and chest with holsters to carry his pistol, dagger, boarding axe and cutlass.

Rackham's thick brown hair fell over his face in ragged curls as he tipped his tricorn hat in a mock salute. He raised his eyes and brushed a thumb along his full lips.

"Take her to the brig," Rackham said to Daniel. "I says no to harbourin' a witch."

Liz made to grab his dagger. Rackham seized her hand. "Make another of yer fast moves, chick, and I will slit the veins of yer arms and use yer blood to warm my rum."

CHAPTER NINE
It's Hard To Believe This Drunken Oaf
Is My Ancestor

Liz was ready to go ballistic. It was nighttime. The dying sun had been replaced by starlight. Daniel dragged her down the deck, while Rackham staggered to his cabin.

"I told you," Daniel whispered, motioning to the device she had hooked around her neck. "You should have kept that thing hidden."

"If I'd left it with you, I wouldn't have it with me now," she whispered back. "You were going to chuck it into the ocean. How dare you!"

Daniel ignored her. He pointed to the brig. It was a hole in the floor planks with a wooden hatch overtop, which he now lifted against its hinge. He told her to lower herself below. She refused. The sounds of footsteps came lumbering toward them. Daniel pushed her and she fell into the hole onto her butt. She was inside a tiny room where she couldn't even stand.

She glared up, expecting to see Daniel, but saw the scarred, one-eyed face of that gorilla, Black Patch, the first mate. He was holding a lighted lamp under his stubbled chin and his head looked like a hideous skull.

Black Patch licked his lips. "A pretty morsel," he said. "But she be the devil aboard this ship. If'n we miss our prize tomorrow, it will be the fault of the she-witch."

Beside the hard-talking pirate mate, Daniel appeared.

Daniel placed a finger to his lips. A quick comeback could be the death of her. Black Patch wasn't exactly Cal Sorensen. The WOMBAT, she could handle. The gorilla was something else.

Black Patch scratched his head and scowled at her. "I be hopin' the captain'll lemme have me way wi' her first. Tis a shame to let a juicy piece like her go without a-tasting her first."

Liz sucked in a breath. Holy crap. Was he a cannibal? What had Daniel brought her to? Then it hammered her on the head like a pile of fish heads—and stank just as bad. The murderous gorilla was talking about rape.

Black Patch rose while Daniel stared at her.

"She be a ripe juicy bitch, me lad," the first mate said. "But don't be gettin' any thoughts o' taking her yerself."

"Aye," Daniel said and watched Black Patch swagger away. He looked at Liz. "Shut up, and not another word if you want to live. If you'd listened to me—"

She cut him off. "I'm tired of listening to you. If that pirate isn't going to eat me, he's going to rape me. And believe me, I think I'd rather be eaten. Let me out of here."

Daniel firmly set his jaw. "Not yet. Wait until they're asleep."

Elizabeth started to her feet. He wasn't that much bigger than her. She could take him. As she shot forward to escape, he slammed a hand to her forehead, knocking her back onto her butt.

"You jerk!" she said, landing at the bottom of the hole.

"Quiet. If Calico Jack hears you, he'll do worse to you than this."

"I should have told the blackguard that he's gonna swing from a gibbet at Gallows Point in a year from now," Liz said.

"Elizabeth. Do not, whatever you do, tell him that." Daniel gave her his two-fingered salute and dropped the hatch, smothering her in darkness.

Liz rose to her haunches and slammed a hand against the hatch. She heard a bolt slide across and a sliver of starlight appeared in the gap between the hatch and the ship's deck.

There wasn't much room to move around in here. This wasn't really a brig. This was part of the hold that had been sectioned off.

Around her she could feel a couple of crates. Were they filled with rum? She peered down to where the sliver of light arrowed onto a label on one of the crates. She sneered. Calico Jack trusted her with his rum? One of the crates was opened and only one bottle of rum was left in it.

Elizabeth scouted around. She tapped lightly on the walls and floor of her prison. No trapdoors anywhere. Below this was the bilge. She could hear the water sloshing. And a chattery squeak. Rats? She took a deep breath. How was she going to get out of here? She was not waiting for Daniel. Look at where trusting him had got her. She was in a box surrounded by rum. And it stank of it and other unmentionables. She swallowed, nervous now. She was thirsty and scared. This really was the eighteenth century and those men up there really were pirates. She remembered reading about their methods of torture. Hanging by the testicles. Thank God, she didn't have any. Slicing off parts of the body. She had plenty of those. This wasn't funny, but there was nothing to do but laugh.

CJ, she thought. Can you hear me?

Arrgh.

Stop it, Elizabeth said. You have to help me.

Mayday, Mayday, Mayday, CJ said.

Elizabeth shook her head. Maybe he wasn't so smart. Maybe she would have to think of another way. If those ruffians treated CJ well, the skank would probably sign their pirate articles and join up with them.

The hold had no portholes. The air inside here was putrid and suffocating. If she breathed too hard, could she use up all of the air and die?

Liz was sure she had been holed up here for hours. There had to be a way out of here.

The only way out was up. The same way she'd got in. Through the hatch.

Liz shoved at the hatch, but it wouldn't give. She was starting to sweat, starting to get claustrophobic. She had never been claustrophobic, but then she had never been trapped in the hold of a ship either. Her heart was racing. She could hardly breathe. Dammit Tess, she thought, how could you do this to me?

It was no longer Daniel she was pissed off at. If her mother wasn't so juvenile, off chasing treasure and adventure, Liz wouldn't be here locked up in this box. If you don't give a rat's ass about me, than what about Lulu? She still believes in you.

There was no point in talking to a mother that wasn't there. But Liz did, might, have a connection to Lulu. Liz pulled the iPocket PC toward her face, stretching its cord from her neck. She knew the pocket computer worked because she'd been able to show Jack Rackham those downloads of the wrecked *Curlew*. How it could possibly work, she didn't know and didn't care. Could it cross time planes and hook her up with her sister in the twenty-first century?

The keyboard glowed in the dark. Liz typed:

> Rebel Goddess from Pirate Hunter
>
> ?

She waited. She got nothing.

Oh, what was she thinking? This couldn't work. How could a signal cross time planes?

She didn't even know why she wanted to connect with Lulu. What could her sister do? She'd only insist on coming to rescue her, and then they'd both be at risk from the pirates and their inhuman tortures. She had to admit, though, right now, she'd give her right arm to see Rebel Goddess and Kung Fu Kid swing through that door. Wang would know what to do.

Liz glanced down. The iPocket was flashing a message!

> Where r u?

Thank you, Rebel Goddess! Liz typed:

> Stuck in Capt J's hold

Lulu replied:

> ?

Liz answered:

> SOS Need map of Caribe

Lu replied:

> OK. Might tk time

Liz typed:

> T+

She had to think positive.

> TMB (text me back)

Lu answered:

> ASAP

Liz let the device fall to her chest. She had figured out how to get out of here. There was a gap about an inch wide between the hatch door and the ceiling to let in air. The hatch was locked by a bolt from the outside. She remembered hearing Daniel slide it across. All she needed to do was find something she could use to shimmy the bolt free.

Once she got out of here, she would find her way across the sloop to a life raft. Did they even have life rafts? No, of course not. But they would probably have a canoe.

She had to make her way to Port Royal and confront Tess. Why was Tess willing to risk her very existence, her kids's existence to stay in this time?

She put a finger through the gap and started to work away at the bolt. It wasn't moving. It had to move. It was the only way.

T+ Think positive, she reminded herself. Maybe when she got out of this hold, she should commandeer Jack Rackham's ship and throw *him* into the brig. It was hard to believe that this drunken oaf was her ancestor.

No, she thought. That wouldn't work. She could maroon the idiot captain. Then—

She sighed. What was the use? She felt like a dehydrated piece of seaweed. Time to rest her brain. She'd figure something out in a minute. She slumped down onto the hard floor planks and shut her eyes. She hadn't meant to, but she crashed, slept like an old mutt for hours, before a crick in her neck woke her up.

A strange sound was coming from above. Liz held her breath. Was it Daniel? She silently sidled to the rum crate and fumbled for the last bottle. She smashed it against the crate, sending the booze fumes into the air, and held the broken end like a sword.

Ok, whoever you are, I'm ready for you. A shadow hovered over the gap in the hatch where Liz could see light from the rising sun.

A flutter of wings landed on top of the hatch and started scratching.

Holy crap, a voice resonated in her head.

Liz laughed. It was CJ.

Where are you? You have to bust me out.

Bust you out, CJ said.

The scratching began again and Liz could see, through the narrow gap, that CJ was drawing the bolt, slowly, away from the hatch.

Arrgh. Bust you out.

Liz kept a grip on the bottle. No telling who she'd meet up top. And she needed a weapon to convince the crew of this ship to take her to Port Royal.

The idea of sailing made her queasy. But she would deal with that when she came to it.

Pirate at twelve o'clock, CJ warned.

Liz braced herself. The bolt slid completely back. Daniel poked his head down.

She raised the jagged bottle to his throat.

"No need for that," Daniel said. "Come. I'll give you a hand up."

Liz let him haul her out, but she didn't let go of the broken bottle. She stood on both feet trying to get the kinks out of her muscles. The heat of the morning sun helped to loosen them. She had spent the entire night in the hold.

Daniel sniffed at her. The fumes of the rum had soaked her clothes. CJ fluttered to Daniel's shoulder and said, "Arrgh."

Liz glared. "Give me back my parrot," she ordered. "Or I'll slit your throat."

Daniel laughed. She had sounded like a true pirate, and at the time, she had meant it. He handed the parrot over and Liz placed CJ onto her shoulder.

"Where is everyone?" Liz asked. "Where's Rackham?"

"Drunk and sleeping like a dog in his quarters. Black Patch is unconscious in his, no help from me. The rest of the crew are ashore, orgying. Don't think they'll trickle back before noon."

Liz scowled. "Why didn't you come to get me sooner. It's already light."

"Rackham was pacing his quarters all night," Daniel said. "You really gave him a scare." He grabbed her arm as she turned to go. "Where the devil do you think you're going?"

He was holding the hand with the broken bottle, crippling her grip so that she couldn't use the weapon against him. She kicked him in the knee to make him let go of her. "I am going to Port Royal."

"No." He bent over to rub his knee but didn't retaliate. If he tried anything, she was ready. He stood up, grinned. "Feisty," he said.

Liz scowled. "Shut up. Or I'll feisty you."

Daniel exhaled. "I think the best plan would be to pay a visit to your great, great, great, great grandmother. Anne Bonney. We have to convince her to escape the governor's clutches and return to Calico Jack."

Liz shook her head. She'd had enough of pirates, male or female. She couldn't imagine the women pirates being any more civil than the men. "I need a boat," she said. She raised the bottle. "I mean it, Daniel."

Daniel leaned against the bulkhead and sighed. "This vessel can't be manned by two people."

"Then get me a smaller one. Or get me a crew. But not that Black Patch creep. I don't want to have to watch my back every second."

"What do you propose to do with the captain?" Daniel asked with obvious amusement.

Liz sneered back. "Leave him on the beach. He's so drunk he won't know what hit him. I can't believe he's a pirate at all. How does he get anything done when he's always drunk?"

Daniel smiled. "Okay. Say we get rid of the captain and the first mate. Then what?"

"We hit the open sea. We go to Port Royal." Liz paused to grab a breath. "Just what part of going to Port Royal don't you understand? I have to find Tess."

Daniel shook his head. "It's no good, Liz. She won't go home. She won't listen to reason. She's willing to risk all on a hunch."

"She'll listen to me," Liz said.

"Why? When she's never listened to you before?" Daniel waited for that bite of reality to sink in before he continued. "After your father died, she quit her job at the University of Victoria. You didn't want her to do that."

Liz clenched her jaw. "How do you know that?"

"She started up a salvage company."

Liz nodded. "And spent all of our money."

"Until she started to find the treasures."

Liz frowned. Daniel had her on the verge of tears.

"Then she got involved with that smarmy Viking," he said.

Cal Sorensen. You mean that smarmy WOMBAT, Liz corrected him in her thoughts.

"How do you know all of this?" Liz demanded. "For the hundredth time, who are you?"

Daniel smiled, shook his head again. "Not yet. One day, you will know me, Elizabeth. But not yet." He turned toward the captain's cabin. He obviously wasn't worried about waking the men on board. "All right then. If you must go to Port Royal, then to Port Royal we will go. Let's go hunt us a treasure hunter."

CHAPTER TEN
Dump The Drunk Captain
And His Vicious First Mate

It was going to be tricky to take this ship. The only sailboats she had ever sailed were catboats and the small sloops at UVic's sailing club. And she hadn't done that since her father was lost at sea. But that wasn't the problem. Calico Jack and Black Patch were big men. Liz did not want to have them on board while she hijacked their boat.

She also had no idea how to get to Port Royal. Daniel knew the way, but she trusted him like she trusted a starving shark.

But first things first. Dump the drunk captain and his vicious first mate. Then figure out a way to overcome her fear of sailing. She stared down at the black skull on her thumbnail. John Latimer had never been afraid of anything, and Elizabeth was her father's daughter.

The audio from the iPocket PC was playing the theme music from *Pirates of the Caribbean*. Liz lifted the miniature computer from around her neck and activated the screen. She opened the message. It was from Rebel Goddess.

> Map of Caribe DL'd

Liz typed:

> THX I'll Tk2ul8r

Lu responded:

> Wait!

Liz typed:

> ?

Lu replied:

> Wang and Cal coming

Liz's mouth dropped open. She was turning into a mouth breather again. She shut her lips. Typed:

2 dangerous

Lu replied:

2 L8

Liz typed:

?

Lu replied:

Found key

Liz choked as she read the rest of Lulu's message. She clamped her lips together. This nightmare was not going to turn her into a permanent mouth breather. She looked up from the iPocket to see Daniel, who had been watching her throughout the entire texting with Lu.

"Lulu just told me something very interesting," she said, giving him an accusatory glare. "She told me that an object from the wreck is the key to travelling through the vortex."

"And you got all of that from a few question marks, letters and numbers?"

Elizabeth scowled. She shook the broken bottle at his chest. "Don't make me threaten you, Daniel. Because I won't hesitate to shove this into your gizzard or brisket, or whatever you pirates call it."

Daniel's head fell comically to his chest in mock defeat. The slimy eel still wasn't taking her seriously. If he didn't stop mocking her, she would choke the life out of his miserable carcass with her bare hands.

She grinned. She was getting almost as good at the pirate talk as CJ.

He caught the moment and grinned back. She immediately changed her expression to a deadly scowl. "Did you think you could keep that a secret from me forever?"

Daniel frowned. "You must tell your sister to keep that knowledge to herself. You have no idea how dangerous that knowledge is. You think you have the key. But do you know how to use it?"

"Well," Elizabeth said, raising the broken bottle to his face. "We'll soon find out. Wang and Cal Sorensen have entered the vortex."

Daniel's face went white.

"Yeah," Liz said. "I think they know how to use it."

"By all that's holy and unholy," Daniel said. "That's not good. They could doom us all."

Liz stared at him sceptically. "Cry me great big cartoon tears," she said. "Don't you think you're exaggerating?"

Daniel looked her square in the eyes. He did have beautiful, sea blue eyes. She glanced away before looking back.

He was still staring at her. "This is not a video game, Elizabeth. Do they have any idea how they're supposed to get back to their own time?"

Liz puckered her brow. "Well, no. But you'll tell us, won't you?" The question was not rhetorical, it was a threat, but Daniel did not look threatened. It seemed nothing she said or did fazed him.

"How do *you* travel through time?" Liz asked. "For that matter, how am I doing it? I don't have an artifact from this time period. Do I?"

Daniel glanced at the dagger earring hanging from her left ear. So she did have an artifact from the eighteenth century. And did he? Did he have its mate?

"You ask too many questions, Elizabeth," Daniel said.

Lulu had finished transferring the marine chart of the West Indies and the Caribbean Sea. Port Royal was in Jamaica, off the southeastern tip of Cuba in the Greater Antilles. Liz could plot her course from this. She wasn't going anywhere, blind, in the hands of a lying, traitorous pirate—who was possibly no pirate at all, but some troublemaker from the future.

Daniel glanced down at the pixilated image on the handheld's screen. "I will take you to Port Royal," he said. "You have my word on it."

"And Wang and Cal. What will happen to them in the vortex?"

Daniel shrugged. "They will be transported into the past. But whose past? That depends."

"Depends on what?" Liz asked.

"It depends on what artifact they took and what date it was made."

"You mean they could end up somewhere else?"

"They could end up on Blackbeard's ship. I told you, Elizabeth, this is not a video game."

Liz's brain was starting to hurt from too much scowling. "There has to be some scientific explanation for how the vortex—" She paused. "For how this time chute works. If we got here, we can get back. I refuse to worry about it."

With that, she spun away from Daniel and started to plan her takeover of Calico Jack's ship.

$$$

It was past dawn. The sun was blazing in the sky. What was that they said about a red sky in the morning?

She and Daniel had spent too much time yakking. They had to get the drunk captain and first mate off the ship. Liz let CJ hop off her shoulder onto a rail, while she grabbed a thin coil of rope from the deck. She still had her broken bottle. Daniel had a cutlass and a dagger. They would tie up the two pirates and leave them on shore, but what would be there to stop them from coming after her when they got loose?

Worry about that later, she decided. She had to get to Port

Royal.

Elizabeth started down the main deck to the captain's cabin. God, she hoped he didn't sleep in the nude.

"Elizabeth," Daniel said.

"I don't have time to argue with you, Daniel. We are taking this ship."

"With what crew?" he demanded.

"I don't know. I'll worry about that later. First, we have to convince Calico Jack to take his shore leave." Liz turned and thrust out an arm. "Give me your dagger."

Daniel handed it to her. She looped the rope over her shoulder, and with the dagger in her teeth and the broken bottle in her hand, she made her way to Jack Rackham's cabin. When she opened the door, his berth was empty. What the hell? she thought.

She swung around and felt a hand grab her throat. It was Rackham. He had leaped out from behind the door. He jerked her face up to his chin so that she could smell his stinking breath.

"So lassie, you mean harm to yer captain, does thee?"

The knife fell out of her mouth and the rope slid off her shoulders. The broken bottle crashed to the floor and shivered into splinters of glass. "You're not my captain," she squeaked.

"Aye. You be an intruder and an imposter. And a liar. So what might ye be up to with the splintered glass and the shiny bit o' steel, eh? The rope? Did ye plan to gag me in my sleep, then do me the Spanish Torture?"

Elizabeth swallowed. No, but that was a good idea.

"I need your ship," she said.

"I should crack ye like a flea," Rackham said, "fer trying to steal my ship. But first I will slice that cankerous tongue o' yours and make you eat it."

Liz wriggled out of his grasp. He was obviously not threatened by her and let her turn to face him. He was dressed in his underwear and he stank of booze and something worse.

"If you would just believe what I told you earlier, it would make this whole thing a lot easier for both of us."

"Ye be nothin' but a saucy, lyin' harlot of a witch. And I will hang ye from the yardarm, if it's the last thing I do."

"You can't do that," Liz complained. "I'm a girl."

"See if I don't," Rackham said.

Liz kicked and punched at him, but he was too strong. Where was Daniel? He was supposed to be right behind her in case anything like this happened.

"Daniel!" she shrieked.

"Aye, Quartermaster," Rackham called, clapping a hand over Liz's mouth. Liz bit him and he shoved her hard into his bunk. "You little claw-cat." He came at her just as Daniel appeared in the doorway, cutlass in hand.

"How did she get loose?" Rackham yelled, hauling her off the bed. "I thought I told ye to toss her into the brig."

"Aye, Captain," Daniel said, looking cool and unruffled. "So you did. She escaped. She's a sly one, she is."

"Swing her from the yardarm," Rackham ordered. "That'll teach the bunter some civility."

"Aye, Cap'n."

Daniel sauntered toward them.

"Wait." Rackham said. He stared suspiciously at Daniel whose belt was missing its dagger.

He glared at the floor where the shiny blade of steel was glinting from the sunlight coming boldly through the windows. It was the weapon that had fallen from Elizabeth's teeth.

He clucked his tongue. "Ye has a thing fer her, don't ye, m'lad?"

"Me?" Daniel shrugged. "Not me, Cap'n."

"Arrgh, I knows that look. I seen it too many times afore. I seen it on me own face when my pearl o' woman-ware, Anne, was aboard ship. Yer not to be trusted." He grabbed his cutlass from where it hung on the wall and turned to the door and bellowed, "Mate, to the captain's quarters!"

Liz didn't wait for Black Patch to appear. She dived for the dagger she'd dropped earlier and raised it against Rackham's own. The captain hammered her with his steel. If ever she had won a fencing bout in a slam dunk, please God, let her win now.

Daniel swung about as the first mate charged through Rackham's cabin door. He rammed a half-foot of steel into Black Patch's shoulder to make him drop his weapon, then he booted him in the gut and watched him curl up like a sowbug in the doorway.

He spun and kicked Rackham in the back of the knees and sent his face to greet the floor. Rackham's dagger skidded aft. Liz ran, leaped over Black Patch, who grabbed at her legs but missed, and raced outside.

CHAPTER ELEVEN
He Doesn't Know A Capstan From An Anchor
Or A Brace From A Sheet

Elizabeth wasted no time in catapulting onto the main deck. CJ squawked from the port rail. "Prisoner escape, prisoner escape! Arrgh!"

Hell's bells, CJ, Liz thought. Whose side are you on anyway?

Elizabeth could hear the clang of steel behind her and footsteps pounding their way through Rackham's quarters.

"Away, aloft girl," Daniel shouted, bursting through the captain's door. Daniel's footwork was leading him backward across the planks of the deck, cutlass flashing against Rackham's blows.

Liz made for the rigging. Everything she'd read about Jack Rackham was true, so he was most certainly a coward, too. Daniel thought so. And he would know. Did Calico Jack really have a fear of heights?

Liz didn't wait to find out. She leaped to the main boom, caught it with her hands and threw her legs over the beam. She shimmied to the mast and clawed her way up the rigging. Daniel was doing hand-to-hand combat with his captain. Daniel was good, but suddenly a chill struck her bones. Daniel was a superb swordsman, but Rackham was better. He slammed his cutlass against Daniel's and the ring of steel shrilled in the air.

She had to help him. But how?

The answer came to her in a blink. Below her, two heads bobbed in the sea. Wang and Cal! And they wouldn't come unprepared. This was pirate country after all.

She swung down from the mast on the halyard, let her boots bounce her off the boom and landed on the quarterdeck. Rackham glanced up from where he jigged with his sword on the deck below. With a vicious two-handed swing, he smashed Daniel's cutlass to the floor and watched man and sword fall. The clatter of steel on the deck planks signalled Daniel's defeat.

Rackham hoisted his sword to inflict the final blow.

"Captain Rackham!" Elizabeth shouted. "I'll be gone before you can deliver that blow. Is it me you want or is it him?"

"You bewitchin' she-snake in ewe's clothing, I'll break you of yer insolent ways. I'll chain ye to the keel. Get below, and sharp!"

Elizabeth saw Daniel roll away safely, but he didn't stand up. Was he hurt? She ran to the rail and looked down. Cal and Wang had disappeared. She could hear Rackham climbing up after her, and she turned to face him.

"I shall strip yer hide and make you wish ye was never born," Rackham said.

He had no idea how close she was to being in that situation— the never-born part that is— if she didn't get to her mother fast.

"Easy, Captain," she said, eyes flitting to his blade. She knew she couldn't kill him. None of them could, not even to save their lives. If Rackham was killed by any one of them, then she and her bloodline would disappear. Besides, she was weaponless.

Rackham waved his cutlass. "Give me one reason to spare yer miserable life, lassie."

Elizabeth said, coolly, "You should spare my life because I am your great, great, great, great granddaughter." Or something like that.

Rackham didn't have a chance to react to that unexpected announcement. He suddenly fell flat on his face. Standing behind him was Wang in his purple wetsuit with his scuba tank held above his head. Without a second's hesitation, Wang had bopped Calico Jack Rackham on the bean.

Liz looked up, stunned. "Oh my God, Wang. You didn't kill

him, did you?"

Wang stuttered, totally confused. "He was threatening to kill you, Liz."

She dropped to her knees and felt the half-dressed pirate's throat. He had a pulse. A strong pulse. It would take more than a bump on the head to kill Calico Jack.

It was just as well that Wang had brained the ruthless pirate. Two seconds more, and she would've had to do something similar to save Daniel's life.

"Help me tie him up and drag him to his bunk," Liz said. "Boy, is he going to be mad when he wakes up."

"Liz." Wang's face was contorted in total puzzlement. "What's going on here?"

"I'll explain after we take care of him. There's another pirate below who is probably bleeding to death, and we have to take care of him, too. Do you know first aid?"

He nodded.

Of course, Wang knew first aid. Elizabeth soaked in the fact that Wang was here and that she wasn't alone. He could do anything. Liz tied Rackham hand and foot with some strong hemp rope, then with Wang's help, they lowered him down the companionway to the main deck. Wang did the rest. He dragged Rackham to his cabin and promised to tend to Black Patch if he wasn't dead. Liz warned him to watch his backside because the pirates were cutthroats.

When Liz returned to the quarterdeck, Cal, cutlass in his hand, stood over Daniel who was trying to crawl to his feet.

"Stay where you are," Cal threatened what he rightly thought was another infernal pirate.

Cal's hand was shaking and his normally puffed-out chest was practically concave. But he brandished the cutlass over Daniel's throat nonetheless.

Daniel knelt complacently, neither scared nor annoyed. Liz smiled at him, then at Cal. "He's okay . . . I think."

She wasn't one hundred percent sure that she could trust Daniel any more than she thought she could trust Cal, but she had to go with her gut instinct because she needed Daniel's help to get this ship underway.

She turned back to Daniel. "Are you hurt?"

Daniel felt his ribs, then his sword arm. He grinned and rubbed his wrist. "I'll live."

"Good," Liz said. She returned her attention to Cal who was standing rigid, holding the sword like it burned, still suspicious of Daniel.

Liz pointed to the cutlass in Cal's hand. "Do you know how to use that?"

Cal, who was no less stunned than Wang after surfacing from the vortex to be thrown headfirst into the midst of a pirate brawl, opened his mouth to protest, then shook his head.

"You'd better give it to me then," Liz said. She took the sword, which clearly belonged to Daniel, and shoved it into the sash at her hip. She stuck out a hand to haul Daniel to his feet.

"WOMBAT," CJ said.

Cal attacked the parrot, disgusted. "You still alive? I thought those ruffians would have boiled you for breakfast."

Liz didn't bother to stop the bickering between Cal and CJ. The wind was picking up. She tucked her fluttering hair down the back of her shirt and faced Daniel.

"We have our crew," she said, meaning himself, Wang and Cal. "You are now officially first mate, quartermaster and helmsman. I, Elizabeth Latimer, am your new captain."

$$$

The sun was fully up. Rackham's crew hadn't returned from their partying, and even if they did show up, they would probably be too hungover to be of any use in sailing this ship. Besides, she hadn't worked out her persuasion tactics yet. Would the promise of more rum convince an already blotto crew to help her?

"Make ready," she said to Daniel. "Prepare to weigh anchor." She turned from the quartermaster(slash)first mate(slash)helmsman and shouted from the quarterdeck. "All hands on deck!"

"We are on deck," Cal said, glancing at Daniel and rolling his eyes.

"But Wang's not. Go get him. Then prepare to make sail. We've got to get this ship under way."

Cal stood, unmoving, legs braced apart, shaking his head. His initial scary encounter with the pirates now past, he was returning to his puffed-up, full-of-hot-air, nostril-flaring self.

"Just who do you think you are?" Cal demanded.

Elizabeth crossed her arms over her chest and glared. "Do you know how to sail an eighteenth century single-masted sloop, Cal?"

"Do you?" he asked.

No. She knew how to sail a catboat, not a tall ship. But she wasn't about to let him know that. John Latimer had taught her how to sail, and by God, she was going to sail.

She grit her teeth, planted her hands on her hips, and glared challengingly up at the tall mast and awesome sails. Cal went below to fetch Wang. The sloop had a mainsail, a main top sail, a fore stay sail, a jib and a flying jib.

Okay, she could do this. First, swallow the queasiness that was threatening to swamp her, and don't barf on Daniel's feet. That would not be a very dignified thing for the new captain of the *Curlew* to do. She had to admit, though, she was terrified. Memories of her father's radio calls for help assailed her. The coast guard had not made it in time and his boat was ripped apart.

Cal appeared on the main deck with Wang, which put a halt to her reminiscences. The two young men had removed their wetsuits and hidden them in Daniel's berth. Dressed in borrowed pirate wear, they glanced up as she yelled from the quarterdeck.

"How are the pirates? Are they going to live?"

Wang nodded and made his way up the companionway with Cal close behind to where Liz stood near the helm with Daniel.

Wang gave Daniel a suspicious look as he approached them, then flashed a smile at Liz. "Rackham is going to have one bugger of a headache when he wakes up," Wang said.

Rackham was also going to be completely pissed off at her, Liz thought.

"And Black Patch?" she asked.

"Is that his name?" Wang shrugged. "He passed out from loss of blood, but I managed to tie a tourniquet around his shoulder. He should live, but he's going to need a doctor."

Liz nodded. The big gorilla would have to wait until they reached Port Royal.

"You want him to live?" Cal asked.

"You never know when we'll need another hand," Liz said.

"More importantly," Daniel cut in, "you don't want to change anything that might alter the course of the future. There's the matter of creating a paradox. Black Patch is not supposed to die yet. He's hanged along with Rackham a year from now."

"So why did you stab him?" Wang asked. "Assuming it was *you* who stabbed him."

"I had no choice," Daniel said, and left it at that.

Liz shuddered. These pirates were cutthroats. The image of her ancestor hanging from the gallows was harsh. But Daniel was right. If they created a paradox by killing Black Patch before he was supposed to die, what other events in history would change?

Cal stared from Daniel to Liz. The paradox thing must have jarred him. Even Liz couldn't wrap her brain around that. Cal's brow furrowed, but he didn't speak a word.

Wang shrugged, looked at Liz and said, "What if the pirates wake up?"

"Like I said," she repeated, "I might need extra hands." Though she hadn't a clue how she'd control the rogues if she *did* need them. Especially Black Patch. He wanted to eat her and worse. Wang scratched his brush cut, nodded and looked overhead at the ominous sails.

"So live they will," Daniel said. "I have some skill with a needle and thread."

Oh do you? Elizabeth thought. What did Daniel do in *his* world? His futuristic universe. Was he some kind of sword-wielding, blinking-in-and-out, vanishing pirate doctor?

Liz squashed her sarcastic thoughts. "Good," she said. "But right now I need all hands. Prepare for . . ." She'd almost said 'takeoff.' The hot Bahamian sun and these unreasonable pirate ruffians were screwing up her usually immaculate vocabulary. What was it that pirates said? "Prepare to man canvas!" she shouted. Yeah, that was it. "There's a good stiff breeze. Clap on sail! We make for Port Royal!"

That sounded good. She took a deep breath and watched Wang race off the quarterdeck, down the companionway to the deck below, then up the mast to the halyards to drop sail from the mainyard. He shouted to Cal to man the braces, but the blonde WOMBAT stood stiff on the quarterdeck until Liz kicked him in the butt. "I want some movement!" she yelled, before realizing that Cal was very likely to misinterpret that command.

"Move yourself," he said.

Liz sighed. "Cal," she wheedled, trying very hard to be calm. "Did you or did you not come with Wang to save me and my mother?"

Cal glared at her. What was his problem? He couldn't captain this boat even though he was the captain of *Tess's Revenge*. He didn't know a capstan from an anchor or a brace from a sheet. He had never sailed a sailboat in his life.

"Cal," she said, trying to cajole him into action. "I know you can handle a boat. You're a terrific sailor or my mother wouldn't have partnered with you. But you have to admit you've never piloted anything without a motor. I know sailboats. My dad was a professional racer. He taught me a lot."

Cal stared at her, huffed and strode across the quarterdeck and down the companionway to join Wang below. He would have to learn to man the sails and he would have to learn fast.

It wasn't as easy as Liz had hoped. Three hands handling the sheets wasn't quite enough, and they found themselves racing from one end of the sloop to the other, trying to keep abreast of the wind.

Wang was a treasure. He raced up the rigging like he was made for it. He knew how to handle a ship.

Liz squinted against the morning sun to the horizon. A ship appeared in the distance. She had no binoculars and had to wait until it grew closer. How was she going to pass this ship unseen?

"Pirate at three o'clock," CJ said.

The ship was hoisting a black flag. Oh crap, Liz thought. That was the last thing she needed. The ship was getting closer. It had changed tack and was barrelling down on them.

"Captain," Daniel shouted from the helm. "Orders?"

Liz couldn't decide if he was mocking her. She stared at the pirate flag but didn't recognize it from this distance. "Telescope!" Liz hollered.

Daniel passed her the telescope, and she shut one eye to view the pirate ship. It was a two-masted ketch with a mainmast, a mizenmast and several triangular sails on a long bowsprit. Great, Liz thought. That's all she needed. She knew from her Archaeology of Piracy class that ketches were used as bomb vessels to take down fortresses.

"Liz," Daniel shouted. "We need a heading."

The ketch's crew was hoisting a square sail on the foremast to make the most of a tail wind. She would be down on them in a matter of minutes.

"Hard to larboard," she shouted below to her crew.

The sloop keeled to the left. "I said larboard," Elizabeth yelled. "Straighten those sails or we'll capsize!"

"Left *is* larboard," Daniel said, correcting the helm.

"I thought larboard was starboard in pirate talk," Liz said.

"You're going to have to brush up on your pirate talk. Larboard is port. Starboard is starboard."

"Stop making fun of me," Liz said. "You're going to sink us!"

"Only taking orders, captain," Daniel answered.

How could he be such a jerk right now? Any minute they were going to be boarded or broadsided by a gang of ruthless ruffians, who would do worse to her than try to eat her.

"All right, Daniel," she said. "I get it. I have no idea what I'm doing. But until we find Tess, I am the captain of this ship. Hoist colours!" she said.

Jack Rackham's skull and crossed sabres went shooting up the mast. Hopefully, the pirates would recognize Calico Jack as part of the brotherhood and let them go on their way.

"Arrgh," CJ said. "Black flag, black flag."

The swift ketch was almost on them. Liz raised the telescope to the colours flying from the other ship's mast.

"Oh-oh," Daniel said.

Liz lowered the telescope. "What do you mean 'oh-oh?'"

"See those colours? That's the flag of Captain Charles Vane."

This was not good. Jack Rackham was the former quartermaster of Charles Vane. In November 1718, Rackham had challenged his captain's decision to let a French frigate go without plundering it in the Windward Passage. The crew tossed out Vane as a coward and made Calico Jack their new captain. Under the orders of Captain Jack Rackham, the mutinous crew had stolen Vane's ship.

The return of the deposed pirate could mean nothing but trouble.

"Nix that first order! Lower the flag," Liz shouted. "Hide the Jolly Roger!"

"Too late," Daniel said. He suddenly became serious. "If we don't do something fast, they're going to board us."

"Strike sail!" Liz shouted.

Daniel spun from the helm to face her. "You want us to surrender?"

"No, no," Liz wailed. She fell silent. Why was he making this so hard for her? They were headed straight for the enemy's ship and he was cracking jokes.

"The captain's hailing us," Daniel said. "He wishes to parley with our fearless leader."

CHAPTER TWELVE
Heave To Or I Will Blast You A Broadside!

Liz stared at the approaching ship through the telescope. He wished to parley with their fearless leader? That would be her—though the *Curlew*'s fearless leader was really Jack Rackham—and that was whom Captain Charles Vane expected to answer his hail.

If only she could read Vane's mind as well as she could read the name of his ship. Across the bow, *Lark* was lettered in bold, black paint. She wondered whom Captain Vane had stolen the ketch from. What did he want with Jack Rackham? Liz slowly handed the telescope back to Daniel who replaced it under the helm. The situation sucked. A sticky situation indeed. Captain Vane would be pissed off to say the least.

He and Rackham were not exactly bros. After Rackham and his crew had stolen the *Curlew*, they had set Vane and a small party of his followers in a canoe, which was capsized by a tornado in the Bay of Honduras. All hands were lost except for Vane. He was washed ashore onto a small uninhabited island where he lived on nothing but turtles and seaweed until he was rescued by a passing brigantine.

What did he intend to do with his treacherous ex-quartermaster? Peel his skin like a mango? Let out his evil soul by the incision of steel? Or merely dangle him from the foreyard by his thumbs?

Liz dismissed the outrageous threats. Talk about drama queens. When it came to melodrama, pirates were the pickle on the burger. And she was starting to think exactly like them.

"Ahoy!" Captain Vane shouted from the *Lark*. "Heave to. Or I will blast you a broadside."

"Ho, there," Daniel replied. "No need for threats. We be right friendly now, we are."

"Where is yer captain, my old friend Calico Jack?" Vane spoke Rackham's name with as much affection as he would've given to a barracuda.

"Oh, crap," CJ said.

Even CJ knew they were in big trouble. Daniel glanced at Liz, waiting for orders. She had to think fast. Mutiny, marooning. Yeah, they could hardly expect help from the enemy of Calico Jack.

Daniel darted his eyeballs at her, then at Vane. She shot a look back. Don't rush me. CJ kept mumbling in her mind, Oh crap. I know, Liz thought. But crap wasn't going to help. First of all, Vane would question her presence aboard Rackham's or—should she say—Vane's former ship. Did he know about Anne Bonny or Mary Read, Rackham's female crew? Could she pretend to be one of them? At least, then, he would know she was a pirate to be reckoned with.

"Stand by to be boarded," Vane hollered.

"Stand by to be boarded," CJ said.

Grappling hooks were tossed to the rail of Rackham's sloop. Vane and two of his pirate company crawled aboard. Vane sent his men to the capstan to drop the *Curlew*'s anchor.

Liz studied the scruffy pirate captain and his burly crew. Was that all he had? Liz wondered. Two men? Maybe things weren't so desperate after all. Liz removed the iPocket from around her neck and tucked it into the sash at her waist. It wouldn't be wise to titillate the captain's curiosity with this piece of twenty-first century technology.

Daniel climbed down the companionway from the quarterdeck and Liz followed.

"Captain Charles Vane at your service," Vane said with a mock salute. He bowed low when he saw that Liz was a girl. "And just who might this dainty bit be?" he asked Daniel. "For that matter, who might you be? You was not aboard the *Curlew* when I was captain."

"I give you good day, sir," Daniel said politely. "I be Daniel Corker, quartermaster of this fine vessel." He bowed in turn. "And this fair piece—" He turned to Liz. "She is Elizabeth Latimer of New Providence."

"I sees. She is yer woman." Vane grinned. "And a fine doxy she is. But I have no quarrel with thee or thine. I want to see the master of this ship. Where is that traitorous, mutinying, ship-stealing snake, Jack Rackham. I want to roast him alive."

Liz stepped forward. "Calico Jack is in his quarters and indisposed." She smiled. "Too much rum, if you get my meaning."

He got her meaning all right. He spat and snorted. "Serves the slime-swilling scupperlout right. I shall haul him out of his sweet dreams and give him a nightmare to think about."

Liz didn't want to think what that meant. All she knew was that she had to get to Port Royal and find Tess. Was surrendering the drunken buffoon such a bad idea? Rackham was no use to her unconscious, and it was unlikely Captain Vane would submit his old mate to some horrific bone-breaking torture if he couldn't feel it.

She wet her lips, ready to bargain. Daniel caught her intent and shook his head. She knew what he was thinking. If she gave up Rackham and Vane killed him, it might change the course of the future. Well, screw the future. There would be no future if she wasn't in it.

Vane noticed the silent exchange between them. He stared hard at Liz, then a gleam lit his eyes. He swung toward Daniel, shot a sideways glance at Wang and Cal, then spoke directly to Liz. "I too have a doxy aboard me ship." His false, gracious demeanor turned ugly. "She has a few years on ye, but she be a right flutterin' dove all the same."

All of Liz's senses came to attention. What did he mean? He had a woman aboard his ship?

"She be the spittin' likeness o' you, gal." he said, speaking directly to Liz again. "P'raps ye knows her?"

Liz froze. Was it Tess? Her mother was no doxy. She was forty years old. A young woman she wasn't. But in the twenty-first century, forty was the new thirty, and Tess looked thirty if she looked a day.

These pirates, most of them were in their twenties, but, where she came from, Vane's sea-weathered face and sinewy sun-browned arms could pass for fifty. This brought her to Daniel. How old was he exactly? She no longer thought that he was in his late teens.

"Well, girl?" Vane asked. "What say you?"

"I want to see this woman you have on your ship," Liz said.

"Oh, does ye, me little flutterin' dove. And what gets I in the bargain?"

You get this in your eye, Liz thought, fingering her sword grip. She glanced at Daniel.

"I needs me a couple o' strong men to join my company. As ye can see," Vane said. "I is a might bit shorthanded these days, thanks to yer captain."

"Is that your entire crew?" Liz asked, waving her hands at his two pirate mates.

Vane squinted at her. "Ye talks a might much for a lass," he said. He gestured at Daniel. "Does yer woman always do the speakin' on yer behalf?"

Daniel looked nervous. For the first time, Liz wondered if he was worried. If she screwed this up, she could get them all killed.

Vane glanced at Wang who had come down from the rigging to stand beside her. Then Vane looked up at Cal who had backed himself up the companionway to the helm, where he was safely out of reach of the pirates. "They looks like two strong lads. What say ye to a trade?" Vane asked Daniel. "I gives yer the doxy fer the Oriental and the Swede."

"These men are not for sale," Liz said before Daniel could answer.

"Aye, but the doxy is," Vane replied. "So what do ye say, me little flutterin' dove? Does thee wish to see yer mama?"

If he called her a fluttering dove one more time, she'd brain him. Every muscle in Liz's body tensed. How could Vane know that his prisoner was Liz's mother? How could Liz be sure?

"What is your woman prisoner's name?" Liz demanded.

Vane squinted maliciously and his expression grew threatening. "Her name? Her name be Rackham, same's yer treasonous captain. I wants yer shiverin' coward of a captain and I wants them men." He glared at Wang, then up again at Cal. "Do we have a trade?"

Daniel placed his hand on his dagger grip. Every muscle in Wang's body was poised to spring. Cal was the only one who stood on the quarterdeck with his mouth hanging open in stunned disbelief, like a dog.

"We do not accept those terms," Liz said.

"Do you know what ye are sayin'?" the pirate asked.

Liz drew the cutlass from the makeshift leather sheath belted about her waist. "I do."

Vane guffawed. It was three against three if she didn't count Cal. But in a pinch, maybe Cal would have a brainstorm and think to drop his scuba tank on Captain Vane's head.

The three pirates from the *Lark* charged. CJ squawked and fluttered away. Daniel sprang forward, dagger swinging. Wang leaped into the air and kicked the first pirate that approached him, knocking the man's cutlass out of his reach.

Wang retrieved the cutlass and fought the pirate who now flashed a dagger. You would think he had the lead in a Jackie Chan movie. Cal climbed behind the quarterdeck to safety. Vane advanced on Liz, and she brought everything she'd ever learned about fencing into fierce play.

"You fight well—for a gal," Vane said. "But not well enough."

He slashed at her sword and she repelled him. She was learning fast. Her most recent bout with Rackham had pressed home that pirates fought dirty.

Elizabeth glared. She grit her teeth. "Come any closer," she warned Vane, "and I will slice you in half and show you the colour of your insides."

Vane chortled. He slammed his sword against hers and she felt her entire body reverberate with the force. Vane pressed her up against the ship's rail and showed her his rotting teeth. Did all pirate captains have bad breath?

"You commit suicide, poppet," Vane warned. "Give the word. Surrender this vessel and crew, and I will let you keep yer pretty face."

Liz knew she couldn't win by brute force. He had his cutlass flattened against her chest, forcing the point of her own sword to lean against her throat.

Liz was desperate. She didn't want to die like this. She resorted to the only thing this pirate might understand.

"I'm only a girl," she squeaked. "It's no honour to kill a helpless girl."

Vane narrowed his wicked brown eyes until he almost had a uni-brow. He wet his lips with the tip of a slimy red tongue. "Who said I wanted to kill you? I might cut off those shell-like ears, put your lights out. Or take that catty tongue o' yours and put it where it can do no harm. But kill ye? Nay. I have a better use fer you in me bunk."

Again. Rather be eaten, Liz thought. She swallowed. This was serious. How was she going to get out of this?

"Rather be eaten!" CJ squawked. The parrot fluttered into Vane's face and tried to claw his eyes. Vane grabbed Liz's throat to hold her in place and swung his cutlass at the bird, almost knifing CJ in half.

"CJ, No!" Liz shouted.

The parrot dodged Vane's second swing, flew into the air and landed on the rail.

"Liz!" Wang shouted, charging toward her. Wang had successfully incapacitated his pirate and now he was coming to rescue her.

Liz shoved Vane off her as he turned to ward off Wang's attack. Wang leaped into the air, feet in Kung fu motion only to have Vane's dagger sling into his chest.

"Wang!" Liz screamed.

All fighting stopped. Daniel turned from where he had disarmed his opponent. The rogue was face down on the deck with Daniel's foot on his head. The pirate Wang had overwhelmed lay slumped against the port bulwark clutching his crotch.

Vane stood over Wang, who lay gasping on the deck planks as Elizabeth wailed and dropped to her knees. "You murderous, cutthroat pig!" Liz yelled at Vane. "You've killed him!"

"To yer feet, girl," Vane said, callously kicking Wang's body. "This be your last chance. Unless you all want to die."

CHAPTER THIRTEEN
All You Have To Say To Me
Is Go Hunt Down A Pirate?

Heart pounding, Liz rose. Vane stared from her to Daniel. He glanced at Wang who wasn't bleeding as much as Liz expected. The dagger was still in his chest, lodged in the breastbone. As long as the dagger remained in place, not much blood escaped.

"Tis a pity," Vane said. "He looked a good strong lad—and a man to be trusted, seein' how he came to yer aid."

"He was," Liz said. "Which is more than could be said for you."

Vane turned on her viciously. "You try eating turtle and sea muck for a month, with naught but yer boots fer pudding, and see how long you keeps yer pretty disposition."

"Then it's really Rackham that you want," Liz said.

"Aye. If you had handed the swine over at the very first, this fine laddie would still be alive and kicking."

Liz scowled. She was ready to implode. "All right, it's a deal. But I want your woman prisoner first."

"You is in no position to be bargaining, gal," Vane said. "Belay that last offer. I changed my mind. I wants it all—the ship, her crew, the woman. And Calico Jack." He glanced at CJ who was still perched on the rail. "And I'm takin' this fine-feathered, wise-crackin' sea lawyer, too."

"No," Liz said. "You can't have my parrot."

Vane twisted his ugly head to look back at the *Lark*. "Ye sees them starboard guns there?"

Liz looked to where the pirate captain was pointing. Four heavy, iron cannon faced the *Curlew* from the ship's right side.

"I has men behind them guns."

Liz didn't know if he was bluffing. If he had men, why would he need hers? But she couldn't take any chances. Vane's injured crewmen were rising and they were flaming mad.

"Tell ye what, gal," Vane said. "Just to shows ye I am no louse, I will let you go. You take the canoe and goes wherever ye likes. P'raps there be a nice deserted island where ye kin sample the local turtle and sea muck." He roared with laughter. "Tis a far better fate than what lies ahead fer yer captain."

Liz glanced around for the canoe. It should have been strapped to the hull of the ship, but it was gone. She looked at the *Lark*, then beyond it, and saw a small boat rowing away with two figures inside.

Daniel caught her stare and frowned. Vane was watching them both. Out of the upper corner of her eye she saw that Cal was no longer cringing behind the helm. The skank. The jellyfish. Cal had abandoned them and taken the canoe.

But wait. There were two persons in the canoe. While she, Wang and Daniel were fending off pirates, had Cal managed to escape to the *Lark*, find Tess and rescue her?

She mustn't give Cal away.

Gotta get off this boat, Liz thought. Gotta get to Tess. Miserably, Liz glanced at Wang. Oh, my God, what had she done? It was all her fault. How was she going to live with this, explain his death to his grandparents?

It could all be moot if she didn't do something fast. She had nothing at stake here now. Daniel could go to hell. He had brought her to purgatory and gotten Wang killed.

Elizabeth stared at the black skull on her red thumbnail. The colour was beginning to chip despite the four coats of clear varnish she had applied. The skull was half-eaten away.

What would John Latimer do?

Well, he wouldn't sit around on his butt feeling sorry for himself. He would rescue his wife.

Liz must rescue her mother.

"What say you, wench?" Vane asked. "Shall I set you free?"

Liz was silent.

Vane snorted in contempt. "There's a reason women are taboo 'board ship. They's bad luck!" He spun on his giant booted heel and looked to the deck overhead. "Where be the big Swede?"

"Hiding," Liz said, to give Cal more time to escape. "He's a craven coward. I don't know that he'd be much use to you."

"Find him!" Vane ordered his men. "And you," he said to Daniel. "Remove this bloomin' carcass afore it rots. Heave him into the sea and let him join his maker and the bones of Davy Jones's locker." Vane plucked his dagger out of Wang's chest.

Liz looked down at Wang in horror.

Daniel hesitated. Vane scowled and hoisted his cutlass. "Obey or feel the bite of my steel."

Daniel hauled Wang's body to the rail. He hoisted him onto his shoulder and dropped him over the side.

Vane grinned and went aft to find Rackham. Elizabeth could not draw her eyes away from the body that was drifting away from the ship. Daniel grabbed her by the arm and shook her. Then he raced to the quarterdeck and returned with the scuba tank that Wang had used to bean Rackham on the head. She would have to swim. She would have to leave CJ and Daniel. The other tanks were in Daniel's berth. But he promised the first chance he got, he would come after her.

Liz watched the speck of the canoe on the horizon.

"They make for Port Royal," Daniel said. "It's not far. You can see it in the distance." He pointed to a thin strip of land. "It's within swimming distance. You can make it."

She had to make it. The future depended on it. Wang's existence depended on it. She strapped the scuba tank over her pirate clothes, tied her boots to her waist and lowered herself quietly into the sea. Wang's body was still afloat nearby. She was tempted to stop and drag him with her, but she knew that would only slow her down. The only way to restore Wang's life was to change everything back to the way it was—before Tess took Jack Rackham's love letter into the past.

Liz swam as though she were in an Olympic competition. She looked back once, saw Daniel staring at Wang's body as it drifted on the current. Where at first Elizabeth had felt like she was swimming in a dream, now she knew she was submerged in a nightmare.

Twenty kilometres as the crow flies, she thought. I can swim that.

$$$

Liz reached shore. She hid her scuba tank between some large rocks beside the pier. She looked up to see the bustling harbour of Port Royal.

She emptied her boots of seawater and tugged them on, listening to them squelch. She plastered back her dripping hair and plucked at the wet shirt that was clinging to her chest. Winning a wet T-shirt contest now was the last thing she needed. She had to pass for a boy.

Where was Cal's canoe? She walked onto the pier, ignoring the rough looks she was getting from the seamen working on the dock.

The Royal Navy used the town as a base, and she passed several armed officers in uniform. Their presence was everywhere. Port Royal was not the haunt and lair of pirates as it was in the late 1600s. After an earthquake devastated the island, the town was rebuilt, and pirates and prostitutes were not welcomed. The governor commissioned pirate hunters to seize and apprehend all piratical vessels and crews. Port Royal was no longer a notorious pirate haven as she had seen it in the movies, but a place where pirates were hanged. Liz had to be careful.

Tess and Cal were here. She knew they were. There was no place else they could have gone. Port Royal was the closest land mass to where the *Curlew* was anchored.

What should she do when she found them? With Cal's help she should be able to convince Tess to come home. But just how were they supposed to go home? That was the one thing that Daniel had failed to tell her.

Liz dropped low beside a stack of oak kegs and logwood. She still had Lu's iPocket PC. She could text her sister and find out if their cousin Stevie had made any progress on investigating the time chute.

Liz activated the miniature device. She typed:

SOS. Need info

Lu responded almost immediately:

Where u been?

Liz answered:

Fighting pirates. Stevie? How get home?

A few seconds passed. Oh no, Liz thought. What happened? Then she got a reply. This time it was from Stevie. Thank goodness Stevie had joined Lu in Nassau.

A video appeared on her screen. Superimposed over a map of the Caribbean, the gaping vortex whirled just off the coast of New Providence.

Stevie texted:

7 days

That meant Liz had seven days before the vortex closed. Seven days to get Tess back to New Providence. Liz texted:

THX

Stevie replied:

B careful

Darned right, she'd be careful. Liz shut off the handheld and looked up. She couldn't believe her eyes. Across the street were

Cal and Tess, and they were entering a dress shop.

How was she going to do this? She hadn't seen her mother in months. She was so angry at Tess for abandoning her and Lulu, and for creating this paradox, that she had to bite her lip and clench her fists before she could bring herself to face her.

Liz tucked the iPocket into her sash. She marched across the street and yanked open the dress shop door. Her mother was behind a Chinese painted screen, being fitted for a new gown. Liz could hear her voice.

"Tess!" Elizabeth shouted. She hadn't meant to shout, but it came out that way.

Tess turned her head and saw Liz over the top of the Chinese screen. Cal, who was sitting on an armchair waiting like an indulgent husband, turned also. He looked like he knew exactly what he was doing, like he had been here before.

Liz narrowed her brows. "What are you two doing?" she demanded.

The dress shop owner came rushing out from a back room, nervously wringing her hands, wondering what this drowned rat of a street imp was doing in her fancy store.

"It's all right, Emma," Tess said. "I'll take care of this."

Emma. *Emma?* Liz thought. Tess knew these people by name? How long had Tess been here? Long enough to get to know the dress shop lady, obviously.

Elizabeth couldn't believe how calm her mother was behaving. You would think she hadn't just seen her daughter drop into an eighteenth century dressmaker's, dripping wet, in an outrageous pirate costume. Good thing she had left Daniel his cutlass.

Tess flung a lightweight cape over her layers of frilly petticoats. She drew Liz by the arm and they stepped outside. Cal followed.

Liz turned on Cal, making him stumble backward on the roadside. "You knew she was here all the time. Damn you. You knew!"

Tess squeezed Liz's arm. Tess was a little shorter than her daughter. She had sun-kissed brown hair, just like Liz's, and wide almond-shaped eyes. With the ringlets she currently sported, she really could pass for thirty.

Liz shook Tess's hand off of her arm. She took a deep breath. She was right on the edge, ready to go ballistic, if her mother didn't start explaining PDQ.

Tess indicated they go around the corner of the building into an alley where they wouldn't draw so much attention. At this moment, Liz could care less. Tess was jeopardizing the future, Liz's future and the futures of all their relatives. And then, there was Wang. Wang wouldn't be dead if it wasn't for Tess.

"You killed him," Elizabeth said.

Tess's mouth dropped open. "Killed who?"

Cal grabbed Liz by the wrist. She flung him off. "Don't touch me, you weak-kneed bilge rat, you hunk of putrid dog leavings. You knew where she was and you didn't tell me."

"Elizabeth," Tess said. "Cal is not to blame."

Liz was shaking. "Then who is?"

Tess waited for Liz's breathing to stabilize. She stroked Liz's arm. For the first time in her life, Liz was repulsed by her mother's touch.

"You're upset, Liz," Tess said. "And with good reason. But it was too dangerous to tell you where I was, and this was too important."

Liz scowled. "Too important than me? Too important than Lulu?"

"You don't understand," Tess said.

"Then explain. Make me understand. Make me understand that Wang didn't die for nothing."

Tess's face went white. She looked like her heart had stopped.

"What do you mean?"

"I mean exactly what I said. Wang is dead. Tell her, Cal. Or did you jump ship before we got to that part?"

Cal's face was turning purple. Liz shook her head in disgust and swung on her mother. "Your student, Jerrit Wang. The one who devoted years to your research was murdered by Captain Charles Vane. A pirate, Tess. A real honest to God, frickin' pirate!"

"Don't shout," Tess said. "You'll bring a crowd down on us."

Liz exhaled. Tess was so stubborn, thick sometimes. Didn't she get it? A boy had died because of her and she was the only one who could fix it.

"We have to find a boat and get back to New Providence. The vortex closes in seven days. If you bring that stupid glassed-in letter back to our time, you can fix it. And maybe Wang will still be alive."

"Is that how you think it works?" Tess asked.

Liz made crazy eyes at her mother. "Well, isn't?"

"Not exactly."

Tess touched Liz's cheek and she pulled away. She was waiting for her mother to tell her how to fix it. "Do you have the letter?" Liz asked.

Tess nodded. It was locked in its bottle in her satchel, tied to her waist.

Liz extended a hand for it, but Tess shook her head. "I can't give it to you," Tess said. "It's the key to my travelling between times."

Liz's jaw nearly fell to her knees. Tess couldn't mean it. After everything Liz had gone through, Tess was going to keep the letter?

"Good grief, Tess. Do you know what you're saying?" Liz demanded. "Do you know what's happened to me since I got here? I've been threatened with rape, with being eaten, with being cleaved in two and other horrible, unspeakable things. I've almost killed people. And you're going to stay here?"

Tess glanced at Cal, motioned for him to leave them alone. He left them in the alley and leaned against the stone wall of the dressmaker's shop to wait for Tess.

Tess looked sincerely into Liz's eyes. But before she said a word, Liz asked her, "Do you realize that if you stay here with that bottled letter and Jack Rackham and Anne Bonny don't get back together, then I, *you*, Lulu and Stevie will cease to exist?"

Tess shut her eyes, opened them slowly. "That's a risk I'm willing to take. Rackham and Bonny are alive. That means they have every chance of getting together."

"He's hanged right here in Port Royal a year from now. You know that. What if they don't get together before that happens?"

"Then make it happen, Liz. That's why you're here."

"No." Liz turned away from her mother for a second, then spun back. "I'm here to bring you home."

"I can't go home, Liz. Not yet. Not while there's still a chance."

"A chance at what?"

"A chance at finding your father," Cal said, coming down the alley toward them.

"What?" Liz jerked her eyes away from Cal and faced her mother. "John is dead."

"We don't know that," Tess said. "He was lost in the storm. His body was never found. There were reports, even back then, of a mysterious oceanographic anomaly. I think he got sucked into the time chute, the same as we did. I think he's somewhere in the pirate past."

Liz slumped against a nearby stone building. If John was somewhere in the piratical past, then that meant he must have had an artifact. *Did* he have one? Her dad was a pirate fanatic, worse than Tess. Was he carrying a charm or something with him that day for good luck?

Tess's smile was imploring. "So you see, Elizabeth, I can't go home. Not yet. Not until I find him."

Liz stayed silent. Liz pushed herself upright from the stone wall. She wanted to believe it, but she couldn't. It was four years. Four years since they had seen him alive. If John Latimer was here, somewhere in the past, how would Tess ever find him?

"It's so thin," Liz said, when she finally spoke. "Such fragile hope. It's as fragile as that glass bottle, as that glass letter that you're hiding in your clothes. It will shatter the minute you drop it."

"I won't drop it," Tess said. "As long as there is hope, I can't. Please try to understand, Liz. I believe he's still alive. Just like you believed that I was. Isn't that why you came? I knew you would, Liz."

Tess slanted her gaze toward the far end of the alley. Tess was going to go. Her mother was going to leave her. Liz stared at her mother in disbelief.

"That is so lame," Liz said viciously.

Tess turned around. "Do you think this choice was easy for me?" Her eyes welled with tears. She dropped her gaze, then raised her lids. "But look at you. You're a pirate hunter. And you can fence as well as a man. And Lulu? Lu doesn't need me anymore. She knows it and so do you. When I find your father, we'll be back and then we'll be a family again."

"Do you really think John wants you to do this?" Liz asked.

"Do you?"

Elizabeth squeezed her eyes shut. Yes. Her mother was right. John Latimer and Tess Rackham had not raised lame children. Then why, at this moment, did she feel so helplessly lame?

Liz opened her eyes. "If you think he's still alive," she said, "then, I'm coming with you."

"No." Tess touched Liz's cheek and kissed her on the forehead. She looked serenely into Liz's face. "Your path lies in a different direction. Find Captain Vane. Hunt him down. Rescue Calico Jack. Then convince him to rescue Anne Bonny. When she knows he's no coward, she'll probably rescue herself. Right now she needs a little incentive. You can do it, Liz. I know you can. You got this far."

"But Rackham *is* a coward, a lily-livered codfish," Liz wailed.

Tess smiled at the colourful epithets. Then shook her head. "No. You wait and see. Jack Rackham will pass the test when he has to. Don't forget. He's *your* ancestor."

"Tess."

Tess studied her daughter's beseeching face. Liz was doing her best to keep her cool. She grabbed her mother's arm. "You can't leave just like that. I haven't seen you in months."

"I *have* to leave," Tess said, gently loosening Liz's grip. "I think you know that."

"No!" Liz lost her cool. "I *don't* know that. I don't know anything. Have you even heard a single word I've said? I haven't seen you in months. And all you have to say to me is go and hunt down a pirate? Well, that plain sucks." Tears were threatening to crack Liz's voice, but she was too angry for that. She glared at Cal, who stepped between them. She thrust him aside and whirled on her mother. "Do you have any idea what you sound like? What kind of a mother are you?"

Tess swallowed, eyes glistening. She gave Liz a moment to control herself, then she answered. "I am the mother of Elizabeth Latimer," Tess said. "And what does Elizabeth Latimer do when the world doesn't go her way? Does she have a meltdown and rant and rave and have a hissy fit? No. Because Elizabeth Latimer is not lame. She fixes things. If the world won't cooperate with her, she finds another way."

Tess softened her voice, blinked away the emotion. "I'll see you soon, Elizabeth. My love to Lu, to you both." Tess looked at Cal, who clearly expected to go with her. Tess shook her head. "Stay with Liz. You have no reason to be here. You've risked enough. Help Liz make things right. Then go home."

"Mom!" Liz shouted.

Tess turned. Liz had never called Tess 'mom' in her life. Tess locked eyes with Elizabeth, waved. She smiled, then ducked down the dark alley.

CHAPTER FOURTEEN
We Are Not A Couple Of Players In A Video Game

Hot tears threatened to explode out of Liz's eyes. She clenched her hands, almost yanked her thumb out of its socket. Parents, she thought. What good were they if they were never around?

Well, this one wasn't going to make her dislocate her thumb.

There was nothing for Liz to do but fulfill her mother's request. She relaxed her hands and watched Tess disappear around the corner of the alley. Was her dad alive? Liz swallowed. For Tess's sake, she hoped so. Liz walked out of the alley and into the brightness of the main street.

Where was she going to get a boat? With any luck, she wouldn't have to hijack a ship. Captain Vane would be hot on her tail. Would he care that she had given him the slip? He was planning to strand her on a deserted island anyway. Turtle soup and seaweed she might get used to, but she didn't relish chowing down on her own boots for dessert. By escaping, she had simply saved the captain the trouble of marooning her.

Captain Vane wanted Cal to sign his pirate articles and join his company. If she knew pirates like she thought she did, Vane would seek revenge because she'd disrespected him and helped Cal to escape. Yeah, with any luck, she wouldn't have to go hunting for Captain Vane. Vane would come after her.

She only hoped that he had kept Calico Jack alive.

Liz marched toward the waterfront. Cal grabbed her arm. "Where do you think you're going?"

"Don't touch me," Liz warned. "You are not my father."

"I'm the only adult guardian you have."

"Oh yeah?" She glared. "Since when?"

Cal sighed, let go of her. "Listen, Liz, I'm only trying to look out for you in Tess's absence."

"And you make just as fine a parent as she does." Liz made no attempt to hide the sarcasm. "Exactly where were you when I had a cutlass at my throat?"

Cal shrugged. "I had to take the opportunity to rescue Tess."

"How did you know she was on Vane's ship?"

Cal sucked in his cheeks, decided not to lie. "We've been keeping in touch."

Liz nodded. Of course. The same way Liz stayed in touch with Lu. No wonder Cal had tried to send them home to Victoria when they first arrived in Nassau. He knew exactly where Tess was all along. He'd only informed them that she was missing because he didn't know how long she'd be gone.

"What's her secret screen name?" Liz asked. "I want to text her."

Cal threw her a suspicious look.

"I know she has a screen name that you use to stay in touch with her. What is it?"

"You can't text her," Cal said hotly. "She lost her iPocket when Vane caught her trespassing on his ship. She had no choice but to get rid of it. It's swimming with the sharks now."

Liz rolled her eyes, sneered. "Was this before or after she asked you to come?"

"After, of course."

Liz frowned. She had trouble believing him. What was Tess doing on Vane's ship? Did she think he knew something about her father? "So did you bring an extra iPocket with you?"

Cal shook his head. "It's too dangerous. Remember, this is the eighteenth century. If you get caught with a gadget like that, there's no telling what they will do. Burn you at the stake for a witch probably."

"Then you know how dangerous it is to be on pirate turf," Liz said. "My mother is alone, without a link to the outside world. We shouldn't have let her go. Just what was she doing on Vane's ship?"

"She didn't mean to be on his ship. One of his sailors promised her information, but I think he said that just to get her in his bunk. When Vane found out, the scallywag was gutted for taking a woman aboard. It's against the code."

Liz rolled her eyes again at Cal's repeated attempts at pirate talk. She twisted her hair and tucked it down into the back of her shirt. "And yet, he kept her aboard."

"It was too late," Cal said. "They were already at sea. She had to ditch the iPocket just in case someone decided to get too close."

Liz swallowed the bile that was building up in her throat. In other words, what Cal meant was that Tess had to ditch the iPocket in case she was raped and the vicious rogue found it in the process.

Liz realized she was shaking. Her mother was willing to risk everything on a hunch.

Liz walked down to the pier with Cal following her like a puppy. She stared at the tall masted ships that were berthed in the harbour. There were brigs and frigates, sloops and schooners, pinks and snows. Even a man-of-war. The pier was bustling with sailors and travellers preparing for ocean voyages. Moored to one of the wharves was a snow with a vaguely familiar name. Snows were the largest of all two-masted vessels. This particular snow was named the *Tyger*, and it belonged to the pirate hunter Captain Jonathan Barnet of the British Royal Navy.

"What are you scheming?" Cal asked. "I know that look and I don't like it."

Liz squinted between the wharves. "You heard my mother," Liz said. "We have to find Vane and rescue Jack Rackham."

Cal stared at her, stepped backward on the wood planks of the unsteady dock as a horse-drawn cart clip-clopped past them to deposit a woman and child on the pier.

Liz frowned at Cal. She didn't like the look on his face. Why was he here? He hadn't tried to convince Tess to bring the letter in the bottle home with them, even though he knew just how dangerous a place this was for a single woman. The truth was, Cal's future was not affected. If Tess and her family ceased to exist, Cal's life might be even better than it was before. He would be sole owner of Marine Explorations Inc, Tess's lucrative salvage company, and he would own her salvage ship, *Tess's Revenge*.

But Tess's fate was out of Liz's hands.

Cal was frowning back at her. Liz couldn't win this scowling competition. Right now, he was the only ally she had and she needed his help. One person could not sail a ship.

"How do you plan to rescue Rackham, steal a boat, and convince a crew of ruffians to sail it for you?" Cal demanded. "And furthermore, once you do get Rackham, how are you going to convince him to do as you ask? You left him at the mercy of that cutthroat, Charles Vane. I'm thinking he'll be so pissed off, he'll just want to filet you like a herring."

"Very funny," Liz said. "You've been spending too much time with pirates."

"I'm serious, Liz," Cal argued. "We are not a couple of players in a video game."

"So I've been told." Liz shrugged. She had no idea how she was going to do anything. She'd worry about transportation later. The first order of business was to find Calico Jack.

Liz stared at the horizon. Against the skyline were two ships. They were close enough she could see that their colours were down. So, she was right. Vane was coming for her.

There was no identification. But she recognized the swift ketch and the even swifter sloop. If Vane was smart, he would hoist the British flag for camouflage, rather than sail into the harbour like crow bait, in clear view of the Royal Navy. The harbour was crawling with officers in blue coats.

"I think we have our ship," Liz said. "I should've known Vane wouldn't leave well enough alone."

Cal stared at the horizon. She saw his face turn pale and his hands start to shake. The *Lark* and the *Curlew* were in full view now, and it looked like they were going to anchor in the harbour, just offshore. She had to get to them before Barnet did.

"I am not going anywhere near those rogues," Cal said.

"Then how are we going to rescue Jack Rackham?" Liz demanded.

Cal turned his stare on Liz. "Don't you realize that Rackham will kill you? He's not going to follow you meekly like the Kung Fu Kid or that smooth-skinned, pirate man-boy you got chummy with so fast."

Liz almost slugged Cal. How dare he mention Wang so callously. And as for Daniel, she was pretty sure now that Daniel was no boy.

"If Daniel is still alive aboard one of those ships, he'll help me," Liz argued.

"I'm sure he will," Cal said. "But you don't know how many men Vane has in his company."

Liz looked around her. There was a dory on the beach, near where she'd ditched her scuba tank. They could take that dory and go . . . to which ship?

WOMBAT, CJ said in her mind.

Liz raised her eyes, startled. She gasped with relief when she realized she still had a telepathic link with her parrot. She frantically glanced around. CJ, where are you?

Man overboard, CJ said.

Liz looked over her head and saw a large red and blue parrot circling the pier. Which boat? Liz asked.

Curlew, CJ said.

So Rackham, Black Patch and Daniel were still on the *Curlew*. That made things easier. She knew the layout of the small sloop and could find her way on board without getting caught. The trick would be to cast off before the *Lark* knew they were gone.

CJ made a nosedive and landed on Liz's shoulder. She twisted around to kiss him on the wing.

"That stupid bird still alive?" Cal asked.

"Spindle-shanked, swag-bellied WOMBAT," CJ said.

Liz grinned. "How many men do you think Vane has?" she asked, smothering the urge to laugh out loud.

"Enough to sail two ships with minimal crew," Cal answered.

Liz had sailed the *Curlew* with herself and three crewmen. That meant there were at least three other men aboard ship unless Rackham had agreed to be Vane's consort.

"I have to get a message to Daniel," Liz said. "CJ, tell Daniel that I'm coming."

"Pirate Hunter coming," CJ said.

"Go!" Liz said.

CJ flew off in the direction of the sloop.

$$$

Liz and Cal left the pier for the beach. Liz lifted her scuba tank from its nest of rock and fallen sea grape, and placed it in the dory. Cal watched the two ships silhouetted against the growing night sky. Hopefully, Vane hadn't skewered his traitorous ex-quartermaster, Jack Rackham, with a pike. If Rackham was still aboard the *Curlew*, Liz could just cast off with him aboard.

"You think you can just climb back onto that sloop and steal it?" Cal asked.

"I did it once before," Liz said.

Cal shook his head.

Liz exhaled, exasperated. "All you have to do is watch my

back. Do you think you can do that?"

"With what?" Cal objected. "We have no weapons."

"Daniel will think of a way to get us weapons."

"The hell with weapons," Cal said. "All I can think about right now is getting some food."

Liz felt a gnawing at her stomach. Yeah, she was starving, too. But her desperation and annoyance with Cal made her callous. "We'll eat later. On board ship."

Liz went back to the dory. She didn't know exactly what kind of a signal she was waiting for. Daniel couldn't exactly text her, could he?

She should probably just row.

"I say we go get something to eat," Cal argued. "There's an inn down the street, not too far from the dress shop."

Liz glanced down at her filthy pirate wear, which was no cleaner after that canoe chase in the open sea. "You think they'll serve us dressed like this?" Liz asked. Cal was also dressed somewhat piratish, except that his clothes were fresher.

Cal rubbed his grumbling stomach. "We could go to a tavern. You'll pass for a boy."

Liz shook her head. "Too risky. Too many lowlifes."

"Then stay here. I'm going to eat."

"Wait," Liz said.

Something was moving in the water. It swam from the ship with ease. Daniel, Liz thought. She walked closer along the shoreline to greet him. She froze. The head that rose from the water had kinky dark hair. The hideously scarred face had an eye patch.

CHAPTER FIFTEEN
I Saw You Dead!

Liz almost screamed. Cal jerked her in front of him like a shield. The one-eyed gorilla of a pirate rose from the sea and stalked toward them. Water rolled off his muscles and gleamed in the starlight. His shoulder was bound with a bandage, but he seemed to have complete use of it. These pirates were tough. They had to be. Or else they'd be dead.

Black Patch stopped and stared at Elizabeth. Oh no, was he going to eat her? Cal hadn't had the pleasure of meeting the *Curlew*'s first mate as he had been indisposed after being literally shish kabobbed by Daniel's cutlass.

"I knows yer face," Black Patch said.

"And I know yours," Liz said, not giving an inch of ground. Her heart was hammering, but she wasn't about to let the fierce pirate know it.

Black Patch drew his dagger. Elizabeth stood firm.

"That yer parakeet?" he asked as CJ fluttered down to land on the one-eyed pirate's shoulder.

Liz stared frantically at her parrot. CJ, what are you doing?

"Avast." CJ said.

"Come here," Liz said, not taking her eyes from Black Patch or his dagger.

CJ didn't move.

Traitor, Liz thought.

"The captain wishes to see ye aboard," the pirate said. He reached around Liz and yanked Cal forward. "You also. Can yer swim?"

He poked his dagger at Cal's throat without breaking the skin. Cal shook his head. He didn't want to swim in the dark. "You two go," he whispered hoarsely. "I'll stay here. I have a reservation over at that inn there." He gestured across the street.

Black Patch scanned the beach, then spotted the dory that was stranded on the sand. He single-handedly pushed it into the water. He ordered them to get aboard. Well, Liz thought. This was one way to get back on the ship. She scowled at CJ, who settled on Black Patch's shoulder as he commanded Cal to row.

Traitor, Liz repeated.

Arrgh, CJ said.

Cal rowed. Liz watched the dark and the gleam of Black Patch's one good eye. She felt like asking him how it had happened. But she was pretty sure she knew. One of his fellow ruffians had sworn to claw out his eye to have a look at his brains—and had made good on the promise.

"Row," Black Patch repeated. His command was directed at Cal, but his eye was on Liz.

She squirmed. She hated the way he looked at her. If she could just kick that dagger from his grasp and put out his other eye . . . .

They reached the sloop in a few minutes. Now what, Liz thought. She'd better have a plan. Maybe Captain Vane would throw her in the brig with Rackham. Rackham would be disarmed, so, unless he wanted to throttle her with his bare hands, he might just listen to reason and she could rescue them both.

Black Patch ordered Cal to make fast to the *Curlew*. Then he motioned for Liz to climb the rope ladder to the deck. He nudged Cal after her and followed with his dagger in his teeth.

"Go aft," he muttered, steel gleaming against his not-so-pearly whites. "The captain is waiting."

Liz swung around. "Where is Daniel?" she asked Black Patch, a cold feeling in the pit of her stomach.

"To the captain's cabin," Black Patch ordered, waving his dagger with a flourish.

$$$

Liz opened the cabin door and saw who was seated at the captain's table. Her jaw nearly dropped to the floor. Daniel was surrounded by food. Luscious red mangoes, black-speckled bananas, fried grey mullet, fresh hard-boiled eggs, salt pork and limes. Not to mention a plate full of hardtack. There were three pewter tankards and plates. So they were expected.

"Daniel!" Liz said. "What happened? Where's Captain Vane? Where's Jack Rackham?"

"One question at a time," Daniel said. "But first, you two look famished. Come sit and eat."

Daniel poured a tankard of wine for Cal. Liz felt like drinking some wine too, but she needed a clear brain. She shook her head when Daniel raised the decanter. She'd rather have some fresh water. To her surprise, Black Patch fetched a bucket of clean drinking water and dipped her tankard into it.

Daniel wiped his lips on his sleeve when he finished eating. Cal couldn't get enough. If he didn't stop eating soon, CJ's swag-bellied epithet would come true.

"I can't stand the suspense any longer," Liz said. "Tell me what happened. Why are you sitting in the captain's seat and—" She turned to see where Black Patch was. He had dragged a chair by the door and was seated like the king's guard. "What's with him?"

Daniel slumped back in his chair and grinned. "Vane has had a change of heart. He no longer wants this ship. We did a trade. Rackham for the *Curlew* and its crew."

"You gave up Rackham?"

"I had no choice."

Liz shook her head, totally confused. "I don't get it. When I left the ship, Vane was prepared to take it all."

Daniel nodded. "We had an unexpected visit from the Royal Navy. A certain Captain Jonathan Barnet offered Vane gold—ten thousand pieces of eight—and a full pardon if he handed the louse over. So he did."

"But the *Lark* is still in the harbour. Why hasn't Vane left?"

"He wishes to be present at the hanging of Calico Jack Rackham tomorrow morning."

Liz froze. She threw her half-eaten banana onto the pewter plate. Oh no. Rackham was supposed to get a fair trial. He wasn't supposed to die yet.

"Daniel," Liz said. "If Rackham hangs tomorrow . . ."

"Exactly," Daniel said. "It's poof for you, Lulu and Tess."

Cal looked up from stuffing his face. He was suddenly very interested in Liz's and Daniel's conversation.

"Do you have the bottle with the letter inside it?" Daniel asked.

Liz shook her head.

"I told you Tess wouldn't listen to you. Now, we haven't much time."

Liz felt like giving up. She stared at the table with the fruit peelings and fish bones from their feast. How were they going to free Jack Rackham? Their chances of getting him out of prison were as thin as those mullet bones. Rackham was being held in Spanish Town jail in St. Jago de la Vega. He was due to be hanged on the waterfront in Port Royal, then his body would be hung from a gibbet and displayed at Deadman's Cay, outside the harbour.

A grating sound came from the door. Liz suddenly realized that Black Patch was still somewhere behind her. She swung to see him rise from his chair, grinning, with his frightening gorilla physique and his one good eye.

"Don't worry. He's with us," Daniel said.

Black Patch kicked his chair away from the door and crossed his arms. CJ landed on his shoulder. "Don't worry. He's with us," CJ mimed.

Liz was too wasted by the awesome futility of her failed

meeting with her mother to question Black Patch's loyalties. She turned back to Daniel.

"Even if we do manage to rescue Rackham, we don't have enough manpower to sail this ship."

"We sailed with four sailors last time," Daniel said.

"Barely," Liz said. "We couldn't get up enough speed. We were caught by Vane."

"Well, this time we'll have six crewmen," Daniel said.

Six? Liz was so tired she had to count on her fingers. Daniel, Cal, Black Patch, herself made only four. Oh, of course. Rackham. That would make five.

But that would still only make five.

"Who's the sixth?" Liz asked.

Daniel tilted his chin at the door. Wang came in at that moment.

"Oh my God!" Liz screeched.

Wang beamed. He had a large cloth bandage wrapped around his ribs, but he looked none the worse for having been Vane's idea of souvlaki.

"How can this be? You're alive! I saw you dead!" Liz turned to Daniel. "You dumped his body into the sea."

Daniel smiled smugly, winked at Wang. "He wasn't dead. I just signalled to him to play dead. If you'd looked closely, you could see he was barely bleeding because the knife only hit bone. And when I dumped him overboard, didn't it surprise you that he didn't sink?"

Come to think of it, Liz thought, it *was* strange that Wang hadn't been swept out to the open sea. But her head had been too messed up to even entertain the idea that Wang wasn't dead.

Liz grinned. On reflection, it all made sense. Instead of watching her swim away, Daniel had kept an eye on Wang.

"As I've proven before," Daniel said, nodding at Black Patch, "I've got a way with needle and thread."

Liz threw herself at Wang and he caught her in a serious public display of affection.

"Thank goodness you're okay," Liz said.

Wang looked slightly surprised at her exuberance and hugged her back, clearly pleased.

"Don't ever do that again," she scolded him.

He smiled at her. Her knees suddenly turned to jelly as the reality of everything that had happened that day finally sank in.

"Liz, you okay?" Wang asked.

She straightened herself. He was still holding her and she realized that she liked it. He wasn't wearing a shirt. Liz found herself ogling his chest. Who did she think she was? Lulu? This was a life-and-death situation. No time for raging hormones. She could be nonexistent tomorrow.

Daniel was frowning at her, hard. She caught his eye and looked away. Oh my God, was he jealous? Liz couldn't help but feel a little satisfied.

"With Rackham back," Daniel said, "we'll be a crew of six. It's a small crew but better than we had before. After we rescue Rackham, we head for New Providence."

Liz nodded. "So what's the plan?"

Daniel stared at her. "As I recall, at our last meeting, you wanted to be captain. I got us the ship and the crew. Maybe *you* should come up with the plan to break out Jack Rackham."

Daniel had reverted to his usual sardonic self. What was his problem? She glanced at Wang, who raised his eyebrows.

Liz still couldn't believe that Wang was alive. Daniel could work miracles. He had more than a way with needle and thread. He was a magician of a healer.

"How far is the Spanish Town jail?" Liz asked.

"Not far," Daniel replied. "We can make it there fast if we have horses."

Yeah, horses would be good, Liz thought. They would help in a speedy getaway.

"Well, what are we waiting for?" Liz demanded. "Shake a leg and bustle! We've got no time to lose!"

CHAPTER SIXTEEN
You Might Try Stealing The Key

The plan was lame, half-assed, but it was all Liz could think to do. Get to the Spanish Town jail at St. Jago de la Vega, then worry about breaking Rackham out. If worse came to worse, she would use her feminine wiles—like they did in the movies—to get in to see him.

Horses weren't a problem. There were horses tied up all over town, and Daniel was not only a clever sea robber, but he knew the ropes on land as well. He nabbed two horses, a black and white spotted mare and a brown stallion. He made her and Wang share the mare. Liz wasn't sure Wang should be coming with them after his injury, but all of his actions proved that he was ready and raring to go. There was only one problem. Liz could sail, scuba dive, fence like Jack Sparrow and even climb rigging if her life depended on it. But she had never ridden a horse.

It couldn't be that hard. She stroked the mare and the mare nuzzled her. So far so good.

Liz saddled up and Wang got behind her. But when the mare took off, Liz couldn't control her no matter how hard she dug in her knees.

Ouch, not like that, the mare complained, bucking her legs.

By the time Liz managed to rein the horse in, her butt was black and blue, and Wang was cursing at her. Daniel, who had followed at her tail, pulled back on the reins and swung the stallion around to check its high spirits.

"Get behind me," Wang told Liz, "or we'll be dead before we get to Rackham. I'll drive."

Daniel laughed, reared his horse like he'd been born on one, and galloped into the night. Liz scowled at Daniel's vanishing, swashbuckling back. *Pirates*, she thought bitterly. She got off the mare and resaddled herself behind Wang.

Why? Liz silently asked the mare.

The mare loosened her muscles. Watch and learn.

Wang was not only the most awesome free runner in Victoria's film-making history, but he also knew how to handle a horse. On occasion, his stunt spots required him to show off his horsemanship. "Comes with the territory," Wang told her, not wanting her to feel bad.

He dug in his heels and the mare leaped forward.

The darkness and unlit road to St. Jago de la Vega hid their movements. Daniel was way out ahead of them and didn't slow to a canter until they reached the outskirts of town. When Liz and Wang caught up to Daniel, they were already near the prison gates. Liz signalled for Wang to curb their horse to a trot. She tugged on Wang's shirt for him to rein in to a complete halt. She studied the small stone building that gleamed in the starlight. Beside the gate was a strangely inappropriate jasmine bush with white flowers.

Two armed guards blocked their entry into the jail.

Liz bit her lip. Prison breaks were not her best thing. In fact, she'd never had to participate in one, no less be the fearless leader.

"Hide the horses," Liz whispered, sliding off the back of the mare and moving into a grotto of thin oleander trees.

Daniel motioned for Wang to tether the horses behind a cluster of shrubs. Liz pointed up. She wanted Wang up the thickest of the trees, swift as a mouse, to play lookout, while she and Daniel figured out a way to get inside.

Daniel stood in front of her, a smug smile on his lips, waiting for orders.

"Well?" he said.

"Why do you stand there with that annoying sneer on your

face? Can't you see that breaking Jack Rackham out of prison is impossible?" Liz complained.

"Since when is anything impossible for Elizabeth Latimer?" Daniel asked.

"You aren't taking this seriously at all," Liz moaned. "Maybe you think *you're* immortal, but I know *I'm* not."

Daniel was no longer smiling. "Immortal, I am not," he said. "I was only waiting for you to ask me for help."

Liz swallowed. Hadn't she been doing that all along? "All right," she said. "I need your help. Help me. How are we supposed to break Rackham out of prison?"

There was only starlight to show them the way to the prison gates. "I wouldn't advise that we slice our way in there with these," he said, patting his baldric that was loaded with a flintlock pistol, cutlass and dagger. "If we do that, all hell will break lose, and we'll have every soldier in that building down on us. We'll have to think of a more subtle way."

Liz exhaled. "You think I could convince one of those guards to let me in with that flintlock of yours?"

"I think you'd do better by placing one of them jasmine blossoms behind your ear and unbuttoning your blouse."

Liz glowered at him. You know where *you* can stick a flower, she thought. "Why don't you try unbuttoning *your* blouse? How do you know those guards don't swing the other way?"

"Don't be a fool, Elizabeth."

"Well, you don't know that they wouldn't be more interested in *your* pretty face."

"So, you think I'm pretty, do you?" Daniel said.

Liz scowled. "Oh, shut up. This is getting us nowhere."

Liz slumped down on the ground to think. She had to create a diversion. But she had to get those guards to open the gate first.

Liz lowered her hand to the sash around her waist. She still had

Lu's iPocket. If she switched it to audio and played a drunken fight scene from *Pirates of the Caribbean* or something like that, it might be enough to get those guys away from the gate.

"Liz, what are you doing?" Daniel asked as he watched her prepare the diversion.

"You aren't exactly helping me, Daniel, so don't ask questions. Wang!" she whispered up at the tree. "Get ready. We're going to have to make this fast. Daniel, get as close to those guards as possible without letting them see you, and get ready to blast through that door. And give me your dagger just in case."

The guards were stirring. Already they thought they could hear something. Liz had to hurry. She snuck along the ground to a palmetto palm and placed her iPocket at its foot, turned the volume on high and ran along the periphery of the grass and scrub toward the jail gates. There was the ring of clashing swords and jumbled pirate talk as the movie played atrociously loud. The guards started cussing and looking around. They couldn't figure out where the brawl was coming from.

Morons, they were going the wrong way. They were headed straight for Daniel and Wang.

"This way you idiots!" Liz yelled.

She ducked under a jacaranda tree and ran back toward her iPocket. This wasn't going to work. It was set on surround sound and the fight sounds seemed to be coming from all directions.

Daniel was at the gates, but he couldn't get the door opened by blasting it with his pistol.

Suddenly the spotted mare was at her side. I know, Liz said. She snagged the iPocket off the ground, switched it off and hid it behind her back, just as one of the guards came down on her with a musket. The mare disappeared.

"Well, what do we have here?" he asked. He squinted at her and gave her an ugly smile. "Dressed like a bloomin' pirate, this one is."

"This one, too," the second guard said, holding Daniel at bay with his musket.

"I'll be damned," the first guard said, hauling Liz around to face him. "If it ain't Anne Bonny."

No, it ain't Anne Bonny, Liz almost said. But Daniel silenced her with a look.

"And you, sir," he said, glaring at Daniel. "I's seen you before. Ain't you the quartermaster for Calico Jack, the pirate we's going to hang tomorrow?"

Daniel stayed silent. Liz's heart was pounding. Where was Wang? She quietly stuffed her iPocket into her sash while the guards waited in vain for Daniel's reply.

"To the pens with you, you scoundrels," the guard said.

Liz locked eyes with Daniel. He smiled ever so slightly as the guards relieved him of his baldric and his weapons.

Liz almost rolled over backwards, laughing out loud, when she realized the irony. Daniel was right. This was one way to get inside the jail.

$$$

"You wants to see yer captain?" the guard taunted, flaunting Daniel's flintlock pistol. "Then you can damned well hang alongside him." He shoved Liz and Daniel down the narrow corridor to a set of wooden steps that led to the cells. "Get below."

There were rows of jail cells, but Liz couldn't see where Rackham was. They threw her into a cage by herself and took Daniel farther along the aisle before locking him up.

Now what? she thought. Was Wang still free? He must be or they'd be bringing him along next.

This really sucked. The rescue had not gone exactly according to plan. Well, on second thought, maybe it had. She hadn't really had much of a plan, except to steal horses and get to the jail. She hadn't exactly figured out how to break Rackham out, and now she was going to have to break herself out as well.

Maybe she could still do as Daniel had suggested and unbutton her blouse and see where that led. But first, she had to link with Lu. Lulu was not locked up in a jail cell. She would have a clearer head.

Liz glanced around to make sure no one could see what she was doing. There were no guards down here. They didn't need any. The cells were escape-proof. There was a tiny, paneless window in every other cell, with excruciatingly, narrowly spaced metal bars, and the front of the cell was barred, too. The ceiling had wooden beams, the walls were impervious stone and the floor reddish dirt. She'd have to be a wizard to get out of this one.

Liz drew out the iPocket PC from her sash. She activated it and typed:

> Rebel Goddess. SOS

Two seconds later, Rebel Goddess replied:

> ?

Liz answered:

> Need ideas. Me, Rackham et al in Jail. Don't want 2 b hanged!

Lu replied:

> LOL :)

Liz replied:

> :(

There was a short wait, then Lu answered:

> Mk like Anne Bonny

Brilliant, Liz thought. She sent Lu multiple electronic hugs (((H))), logged off, and stuffed the iPocket into her sash. In a year from now, when Rackham and his crew were caught by Captain Jonathan Barnet and sentenced to be hanged, Anne Bonny and fellow female pirate Mary Read both 'pleaded their bellies.' If she told the captain of the guard that she'd been knocked up by Rackham, her sentence would be reprieved. Thank goodness pregnancy tests wouldn't be invented for another two hundred and fifty years.

The guards already thought she was Anne Bonny. In November 1720, they allowed Anne Bonny to see her lover one last time before he was hanged.

"Guard!" Liz picked up a loose stone from the floor and rattled it across the bars of her cage. "You cannot hang me. I am with child!"

The guard came stumbling down the wooden steps to her cell. He stared at her, then looked at his mate who had followed to investigate the ruckus.

The first guard stared at her squinty-eyed. "And just whose child did yer happen to be with?"

"Why, Jack Rackham's, of course. Who else's?"

The second guard scowled. "She cannot be hanged with her captain if that be the case."

"It be the case," Liz said boldly.

"Pah!" the first guard said.

"And I request that I be allowed to see my poor Jack before he dances the hempen jig."

"That be tomorrow," the second guard said.

"That's correct," Liz said. "I know my rights. Let me out. I want to see the pirate who is the father of my babe."

The first guard shook his head, miffed. His plan to hang Rackham's gang was being thwarted by a girl.

"It's her right," the second guard said.

"Darned right," Liz said.

The first guard glared at her, then opened her cage with a skeleton key.

"This way then," the guard said. "You have five minutes."

Five minutes was long enough.

They brought her to Rackham's cell and she was delighted to see that Daniel was holed up with him. She was outnumbered, so she couldn't exactly plough her way through these guards. But she did have brains, which these guards seemed to be slightly lacking in. She was hatching a plan. A good one. It might work if she could just get word to Wang to bring Black Patch and CJ to the gallows on Port Royal's waterfront in the morning.

"Jack, my love," Liz said when the guards deposited her in front of the unruly pirate. "I take it that bump on the head is feeling slightly better today?"

Jack Rackham scowled at her. "I knew from the first ye was a witch. You've cursed me and brought the devil down on me at last."

Liz looked around her to make sure the guards were out of earshot before she answered. "You could stand off a ways there," Liz said to the scowling guards. "After all, these are our last moments together." The guards scowled even more and backed down the aisle out of earshot, but stayed within musket range.

"The devil my butt. I've done no such thing," Liz said, lowering her voice. "I'm here to break you out."

"Indeed?" Rackham snorted. "And why would ye be doing me such a favour."

Liz exhaled, exasperated. *Pirates.* You had to tell them something ten times before it sank in.

"Well?" Rackham wheedled.

Liz wanted to slam her fist onto something out of frustration, but there was nothing except the iron bars of Rackham's cell. She said, "I told you from the beginning. I need you to get back together with Anne Bonny." She dropped her voice even lower in case the guards were creeping to Rackham's cell to eavesdrop.

Rackham arched his brows. "If yer kin get me out of here, I will forever be at yer service." Rackham bowed low and deep, and Liz wondered if he were mocking her.

"Good," she said. "You just do as Daniel here tells you to, and you won't be swinging from a rope tomorrow."

Daniel moved nearer to her. The guards had not opened the cell to let her inside in case the pirates decided to rush them. She clung to the bars and beckoned Daniel even closer. She whispered her plan into his ear. It would be close. But it was the best thing she could come up with, provided they let her witness the pirate hangings—and she was going to make damned sure that they would.

"That will be cutting it closer than I would like," Daniel said.

"Well, can you think of a better plan?" Liz asked.

Daniel frowned. "You might try stealing the key."

"I might," Liz said, "and be killed in the process. Don't forget, Wang is still hiding out there somewhere. I think my plan will work."

"It better," Daniel said. "Or all my efforts at getting you here will be lost."

Now it was Liz's turn to frown. "Yeah," she said. "And that's another thing. Just exactly what, for you, will be lost? Other than your life, that is?"

"No time for that, Elizabeth." Daniel shot a sideways glance at the approaching guards. "Or should I say Anne Bonny. It looks like our time is up. Until tomorrow then."

Liz nodded. And then just for emphasis and for the benefit of the guards, she turned on Rackham. "If you had fought like a man, you wouldn't be hanged like a dog!"

With that, she spun on her heel to meet the guards.

"Lover's spat?" the first guard said smugly.

"I insist on seeing this cur hang in the morning," Liz demanded.

The guard glanced from Rackham, who was cowering in the

back of the cell, to Liz who stood firmly, hands on hips.

"Aye," he said. "I shall see that it is arranged at the morrow."

Daniel shot her a satisfied look and Liz winked.

CHAPTER SEVENTEEN
See You At The Gallows

"Wang!" Liz whispered through the barred window of her cell. "Are you out there?"

Was she ever lucky that the cage they had put her into was one with a window. The iron bars of the window were spaced only about an inch apart. Too narrow for Wang to slip her a knife or a pistol.

Liz strained on her tiptoes to see. The window was so high, she could barely get her eyes level with the windowsill. She grabbed the bars and hoisted herself up until her biceps crunched, like she was doing chin-ups on the monkey bars back home.

She caught a whiff of jasmine from the bush that grew outside the gates, then the smell of horse. Her muscles gave out and she dropped her feet back to the ground. Where was Wang? They hadn't caught him, had they? No. They couldn't have caught him because if they had, they would have thrown him into a cell.

She heard a scraping sound, then soft footsteps. She couldn't decide whether to call out or keep quiet. Those footsteps weren't necessarily Wang's. Whoever was out there could be the prison sentry.

Someone was definitely out there. They were doing something at the window. She heard a snuffling, then a low whinny. It was the mare. Liz silently thanked her for coming.

"Wang?" Liz whispered, standing on her tiptoes. Had he followed the mare?

"Liz," Wang said. "Thank goodness Fancy here found you. Are you okay?"

"You've named the horse Fancy?"

"Suits her, don't you think? All those fancy black spots on her back?"

Right. Liz deliberately rolled her eyes, but she was smiling. That dappled effect was what had kept the horse camouflaged in the starlight.

"Did those filthy rats hurt you?" Wang asked.

"No, I'm fine," Liz answered. "But I won't be for long if I don't get Rackham out of here ASAP. Do you still have Daniel's horse?"

Wang grunted. "Yeah, Fancy has gone back into the woods to join him. I swear she knew exactly where you were."

Wang was trying to shove something between the iron bars of the window. He cursed.

"It's too bloody big," he complained. "Why do pirates have to carry such stupidly large weapons?"

"What is it?" Liz asked.

"Daniel's dagger. Stand back. I don't want to stab you with it. You dropped it when that maniac shoved his musket in your face. I would have leaped on his back, but I didn't want to risk getting killed again. Thought I'd be of more use to you alive."

Liz sank back to her heels and grinned despite her grim situation. "Good thinking, Wang."

Liz heard some more grating sounds, then an oath in Chinese.

Liz giggled and Wang blustered when he realized she'd understood. "I can get the blade in between the bars but not the hilt. Dang it, I was hoping you could use it to jimmy the lock. From what I can see through this teeny window, that's a standard lock that can be opened with any old skeleton key."

"Never mind. Keep the dagger on you. You'll need it tomorrow. Now listen. I've got a plan. Everything counts on perfect timing." Liz paused. The one thing she hadn't reckoned on was having to use Black Patch. "Can we trust that one-eyed gorilla?" Liz asked.

"Huh? Who?" Wang snickered after a pause. "You mean Black Patch? He's not so bad. We sort of became chummy after Daniel stitched us up and threw Rackham to the wolves. He thinks old Calico Jack is a bit of a tool."

Great, this was her ancestor the brute of a pirate was calling a tool.

"He actually called him a tool?"

"Not exactly. He called him a dawcock. That's pirate for fool. Same difference."

Liz frowned. "He thinks his captain is a fool, yet he followed him when he commandeered Vane's ship."

"I don't think he thought Rackham was a fool at first. But after seeing you dog-whip him, he sort of changed his mind."

"That's not good, Wang. We need Black Patch's loyalty to Jack Rackham and to no one else."

"Black Patch has absolute respect for your friend Daniel."

Even after Daniel had stabbed him?

Liz flinched at the way Wang had spoken Daniel's name. Was that a hint of sarcasm in his voice?

No time to decipher this romantic threesome triangle that seemed to have transpired around her. The only thing that mattered was saving Rackham's neck.

"Will Black Patch help us rescue Calico Jack?" Liz asked.

"I think so. What did you have in mind?"

Liz rose on her tiptoes again and whispered through the iron bars of the window to Wang. Her plan would work provided everyone cooperated, including her traitorous parrot. Now that Fancy had taken a fancy to herself and Wang, that was even better. The horse was one more ally to count on. Wang thrust his thumb through the tight bars and Liz did likewise. They hooked thumbs to seal the deal. Liz's red-painted nail with the chipped skull gleamed in the starlight.

"See you at the gallows, Liz."

Liz nodded, but Wang was already gone.

$$$

The procession that took Liz, Daniel and Jack Rackham in a horse-drawn cart to the waterfront at Port Royal consisted of Jamaica's deputy Admiralty Marshal and twenty soldiers. Liz was impressed they thought Calico Jack was worth that much security.

When they reached the town, the harbour was packed, sardine style, with curious looky-loos. Ships were moored tight to the wharves, creating a forest of masts and sails like they were saluting the execution of one of piracy's greatest scoundrels. Liz knew better. Three centuries later, Jack Rackham would only be remembered for having history's most notorious woman pirates among his company.

The gallows was set up on the shore near the low-tide mark. This was where Rackham and Daniel would be hanged if her plan didn't work. Their dead bodies would be submerged by the incoming tide three times before being taken away. She couldn't risk that. Couldn't consider the possibility.

The prisoners were escorted under military guard to the gallows, which were two tall structures made of double wooden uprights joined at the top by a crossbeam to form an arch. A ladder leaned against each of the gallows, and the ropes with the nooses were suspended from the crossbeams.

Liz glanced around her. She was allowed to remain in the crowd to witness the hanging of her supposed lover, Calico Jack. In the audience, the governor of Jamaica was present, and so was Captain Jonathan Barnet, the pirate hunter. She sighted Charles Vane and two of his men. In the bay she saw two islets, Deadman's Cay and Gun Cay, the future respective resting places for Rackham's and Vane's bones.

Off in the distance a horse whinnied. Liz clutched her hands and hoped that Wang and Fancy were in position. Black Patch, too. In the sky, CJ circled the pier.

Daniel and Rackham stood at the base of the gallows with the prison chaplain. The chaplain was an old codger who looked like he wasn't long for this earth.

"Any final words before the Lord takes your devil's souls?" the chaplain asked.

Daniel shrugged. He looked remarkably cool for a guy who was about to die. If Liz's plan flopped, his death would not be pretty. Being dropped from the gallows was not always enough to cause instant death, and the poor bugger would gag until he expired. After that, he was swamped in the tides. Then he was lugged to the Surgeon's Hall and dissected or hung in chains and put on display. Liz was the only thing that stood between Daniel and this horrific fate.

And it was too soon for Jack Rackham to swing from a gibbet on Deadman's Cay.

It suddenly occurred to Elizabeth that Rackham's real lover, Anne Bonny, was a captive of the governor of New Providence and, at this moment, was probably pacing her frilly bedroom in his lofty mansion, with nary an inkling that Calico Jack was at the brink of the hangman's noose.

"What of you?" the chaplain asked, turning to Rackham. "Repent your sins of this world and p'raps the good Lord will welcome you into his fold instead of sending you to Satan's lair."

Liz swallowed. Timing was everything.

Fancy, CJ, Wang, but especially Black Patch.

"Goddamn my soul," Rackham spewed, "for trustin' a witch!"

The hangman offered Rackham and Daniel a black hood so that they wouldn't have to see the horror or pleasure on the faces of the crowd as they choked to death. Both men refused the hoods and climbed the gallows with their eyes wide open to stare death straight in the face.

As for the hangman, his identity was unknown. He wore a black hood with cutouts for eyes. A single white gleam was the only bit of his face that showed.

The hangman forced Rackham, then Daniel, to the top of the twin gallows.

He climbed onto a crate between them and placed the nooses around their necks.

CHAPTER EIGHTEEN
To Sea, To Sea!

The chaplain shouted from below the tall ladders. "Blasphemy will not appease God's wrath, ye evil-doers, ye sons of serpents. Find the barest humanity in your soul, show the slimmest feeling of remorse, find the Lord that you have so long forsaken and beg his forgiveness, and ye may yet escape the fiery flames of hell!"

Rackham spat to the ground, but Liz knew the gesture was not directed at the chaplain. Rackham thought she had abandoned him, and his hooded eyes were scouting the crowd for her. Daniel smiled. Liz was sure that Daniel had never feared the flames of hell in his life. In fact, she wasn't totally certain that *that* wasn't exactly where he came from. He was certainly putting her through hell now.

All right, she thought. The hangman jumped off the crate and booted it aside. He moved between the two pirates who stood helpless above him. Those were awfully high nooses, but Liz knew that the height was to allow the audience a superlative view.

Liz made a fist. She wet her lips, tried not to count the beats of her thumping heart.

Five, four, three, two . . . She lifted her red-painted thumb.

Black Patch kicked away the ladders and the men fell. A black and white spotted horse suddenly galloped onto the pier, shot under Daniel before the rope could tighten, while a large red and blue parrot lifted his noose. Daniel, on horseback, caught Jack Rackham, who unfortunately had to swing for two seconds by the noose before Daniel could reach him and slice away the rope with a dagger the hangman tossed to him, hilt first. In the confusion, no one saw that a one-eyed man was the hangman, and that a brown stallion, with a cavalier Chinese boy in pirate's clothes, swooped through the raving crowd and swept up a long-haired girl who looked exactly like Calico Jack's lover, Anne Bonny.

"To the beach," Wang shouted. The black and white mare with Rackham and Daniel leaped off the pier, followed closely by the brown stallion. CJ flew high in the sky, circled and darted down to the shoreline.

The governor's men and the Royal Navy, with Captain Jonathan Barnet, were flush on their tails. At least they were trying to be. Luckily for Liz and her accomplices, the hapless soldiers had to find their horses and untether them before they could join the chase.

At the appointed place, Liz slid off the back of the stallion. Wang dismounted and slapped the stallion to send it off to freedom. There was a dory on the beach and already Daniel and Rackham were pushing it into the sea.

"Fancy!" Liz called out to the mare.

The mare knew her new name. Liz covered one eye, mimicking Black Patch, and shouted, "Go, quick!"

The mare darted back toward the pier where Black Patch was trying to blend in with the crowd. He leaped onto the mare and was catapulted onto the beach, but the soldiers were on to him. Several of them wheeled their horses to check him.

Liz turned and joined the others in the dory. They couldn't wait any longer. Rackham and Daniel were already rowing, crashing into the breakers, blindly plowing out to sea.

The *Curlew* was not far. She was still anchored in the bay. The stupid Navy hadn't anticipated an escape by sea and had no ships at the ready.

Liz looked back to see Black Patch and Fancy rearing in circles, fenced in by a quad of soldiers.

To sea, to sea! Liz frantically waved in the direction of the anchored sloop.

Black Patch didn't understand. As the target of the fray, and in the confusion of horses and men, it was doubtful the one-eyed pirate even saw Liz flailing her arms like a lunatic. But Fancy did. She whinnied loud enough for Liz to hear her. Then she reared up on her hind legs, bucked at the resisting soldiers, almost ejecting her rider like a slingshot, and vaulted over the heads of the Royal Navy and the governor's men.

Did Black Patch know how to swim? It seemed not. He clung to the mane of the black and white mare while she paddled swiftly toward the dory and the *Curlew*.

"We can't take the nag aboard," Rackham shouted, spraying spittle all over the place.

"Why not?" Liz asked, hoping the spray on her face came from the sea. "She saved your first mate!"

Rackham fumed. But there was no time to argue. They had to get to the *Curlew* and set sail. Cal had better be on the ball and get ready to weigh anchor.

Hoist sail, Liz signalled to CJ, who was riding an air current above them.

CJ took off to the sloop, squawking, "Hoist sail!"

It was a matter of minutes before they were safely aboard the ship with the dory fastened along her port side. Black Patch and Fancy caught up in a crest of foam. The one-eyed pirate hauled himself aboard, his good eye gleaming. Apparently, there were no hard feelings between Daniel and Black Patch despite the fact that Daniel had skewered him earlier. Pirates. Liz would never understand them. The rescue had gone according to plan and Black Patch had proven true.

Fancy was still floundering in the waves alongside the hull. Dripping wet from sea spray, Liz had hold of the mare's reins that were fastened to a long rope. Liz couldn't figure out how to get

Fancy aboard. Finally, Daniel said, "We have to let her go."

"We can't," Liz said. "She's exhausted. She won't make it back to shore."

Black Patch, Wang and Cal were making the ship ready under Rackham's orders. The captain occasionally clutched at his throat and coughed as he forced out commands in a froggy voice, making Liz fully aware that Calico Jack Rackham held Elizabeth Latimer responsible for almost choking him to death.

"Helmsman. Make ready," he shouted. "Crowd that canvas!"

The anchor was already up. The sails unfurled. Liz was not going to abandon this horse to a murderous death by drowning. "Cut loose that rigging!" Liz demanded. She was going to make a harness and haul the horse up by the capstan to the deck.

Daniel glared at her.

Liz glared back. "If you don't cut me a piece of that rigging big enough to wrap around this horse, I am going back down there with her, and we'll take our chances with the slimy deep."

"All hands!" Rackham yelled, glowering down from the quarterdeck at her and Daniel. He shot a look to the shore where the soldiers were frantically hatching a plan. "If yer don't wants yer blood to be washing this deck, shake a leg!"

"Captain Rackham," Elizabeth shouted up to him. "We are missing one of our crew. Fancy, the horse that saved your life, must be hauled aboard this ship!"

"No time!" Rackham replied. "Look yonder. The Royal Navy is massing her fleet. She be out to get us!"

Liz planted her feet firmly on the lower deck. "I am not leaving without the horse."

"Cut the nag loose," Rackham ordered Daniel. "And whiles yer at it, cut the chick loose as well. She be more trouble to me than the bluecoat, Cap'n Barnet, who's been after me neck fer months."

Liz ignored him. She cut a large piece of the rigging to his utter

jaw-dropping astonishment. She twisted her damp, stringy hair
down the back of her shirt and lowered herself and the ropes into
the dory beside Fancy. The mare seemed to know exactly what Liz
planned and wasn't the least bit worried. Liz rigged a harness
around the mare's torso as though she were a beached whale that
they were rescuing. Then she towed the remaining rope up to the
deck with her where she wound the two ends around the capstan.

Daniel suddenly realized what she had planned and joined her
at the capstan.

"Black Patch," Daniel shouted. "Your faithful mount is a
needin' yer help!"

Black Patch leaped from the mainmast and grinned. He took
hold of the crank on the opposite side of the capstan and heaved
along with Daniel. As they hauled up the horse, Liz knew that they
were simultaneously dropping the anchor, delaying them precious
minutes of escape time. But Fancy was more precious, and Liz
wasn't leaving her behind.

Rackham cursed as every member of his crew, except Cal, of
course, dropped their tasks to help reel in the spotted mare.

When Fancy was aboard, Rackham scowled. "You be paying
for this lass, with your blood, if we don't cast off at once. Cut
anchor!"

Immediately, Daniel tossed Black Patch his dagger to cut the
anchor cable.

"That'll cost Rackham a pretty penny when he goes to replace
it," Daniel said.

Liz nodded. She had no idea how much an anchor cost and she
had no intention of paying for it.

"Draw on every rag of canvas the yards will hold and let her run
before the wind!" Rackham ordered.

Liz rushed to secure Fancy to the rail. CJ fluttered down to the
deck and decided it was safest to stay on the floor even though he

rolled back and forth like a drunken sailor. Cal ran to man the foresheets. Only fear got his feet flying so fast. Wang stood by the aft sheets. Black Patch climbed the mainmast to let out the sail.

The wind caught. They flew out of the harbour into the open sea. And just in the nick of time. The man-of-war, a Navel ship that had been berthed in Port Royal's harbour was making ready to follow in cold pursuit.

When the vessel was steady, Daniel and Liz joined the captain at the helm. They took turns watching the activities on shore through a telescope. "It will take that ponderous warship a few minutes to manoeuver out of the bay. We have the advantage in that this sloop is light and fast," Daniel said.

"Aye," Rackham agreed. "But what course be best to ditch those dithering bluecoats?"

"Set a course for New Providence," Liz said.

Rackham frowned at her.

"You promised you would do as I asked if I got you out of that jam, and I did. You're alive, aren't you?" Liz asked.

Rackham fondled his neck, coughed and made a big production of clearing his poor tender throat. There were red marks around his neck, burn marks from the noose, but he was alive and kicking and not dancing the hempen jig. "Two blinks of an eye more," Rackham cursed, "and I be a goner."

It would have taken longer than two blinks of an eye. In fact, it would have probably been an interminable two to ten minutes while he writhed and kicked and gasped, and his eyes bulged out of his head and his face turned purple and the veins in his temples threatened to explode.

Liz winced. Not an image she wanted to stick in her mind. She didn't particularly enjoy the company of this fool of an ancestor of hers, but she didn't want to watch his brain explode either.

Black Patch chose this moment to exit the captain's cabin with

Rackham's tricorn hat in his hand. The one-eyed pirate handed the hat to his captain and grinned at Liz. Liz did her best to squash her smile as Rackham slapped the hat on his head.

"I am the captain of this vessel," Rackham said. "We goes where I says."

Liz stared Rackham straight in the eye. Rackham glared back.

"Set a course for New Providence," she ordered. "You have a date with your significant other, Anne Bonny." Liz just hoped that this other ancestor of hers had more backbone than the tricorn hat-toting buffoon.

CHAPTER NINETEEN
I Want You To Write A Letter

Liz tried to sleep. She hadn't slept since that ill-fated night she spent in Rackham's brig. How many days had passed? She didn't know. She only knew that there was a time frame within which the vortex would stay open, then they'd be trapped until the cycle repeated itself and the time chute reappeared.

She lay resting her head on Daniel's bolster. The thing was hard as a rock, but it was all she had for a pillow. The bunk was hard, too. She looked out of the porthole. They were still on course, still headed for New Providence.

Good.

She got up and went to the captain's cabin.

The captain wasn't in there, so he must be on deck. Liz went outside, glanced aft at the quarterdeck, and saw Rackham, in all his calico glory, standing at the helm with Daniel.

Liz climbed the companionway and joined them.

"I give you good morning," Daniel said, flashing his two-fingered salute.

Liz grunted. She stretched and yawned and combed out her slept-on hair with grimy fingers. If she didn't get hold of a bottle of Clairol Herbal Essences shampoo pretty soon, she'd have to hack off this mouse's nest.

"More like good afternoon," Rackham said.

"Okay, so I slept in a bit," Liz argued. "Is that a crime?"

Rackham turned to his quartermaster. "This one speaks like a witch."

And how would you know what a witch speaks like?

Liz decided to zip it. Insulting Rackham first thing in the

morning—oh yeah, it was afternoon—was not so smart.

"We'll see land soon. It's time to plot our move," Liz said. "Come below with me."

Rackham's eye gleamed with mischief. "Yer wants me below, does ye, lass?"

Oh, for crying out loud. Liz clenched her teeth. *Pirates.* They either wanted to rob you, rape you or eat you.

Liz planted her hands on her hips. "I want you to write a letter to Anne. I want it sealed and sent to her at the mansion as soon as we anchor."

"Aye, cap'n," Rackham said sarcastically.

Elizabeth exhaled. I will not let this moronic, dipstick of an ancestor of mine make me lose it. She smiled sweetly. "Let's go."

They went below to Rackham's quarters. The cabin was the same as she had seen it when Daniel was playing the part of Fearless Leader. The room was dim with the sun overhead and not yet reaching the stern windows.

Rackham lit a lantern and set it down on the table. He stared at her. "What makes ye think ye can remove my Anne from the governor's mansion so easy?"

Liz shrugged. "She loves you, doesn't she?"

Rackham chuckled. "Aye, she did. Until I did a stupid thing."

Oh, crap, Liz thought. What did he do?

She waited for the bomb to fall, but he merely smiled. "There is something you do not know," Rackham said. "I been dallying with the likes o' Molly O'Leary." When Liz didn't react, he explained. "Madam O'Leary owns the cathouse by the same name."

Cathouse? Liz thought. Oh, right. A whorehouse. Great. You philandering piece of monkey doo. Just when she thought it was smooth sailing . . . . Out of the frying pan and into the fire.

"A stubborn claw-cat is my Anne," Rackham continued, "and she won't forget it, though she cuckolded her own husband."

"You mean you don't think she'll cooperate because you cheated on her?"

Rackham shrugged. "She's a better pirate than I. Had she wanted to escape, she'd have done so by now."

Liz stared at him. That may be so, but there was still a chance. And as long as she could swing a sword, she would try.

"Write the letter," Liz said. "We'll worry about Anne's response to it later."

Rackham tipped his head in a mock salute. He tossed aside his tricorn hat, which landed on his bunk. He removed a sheet of vellum from the top drawer of a walnut-tree box. From an ivory pen holder, he extracted a goose feather quill.

Rackham's shadow bounced as he fiddled around with the writing materials. What was the matter? Don't tell me he had writer's block? Liz raised her hands in a 'What gives?" gesture. He wasn't even looking at her, so he didn't see her eyes roll.

In profile, his face was actually kind of handsome. Thick brown hair fell to his jaw in ragged curls, just like her mother's.

"Make sure she knows you care and that you're coming for her," Liz said.

Rackham scowled.

Liz had to be careful how she ordered him around. After all, as far as he was concerned, he was head honcho. She would have to keep him thinking that way until Anne had safely returned to his powerful, but somewhat grubby arms.

Liz watched him make his quirky flourishes with the quill pen.

Rackham raised his eyes and brushed the goose feather along his full lips. He watched her, amused at her watching him.

"Sign the letter," she said.

Rackham leaned on his elbows, peering at her, his breath reeking of rum. Liz held her breath without being too obvious about it. So he'd had a liquid breakfast?

Rackham scratched his nose. He tapped the letter. "I wants to know more about this future we is tryin' to save. You told of the scuttlin' of my ship. Does ye means to tell me you captain a vessel yerself and hit me a broadside?"

Liz shook her head. How to explain underwater archaeology and a salvage operation to a lame-brained pirate? "My mother raises sunken ships for a living. Yours was one of them."

Rackham scratched his head. "And why would she be wantin' to do that unless the ship was seaworthy? I be a chunk o' rotted seahorse afore I believes a sunken ship could be made seaworthy. Is this something ye does in the future?"

Liz blew out a gust of exasperated air. "No. We raise them, we don't sail them. Now, sign the letter."

Rackham dipped the quill into the ink once more.

With a flourish he scribbled, *There be better days ahead, Jack.*

Grinning, he passed the vellum to her.

Liz read it over. It was the same letter as the one her mother had stolen from the shipwreck. She handed it back. "Now seal it."

He folded the letter and flattened it. He removed a gold seal ring from his finger, melted a wand of red candle wax, and dripped the wax onto the fold. He pressed the insignia of his ring into the red wax to leave an impression of his seal.

"How did you get the letter to her the first time?" Liz asked.

Rackham frowned. "The *first* time?"

Liz suddenly realized that for him, this *was* the first time.

"How well guarded is she?" Liz asked. "Can we climb the walls to her room?"

"Her bedchamber is heavily guarded, as are the grounds," Rackham said. "To attempt a rescue from the walls is asking fer a musket ball between the eyes." He added with a heavy lacing of sarcasm, "P'raps we needn't be so bold. P'raps we will be most cordially invited to the governor's ball tomorrow night."

Liz clapped her hands to her mouth. Why not? That was brilliant. Woodes Rogers was giving a fancy party in honour of Anne's husband, the man she had left for Jack Rackham. The husband's name was James Bonny, and the governor was inducting him into his ring of privateers.

"Will Anne attend the governor's ball?" Liz asked.

"I should think so," Rackham said.

Liz nodded. "Perfect. We'll disguise ourselves and attend the governor's ball. I'll slip in as Anne. You can come as a Naval officer. As long as she and I are never in the same room together, who would know?"

Rackham scowled. "As I said afore, you speaks like a witch with twisted words and makes as much sense. Don't ye know I'll be gallows meat if I walk boldface into the governor's house? They'd know me in the blink of a catfish's eye. I'll be dancing the hempen jig afore you can say Imp o' Satan."

"You have to be there," Liz said. It was clear to her now that getting the letter to Anne Bonny wasn't enough. Rackham had to show his face to convince her to cooperate.

Liz drummed her fingers on the wooden top of Rackham's table. If only they could simply whisk the woman away through her open window despite the guards. Calico Jack was a pirate, wasn't he? Wasn't that what they did?

Liz looked at Rackham and sighed. She met him square in the eye. "The first matter of business is to get the letter into Anne's hands."

"Then what?"

"Then we swing through the windows or down the spiral staircase, cutlasses blazing. I don't know. First things first. We need costumes. I need a gown. What will she be wearing?"

"I can hardly escort you to the mercer's to buy a piece of silk to be fashioned into a gown," Rackham argued. He paused, then said,

"Of course, there is Molly's."

Rackham glanced out through the porthole at the sun, then sighed. He vehemently shook his head. "The lark will never work. If people thinks you is Anne and the king's soldiers sees ye on the streets, they will think ye escaped, and you will be hauled off to the governor and flogged."

"Do you have a better idea?" Liz demanded.

Rackham rubbed his eyes and blinked at her.

He massaged his throat, coughed. "If only ye was just an apparition of the drink after all."

Liz seized his wrist, dug in her nails. "But I'm not. I'm real!"

Rackham yanked his arm away, sending her flying to the floor. "Tis the grip of a shark ye has. And if ye does that again, I will flog you myself."

Liz crawled to her knees apologetically. "But what about Anne?" she implored. "Don't you want her back?"

"Whether I want her back or not is moot. As I said afore, had she wanted to escape, she would have done so by now."

He grimaced, threw himself onto the bunk and shut his eyes. Liz tossed up her arms in despair. This was no time for sleep. She exhaled in total exasperation and clawed her hair. *Pirates.*

"Captain Rackham," she said. "Wake up. You wrote the letter. You *have* to deliver it."

Rackham opened his eyes. "Is the only way I kin get yer claws off my back to agree?"

"Yep," Liz said, standing tall over his bunk.

Rackham smiled at her. "Aloft then, girl, and set a course for Molly's."

$$$

They reached Nassau harbour on the island of New Providence before nightfall. Liz gazed at the long stretch of blue water that shimmered between the wharves lining the town's waterfront.

There was a low, offshore island of palm trees and sandy beach. This was where they headed to spend the night. A small cove on the other side of the island hid them from the eyes of the bluecoats.

The next morning, Rackham was more hungover than ever. He had finished what rum was on board and was in a pretty good mood. Rackham assigned tasks, and he, Liz, Daniel, Black Patch and Wang took the dory ashore.

Liz's first stop was Molly's.

Molly's fit exactly Liz's image of a whorehouse. Women with different skin tones, from pink and ivory, to caramel and molasses, strutted around in rib-cracking corsets and frilly bloomers. They ranged in age from thirteen to forty. Apparently, Calico Jack had spent a good deal of his shore time here before he had taken up with Anne Bonny.

This was no pleasure outing. Rackham's eyes repeatedly flitted to the window as Liz stood beside him in her borrowed pirate wear.

"Stop looking around like that," Liz complained. "You're making me nervous. What's wrong? You're more jumpy than a condemned man waiting for the gallows."

"I has a feelin'," Rackham said. He glanced around fretfully. "We best not tarry too long. I sent the boys to lay in supplies so that we can make haste soon as this distasteful thing is done."

Distasteful? Liz thought. Rescuing his beloved was distasteful? Did he even like Anne Bonny anymore?

Rackham's eyes shot toward the window again. Daniel was waiting outside, as lookout, in case any of the governor's men got a notion to pop in for a quicky. Wang had gone with Black Patch to get food and water and, Liz assumed, more rum. Cal had been left behind on the *Curlew* to make ready to sail.

"Hello, luv," Rackham said to the madam who sashayed over to hug him.

"Jackie Boy," she said. "What do we have here? Is this your latest, Jackie Boy? I thought you was still carousing with—" She stopped as the resemblance between Liz and Anne Bonny struck her. "Anne has a sister?"

Rackham nodded. "Aye. This be her."

Molly took Liz's hand and swung her around. She pulled aside her blouse and fingered the strap to her orange bikini. "What manner of dress is this?"

Three gold teeth flashed in Molly's mouth. "If she be trying to look like the cabin boy to a pirate master, she best be wearing something less eye-catchin'."

"I would like to borrow a dress," Liz said boldly. "In yellow, if you've got it."

Molly released Liz's shirt. She tugged on one of Liz's sun-kissed—albeit somewhat straggly—strands of brown hair like she was measuring Liz for a wig.

"She's a sassy lass. Yer wants to sell her?" Molly asked.

"I am not for sale!" Liz objected.

Rackham guffawed. "No, she ain't. And she means it. We need a gown, if ye please."

"I'll say she be needin' a gown," Molly said. "If she goes walking the streets like that, she'll end up here faster than a cock to a hen."

"I'd be indebted to ye, Molly," Rackham said.

"You knows I'm always pleased to help ye, Jackie Boy. I'll see what I can do."

"Yellow," Liz called after her. "That's my colour." Molly turned her head for a second and scrunched her eyes.

"Bone lace," Rackham corrected. "Yeller is no colour for a pirate. Anne will almost certainly be wearing bone lace."

CHAPTER TWENTY
I'm Afraid We Be A-Mutinying Again

Molly found the perfect dress, a smooth satin number trimmed with bone lace. It wasn't exactly Liz's taste, but hey, when in the eighteenth century, do what the Georgians do. George I was the king of England, wasn't he?

Now, they had to hope that Jack Rackham knew his lover as well as he thought.

"So far, so good?" Daniel asked, as they came out of the whorehouse with a large package.

"I got a dress if that's what you mean," Liz said.

"What about us?" Daniel asked. "Rackham and I will be needing a disguise, too. We are not letting you handle this charade by yourself."

Liz nodded. Daniel had a point. She needed backup and Rackham had to be there for Anne to see him, if at all possible. "You need uniforms," Liz said. "How are we going to get you official uniforms of the British Royal Navy? And what about Wang? He's Asian. He'll stand out like a pretty peacock amongst all of those ugly ducklings."

"The lad stays behind," Rackham said.

Liz made a face. Unfortunately, Rackham was right. They couldn't take the chance of being noticed. Cal was useless, so he would stay behind as well. The pair of them could make the ship ready for their getaway.

Liz, Daniel and Rackham waited at the dory down by the water. Liz spotted Black Patch and Wang above the beach on the other side of the street. They were coming with arms loaded.

The dory was already crammed with sacks of fresh fruit and

dried goods, as well as a cask of fresh water and a small keg of wine. When Black Patch and Wang arrived, they stacked the remainder of the supplies and shoved the flat-bottomed dory into the sea.

The five of them climbed into the overloaded boat, sinking the hull to six inches from the surface. Daniel rowed.

Rackham was nervous even though they had left Molly's cathouse without incident. He tugged anxiously at his ear. Liz locked eyes with Daniel, but Daniel shrugged and kept rowing. They circled the islet and approached the *Curlew*'s starboard side. The closer they got to the sloop, the more nervous Rackham became.

"What is it?" Liz demanded. "You're driving us all crazy."

Rackham shot his eyes to the quarterdeck, then to the main deck where the ports for the cannons opened. He squinted and Liz squinted, too.

CJ was circling the air above the sloop, squawking. He was so excited he wasn't making clear words.

What's happened? Liz asked her parrot.

WOMBAT! CJ screeched.

Now, she could see. What Liz had thought was a cover over the third gunport was a figure strapped over the mouth of the cannon like a human X.

"It's Cal," Liz screamed.

"Shut yer yap," Rackham ordered. "I sees that. And so does everyone on this boat. You'll do him no good, bringing the ghoul down on us who done that dastardly deed."

The ghoul who done that dastardly deed now saluted them from the *Curlew*'s helm.

"Ahoy, Calico Jack, me boy. It's yer old chum, Charlie Vane!"

The man has truly flipped out, Liz thought.

Vane swaggered over to the rail and glared. "I will blast this bloke to smithereens if ye don't surrender to me now!"

"Come about," Rackham ordered the crew. "We're going back to shore!"

"Stowe that," Liz countered. "We are not going back to shore. We will parley."

"Parley?" Rackham said. "Parley with that unreasonable son of a dogfish? He wants me skin and nothing less. Look you around. Does ye sees a ship? Where's the *Lark*? I'll wager me own miserable life that them bluecoats, that smooth-faced codfish Jonathan Barnet, has taken Vane's ketch and threatened him with the gallows if he doesn't bring me in."

Liz shook her head. "I think he just wants your sloop and your crew. I think we can bargain with him."

"Does ye recall what happened the last time we bargained with him?" Rackham spewed. "I found meself with a squid of a headache, locked in the putrid dungeons of Spanish Town. It be the death of me, it will. You be the death of me."

Oh, stop being such a drama queen, Liz thought.

Liz called out to the maniacal captain. "Captain Vane. We wish to parley!"

Vane shook his head. "Ye sees the poor bloke over the cannon? I has a gunner behind that cannon, and I will blow the bastard to hell and back unless ye hands over yer rascally captain."

"And if we do," Liz shouted, "will you cut down that man?"

"I will," Vane said, tossing her some frayed rope. "But no afore ye ties the slimy eel with these braces and hoists him shipboard."

Rackham glared at her, his hand on his pistol.

"Captain Rackham," Liz said. "Charles Vane wants your crew. That means he has no crew or very little crew, and I doubt that he even has a man behind that cannon. However, I can't take any chances. So we are going to turn you in. Then, we will rescue you. *Again.*"

Liz knew her voice sounded just a teensy bit impatient, but for the love of God, she *was* impatient. This whole thing was taking entirely too long.

"We're agreed," Liz shouted to Vane. "Permission to come aboard, sir!"

Vane grinned. He was a cocky, foolish, joke of a pirate, just like Calico Jack. But unlike Charles Vane, Liz needed Jack Rackham.

Liz turned to Daniel before making the move to board.

"What do you think?" she asked. "Do you think he has any men?"

Wang stared at Daniel, then at Cal who was shrieking in terror. "God, we better get him down before he has a heart attack," Wang said.

Daniel shrugged. "I think Vane is bluffing, but obviously, old Cal doesn't think so. I think we best do as Vane asks."

"Sorry, Cap'n," Daniel said to Rackham. "But I'm afraid we be a-mutinying again."

"Ye shall have to kill me first," Rackham said, drawing his pistol on Liz.

Liz did an eyelock with Wang who was sitting behind Rackham. Carefully, and without upsetting the already precariously loaded dory, Wang picked up the keg of wine and bopped Captain Jack Rackham on the bean.

"This is starting to get boring," Wang said.

Liz leaned over to check Rackham's pulse. "He's alive. But one more bump on the head like that and I think he'll have permanent brain damage."

$$$

Liz would have preferred an alternative to knocking out the poor blustering pirate captain again, but he had left her no choice. There had to be a better way to resolve this mess. What did Vane want? Revenge on Rackham? Or could he be bought?

Jonathan Barnet had bought him. She wondered if the governor of Jamaica had reneged on the promised bounty when Rackham escaped the noose. Ten thousand pieces of eight was a cool fortune. The governor would have eschewed handing over the prize until Jack Rackham's body was clamped in irons and swinging over the pristine waters of Deadman's Cay.

Likewise, the pardon would have been retracted. Vane's reward for handing over the comical, nuisance of a pirate would have been to have his ship confiscated and his crew running for the hills. So maybe Vane was willing to barter.

The question was, What did Liz have, other than Rackham, that could make up for all that lost loot?

Vane was still waiting for her to tie up Calico Jack. He hardly needed to be bound now. He wasn't going anywhere on his own steam.

Liz glanced back to the shores of New Providence. There was a ship berthed in the docks that she had noticed while she was waiting for Rackham and Daniel to be hanged. The ship was a sloop, exactly like the *Curle*w. It was called the *William* and its name rang a freakishly familiar bell.

Why?

Liz turned her back on Vane and yanked out her iPocket. She hunched over the keys so he couldn't see that she was sending a request to Rebel Goddess.

Need info on sloop. Re: *William*

Lu answered almost immediately:

TG your alive!

Liz typed:

Ditto. Need info now!

There was no answer for awhile, then Lu replied with all the details of the *William*, including her cargo. The sloop was stolen by Calico Jack just prior to being caught by Jonathan Barnet in

October of 1720. Okay, Liz thought. So it won't matter too much if it's stolen a little ahead of schedule.

Liz typed:

THX B home soon! (She hoped)

She sent Lu multiple electronic hugs (((H))).

Liz stowed her iPocket back inside her sash. She told Daniel and Wang what she planned. If Vane agreed, she would hijack the *William* and her crew, force them to sign the pirate's articles under threat of torture, and consign the ship to Vane.

"But won't that create another paradox?" Wang asked. He was really getting into this paradox thing now. "If the *William* is stolen too early, doesn't that mean we're sending Rackham to an early grave?"

Daniel cut in. "No. No, I don't think so. Liz is onto something. The ship will be stolen by us, not Rackham, so the time line won't be affected." He glanced at the poor pirate captain, who was slumped over, drooling on his chest. "Odds are, the first chance they get, the crew of the *William* will mutiny and maroon old Vane on another turtle-infested island where he'll feast on his boots and seaweed for another week."

"Boy, will he be mad," Liz said, snickering.

"It's a hare-brained scheme, but it just might work. The cargo on that sloop will certainly make up for the loss of the governor's gold," Daniel said.

Charles Vane suddenly roared at them. "Is ye coming aboard? I thought we had an agreement. Or did ye wish that I should blow yer shipmate here to atoms?"

Liz looked to see poor Cal renew his shrieking. He was still tied to the cannon's mouth and, any minute, it looked like he was going to pass out from corporeal fright.

"I have a proposition for you," Liz shouted up to Vane. "We're coming aboard."

Liz climbed the rope ladder to the main deck of the *Curlew*. Daniel and Black Patch followed with Rackham between them. Wang took up the rear with the supplies.

Vane sneered at them from the quarterdeck as they approached with their unconscious captain. Then he descended to the main deck to meet them.

"So, the poor snivelling coward needs to be put ter sleep afore he can meet his fate."

Daniel and Black Patch dropped Rackham at Vane's feet. Calico Jack looked a sorry sight. He was a ridiculous excuse for a pirate. He hardly looked like he was worth his weight in Spanish gold.

"I don't get it," Liz said, staring Vane straight in his wicked uni-browed eyes. "Jack Rackham is a small-time pirate. Your reputation, Captain Vane, precedes you. Your name is by far more widely known and feared than this calico-sporting jack-in-the-box. Why would the governor reward and pardon you for turning him in?"

"He is what we in the business calls a pest. He slips in and out of bays and coves on his swift sloops like a rat dodging a cat. He boards small craft and he strips them, and he is on his merry way afore anyone knows they been pilfered. He is a sly, crafty devil. And no one likes a crafty pirate."

So Rackham was considered clever? Ha, ha. Liz couldn't wait to see that. She pinched her lips together and sized up the rugged sailor. Charlie Vane looked fifty if he looked a day, but she knew it was only the weather and hard living that made him look so old. He was very likely only in his thirties.

"I have a proposition for you," Liz said.

"You wish to parley?"

Well, not exactly. Didn't 'parley' mean to discuss? She really had no intention of discussing anything with Captain Vane. Vane would accept her terms. Or else.

Or else what? CJ cut into her thoughts.

Liz scowled. Or else . . . She didn't know. She'd worry about that later.

"Here is my proposition," Liz said.

She told him about the *William* and its cargo. "She arrived in Nassau harbour last night," Liz said. "I saw her berthed, loaded down with gold, sugar, tobacco and silks from the Indies."

Vane's brown eyes turned amber in his pleasure, and the unibrow separated into two hairy caterpillars.

"What do you say?" Liz asked, smiling brilliantly. "I give you the *William* for the *Curlew* and her pathetic excuse for a captain."

"Elizabeth," Cal shrieked from the starboard cannon. "Quit your yakking and get that sadistic, bloodthirsty savage to cut me down!"

Liz turned back to Captain Vane. "You will, of course, cut down that paltry imitation for a sea hand. He's hardly worth it."

Vane snickered at the terrified man plastered to the hull. He glanced down at the helpless Rackham, who was no longer a nuisance. "A'right then, cut the snivellin' cockroach down and hoist him aboard." He gestured to Black Patch and Wang who went to extricate Cal from his mind-breaking living nightmare.

"I wants Rackham as collateral," Vane said. "How does I know ye'll succeed in gettin' me the *William* and her crew? What makes yer thinks ye kin sway the young sea dogs aboard her to accept my command?"

"You have my word," Liz said.

Vane scoffed. "Yer word? Yer word's as good as a pirate's."

So true, Liz thought.

"Well, Rackham will be of no use to you unconscious, and I'll convince the sailors aboard the *William* to join your company by bribing them with rum. You'll have their John Henry's before they even know they've signed your pirate articles," Liz insisted.

"Aye, the rum," Vane said, smacking his lips. "Where be this rum?"

Another quandary for later.

"Don't worry," Liz said. "I'll get it." She was pretty sure Molly and her girls could help—not only with the rum, but with persuading any of the young sailors who rebelled against the idea of pirating. As soon as Molly heard that Rackham was in trouble . . . Hadn't Molly said she was always pleased to help Jackie Boy?

"We'll leave Rackham in his bunk. You don't need a hostage," Liz said. "How's this for a plan. You come with us when we take the *William* and convert her crew. We're without a captain now, and we need your expertise."

Vane obviously liked that idea. "Agreed," he said. He glanced at the keg of wine that was lying at her feet among all their other provisions. "Is that the grog? Then we must drink to our contract."

He fetched a spigot for the keg and some pewter goblets from the captain's quarters, then led Liz and Daniel to the quarterdeck. On the main deck, Liz could hear Cal screaming at Wang in terror and total ingratitude. "I am not staying with these depraved maniacs another second. These pirates are inhuman. They're psychopathic, vicious and insane." Cal couldn't think of enough epithets to describe their ungracious host. He was tripping over his tongue with uncontrolled verbal vomit.

Well, what did you expect? Liz wanted to screech at him. They're pirates. They don't call them bloodthirsty for nothing.

CJ rose from the port rail and fluttered his wings at Cal. Cal brutally swatted the parrot away. Wang grabbed Cal's wrist before he could actually bat the annoying bird like a ball. Wang smiled sheepishly and helped Cal below.

When Wang returned to the main deck, he was alone. He joined Black Patch at the port rail where Fancy, the spotted mare, was still tethered.

Liz was just about to accept a goblet of wine from Captain Vane, when Wang yelled from the main deck. "Elizabeth, Daniel. It's the vortex!"

The pirates were clueless as to what all the hollering was about. Daniel frowned and Liz stared in awe as the vortex, the whirling mouth to the time chute, swirled half a kilometre away.

"What Devil's sorcery is this?" Vane asked.

Liz dropped her goblet as a tall, blonde figure exited the crew's quarters in a black diving suit, replete with oxygen tank. "I've had enough, Elizabeth Latimer," Cal shouted to the quarterdeck. "You are on your own!"

Cal climbed the rail and tumbled over the side.

"Man overboard!" CJ squawked.

Cal headed straight for the vortex that looked as though it were moving north. As the wine from Liz's cup spilled over her feet like blood, Cal disappeared in a swirling mass of water.

CHAPTER TWENTY-ONE
The Name Is Noah Harwood

The skank, Liz thought. WOMBAT, triple WOMBAT. Cal Sorensen was truly a waste of money, brains and time. She should never have let him stay in the first place. Or she should have insisted he go with Tess. It was all Tess's fault anyway. Why should Liz be saddled with this dirtbag?

Cal had jumped ship just when they needed all hands. Well, screw him. She knew she couldn't trust him. She only hoped that, with what he'd seen and heard, he wouldn't use the knowledge to the detriment of them all.

Okay, she was being a drama queen. But she had this prickly feeling. She felt exactly the way Jack Rackham had felt in Molly's cathouse—and look what that had got them.

"We don't have much time," Vane said, breaking into Liz's fuming. "Captain Barnet of the Royal Navy is on our tail. As we speak, his ship be docking in the harbour. How are you going to get around that?"

Liz stared at Charlie Vane. He was actually making sense right now, and he was speaking to her with respect. If there was one thing she'd learned about pirates, it was that they were never consistent. Not in action, speech or thought.

Liz had to think quick. How to steal the *William* while avoiding Jonathan Barnet, attend the governor's ball and get to Anne Bonny with Rackham, whisk Anne away, and find the vortex so that Liz could get home?

"Captain Barnet will not be suspecting the commandeering of the *William*," Daniel said. "We can take her in broad light. Much of the crew will be ashore. Those who remain will be politely coerced to join the pirate company."

"Yeah," Liz said. "But what about Barnet's ship, the *Tyger*? Won't she be in the harbour, too?"

"Tonight is the governor's ball," Daniel said. "Captain Barnet will be in attendance. Of that much I am sure."

"We will need uniforms for you and Rackham," Liz said.

Vane cut in, "Calico Jack is not going anywhere until I get me ship and me gold."

"Of course," Liz replied. "You will get it."

Hijacking the *William* was the least of her problems. Maybe they should hijack Barnet's ship instead. A snow was as good as a sloop to a pirate, wasn't it? That would save them the trouble of encountering Barnet at the ball. But there was still the problem of what to do with him if they took his ship.

No, she decided. Capturing Barnet and his ship would never work. The *Tyger* was not loaded with valuable cargo. Vane would never go for it.

All right then, they would take the *William*.

The hijacking party consisted of her, Captain Vane, Daniel, Black Patch and Wang. Rackham was towed to his bunk and left to sleep off that bump on the head. Liz hoped that he would feel well enough tonight to attend the governor's ball.

The long sheet of brilliant blue water that was Nassau harbour seemed suspiciously quiet. Few boats were anchored offshore. But the wharves lining the town's waterfront were bustling as usual. The treed islet, where the *Curlew* was anchored, hid the sloop from the town's view.

Elizabeth and her gang of merry hijackers boarded the dory. Daniel rowed them around the islet to the sheltered bay where a single, small trading vessel sat anchored. The vessel was the *William*, and, not too far from it, Liz recognized the *Tyger*. Liz's iPocket suddenly vibrated under her sash. From his seat at the bow,

Vane saw Liz jump and frowned at her. She put her hand to the small electronic device but didn't dare open it. How would she explain a palm-sized computer, or any computer for that matter, to an eighteenth century pirate?

Thank God, she had switched it from audio to vibrate.

Daniel rowed the dory with his back toward New Providence. Vane scowled where he sat at the bow with Wang in front of him. Black Patch sat in the stern behind Daniel with his back to the harbour. Liz sat facing Wang, who was also frowning at her. The iPocket was still vibrating. How to see the message from Lu without Vane catching a glimpse of it over Wang's shoulder?

Liz got Wang's attention, motioned with her eyes to her sash where the iPocket was stashed. Wang's eyes blinked wide, then he nodded. He leaned slightly forward. Liz curled like she felt seasick and passed the iPocket to him. He opened it with his back hunched just enough so that the pirate captain behind him saw nothing.

Wang's face went still, and his sun-darkened, medium complexion paled.

Liz wanted to grab the iPocket from him but restrained herself by hooking her hands under her seat. Slowly, she leaned toward Wang. "What is it?" she mouthed.

Wang turned the small screen to face her and held it at his chest. The text was from Stevie, not from Lulu.

What Elizabeth read on the miniature screen made her heart do triple flips. Stevie was wrong about the time frame. The vortex was moving north. It would close tonight.

Liz indicated for Wang to slip her the iPocket as secretly as he had received it.

Shit, Liz thought. She had never said 'shit' in her life.

$$$

Elizabeth Latimer and her company of four targeted the single-masted sailboat that was anchored in the middle of the channel.

The ship was a twelve-ton sloop like the *Curlew*. On its bow was painted the name *William*. The *William* had four guns on her broad, sun-bleached decks and two swivel guns mounted on her rails. She was fitted out exactly like the *Curlew*. If she held the cargo Liz had promised, then she truly was a prize. Vane grinned in anticipation. He informed Liz that merchant ships were well equipped with ammunition, so they must be cautious.

They were in luck. The canoe lying alongside the vessel was gone. That meant some of the crew, at least, were on shore. As the dory drew closer, it was clear that no one was keeping watch. Black Patch, Liz and Wang slipped aboard.

The decks were empty. Liz peeked into the captain's cabin. Daniel's dagger hung in a leather sheath at her hip. She didn't need it. The captain was not aboard.

She returned to the main deck and looked up. On the quarterdeck, someone was looking at her. The figure was slight, like Liz. It was either a cabin boy or a woman.

Liz placed her hand on the grip of the dagger. You could never be too careful.

"Ahoy," she shouted. "Is your captain aboard?"

"You saw yerself that he was not," the boy or woman said.

So the boy or woman had seen her sneak into the captain's quarters.

"Don't be afraid," Liz said. "Are you alone? I won't hurt you."

The boy or woman leaped from the quarterdeck and landed in Liz's face, cutlass flashing.

"Aye, you may wish me no harm, lassie, fer I kin sees you is a woman. I, on the other hand, will slice you without hesitation if ye don't tells me why you have boarded my master's ship."

Didn't see that one coming, Liz thought. Liz stared at the boy or woman. He or she was dressed in a man's jacket and trousers with a red kerchief tied around his or her skull. The face was plain and browned by sun and wind, but the features were small and the eyes fierce.

"You're a woman," Liz said.

A moment of hesitation passed before the woman got it together and answered. "As are you. How did you know? No one aboard me ship knows, and I will give you a bellyful of pickling brine if you speaks of this again."

As far as Liz knew, a bellyful of pickling brine meant that the sailor woman intended to cut her open and toss her into the salty brink if she let on to any of her crew that she was female.

"No worries there," Liz said and zipped her lips with a flourish.

The woman smiled. "Who is your master?" she asked.

"I have no master," Liz said. "My name is Elizabeth Latimer, and at the moment I am with Captain Charles Vane's company and we intend to commandeer this ship."

The woman laughed.

A lightbulb flashed in Liz's head. "You're Mary Read."

This time the woman's jaw dropped to her carefully flattened chest. "How could ye know that? No one knows that."

Elizabeth sucked on her upper lip, thoughtfully. Of course, no one knew that. Mary Read was not yet part of Rackham's crew. She soon would be. But first she had to join Charlie Vane's.

Liz hated to lie, but she had no choice. She had to get Mary's cooperation. "I'm a witch," Liz said. "I know things. If you want to live, you must join Captain Vane's crew. But don't worry, Mary. There be better days ahead for you."

Mary Read could have lopped off Liz's head then and there if she'd wanted to. She didn't. She stood in open-mouthed shock, maybe even fear.

Mary swallowed as Black Patch and Wang came onto the deck from the crew's quarters with eight drunken sailors in tow.

It looked like they wouldn't be needing Molly's help or the rum after all.

"It was that easy?" Liz asked Wang.

Wang shrugged. "They're merchant seamen, not pirates. They weren't expecting us and didn't have weapons on them." He waved Black Patch's flintlock pistol. "None of them wanted an iron ball in the eye." Wang glanced briefly at the weapon. "I have to admit, though, I didn't feel all that good pulling this on a bunch of hammered, unarmed men. Mind you, I don't think any of them knows what's happening. They probably think they're having hallucinations."

Liz nodded. She felt the same. This was one escapade that she'd taken on reluctantly. But it was a matter of life and death. Her life—and the life of whatever she did or affected that would shape the course of the future. Wow, was that ever egotistical. But no one was giving her a choice.

She stared at the hapless bunch of sailors. Wang was staring at Mary.

Liz finally found something to smile about in this whole fiasco. "Wang, meet—"

Mary glared, her fist whitening at the knuckles where she gripped her half-sheathed cutlass.

"The name is Noah Harwood," Mary said.

"Yeah." Liz nodded. "Noah Harwood."

Wang glanced at Liz. Liz arched her brows, nodded again.

"Pleased to make your acquaintance, young sir," Wang said.

Liz grinned. Great save. But she knew that Wang knew. And as a promising, young Archaeology of Piracy scholar, Wang was thrilled to have met the notorious Mary Read in the flesh. It was too bad that he was not going to meet Anne Bonny. Liz decided that Wang's sacrifice to Liz's crusade was over. Vane had his ship and his crew. The vortex was disappearing. It was time for Wang to go home.

$$$

Liz turned away from the sea. No time to lose. Barnet's ship was in the harbour. The sailors of the merchant vessel signed Vane's pirate articles under threat of death. Liz hated what Vane was doing, loathed being an accessory to the despicable crime, but Daniel assured her that Vane would get his comeuppance in a matter of months. Meanwhile, the sailors would not be tortured. Vane was a blowhard, so full of hot air that he was scary, but he was not known to be a viciously cruel pirate like Blackbeard or Edward Low. Daniel predicted that in a matter of weeks the men would mutiny and return the ship to her captain.

The last of the *William*'s men signed the articles. Now it was Mary Read's turn. She stared at the document and threw the quill pen down. Her shipmates were so drunk they simply laughed. "I will never be a pirate," Mary said. "I will die before I sign your articles."

"Then die you will," Vane said, drawing a musketoon.

Liz drew her dagger, but she didn't have to. Mary wasn't stupid. She was standing at the starboard rail, and it was just a matter of a swift leg over and she was in the sea and swimming toward Barnet's ship.

A shot From Vane's musketoon fired after her and missed.

Oh no, Liz thought. Mary Read was going to turn them in to the Royal Navy.

"Back to the *Curlew*!" she shouted.

"A minute, gal," Vane said.

Liz turned and found herself staring down the barrel of Vane's musketoon. "I just lost one of me crew. I wants him back or I wants one of you to replace him."

Liz exhaled. She'd had enough of this blowhard. "Captain Vane," she said. "That sailor was a mere boy. He obviously can't be bought and would rather die than become a pirate. You have eight strong men. You're better off without the boy. If he'd stayed, you'd always be watching your back."

The chill in Liz's stomach ebbed as the pirate captain absorbed her words. She exhaled. He was buying it. Captain Vane was even more of a pill-head than she had thought.

"Gets off me ship afore I change my mind," Vane said.

"Aye, sir." Liz said.

CHAPTER TWENTY-TWO
They's Boardin' Us, Cap'n

Rackham was returning to consciousness from that whack on the head. He lay, limbs akimbo, on his bunk, moaning in his sleep. Wang stood at the door with CJ on his shoulder, while Liz knelt on the floor and bathed Rackham's hair and scalp with a solution of rum and seawater. The alcohol would numb the pain in his skull, and the smell of liquor would make the pirate think he'd simply been drinking. For good measure, she poured two fingers of rum down his throat and watched most of it trickle along his chin.

"When you look at him like this," Wang said, "he doesn't look so fearsome."

"He's not so fearsome," Liz said. "His greatest crime is probably that he drinks like a squid, likes women too much, and loves spending large sums of money more."

Wang nodded. Very little was written about Calico Jack Rackham in the history books. And it looked like he and Liz had nothing to add.

"He's coming to," she said. "In case he remembers what happened before he blacked out, you better make yourself scarce."

Wang left and CJ fluttered onto the back of the captain's chair and stared at Rackham. Liz corked the rum and rose to her feet.

"Wasn't that a party?" she said, as Rackham cussed back to life.

"God rot my bones, what happened?" Rackham rubbed his eyes and glared at her, then tested his balance on his elbows. "Me head feels like the thunder of forty guns."

"Forty guns," CJ mimed.

Liz smiled. No, just one keg of wine.

"You don't remember?" she asked. "We swung a deal with your

old pal Charlie Vane. We have the *Curlew* and her crew. And old Charlie is as happy as a lark." Liz grinned.

"He got the *Lark* back?" Rackham bellowed, then sank back to his bolster, gripping his head.

"No. I believe Captain Jonathan Barnet has custody of the ketch. We got Captain Vane the *William*."

Rackham rose to his elbows again. "The *William*? You captured the *William*? And how many men did that cost ye?"

"Not a one. They was a-partyin' hardy. And gave up the sloop with nary a fight."

Rackham scowled. "Aye, and ye still speaks like a bloody foreign witch."

Liz stepped back from Rackham's bunk and glanced around for where he hung his clothes. He needed a uniform or at least something presentable to wear to the governor's ball.

"How's the head?" Liz asked.

"I been better."

"Well, you're not dead," Liz said. "So be grateful for small mercies."

"Not dead," CJ repeated.

Shut up, Liz thought.

Rackham frowned. "Should I be?"

Liz bit her lip. "No. I just meant—that was some party, huh?"

Rackham tasted his breath, smelled the rum in the air, and acknowledged that it was coming from himself.

"Where did yer get the rum?" he asked. "We brought none aboard."

"I borrowed a bottle from the *William*."

Enough of the small talk, Liz thought. They had no time to lose. She went to the captain's table and lifted the letter that he had written last night. The bright red seal was unbroken.

"Is Anne allowed to receive mail?" Liz asked.

"Mail?" Rackham asked. "What is this mail?"

"The post. Letters. You know, correspondence. Is she allowed to receive correspondence from outside the mansion?"

"Aye, she is. But the governor's men opens the letters afore she reads them."

"So they know who and what she's corresponding about."

"Aye."

Liz paced up and down Rackham's cabin. Crap, crap and double crap. How were they to get word to Anne Bonny that Rackham was coming?

"She must be really pissed off at you to put up with being a prisoner in the governor's house," Liz said.

He grinned. "Pissed, that she is."

"It's not funny," Liz said. "You really have no idea how serious this is."

Rackham rose from his bunk and stood towering over her.

"I have a mind to remove your mealy mouth jib from me quarters and get back to pirating like afore I ever laid eyes on you plague o' the seas."

"Well, that won't happen unless we rescue Anne Bonny," Liz said.

Rackham sank back onto his bunk and stared at her. "You really is her seed. A claw-cat like I never saw afore my Anne—and yer got the same yap on ye."

Liz smiled. This was the closest thing to a compliment that Jack Rackham had ever given her.

"And just as stubborn," Liz said.

"Aye, that also." His blue eyes twinkled.

"But I can be swayed, and so can she," Liz said, waving the letter in his face. "We just need to get this letter to her."

Rackham sighed. "To resist yer will is to condemn myself to me grave."

Resistance is futile, Liz agreed.

"We need a uniform for you," Liz said. "I need you to escort me to the governor's ball. Once inside, I'll find a way to get the letter to Anne. Then, we'll fix a rendezvous for you and her."

"I cannot enter the mansion," Rackham said.

Liz frowned. "Well, maybe you won't have to."

"There be extra soldiers to protect her and to keep her from trying to escape. But she will be expected to stand by her husband when he accepts his commission."

Little did the governor or Rackham know that James Bonny never did take up that commission. He chickened out and returned to his sorry occupation of turtling. He died in a hurricane while hunting sea turtles.

Liz was about to hatch her plan when Black Patch came stumbling into the captain's cabin shouting, "Captain, we is being hailed!"

Rackham cowered for an instant. Liz glared at him. He caught her look and slowly straightened his back. "Who hails us?" he asked.

"It be the captain of the *Tyger*."

Captain Barnet. Liz wasn't surprised. So, Mary Read had got to him.

Liz exchanged looks with Rackham. What was he going to do? Hide down here?

"How many men has he?" Rackham asked.

"An entire ship's complement," Black Patch answered.

Rackham fell silent.

"We stand and fight, Cap'n?"

"No." Rackham shook his head. "You tells the captain of the *Tyger* that the captain of the *Curlew* is not aboard."

The expression on Black Patch's face reflected Liz's own thoughts. White-livered coward.

Rackham saw the looks. "If we fights, we dies. If I turns meself in, yer plans, me pretty poppet, are finished."

Liz swallowed. Of course. What was she thinking? He was right. It was the only way. They had to hide Rackham until Barnet left the ship.

"They's boardin' us, Cap'n," Black Patch said uneasily. Liz could hear the thunder of footsteps on the deck.

"Save yerself, Patch," Rackham said.

Black Patch drew his dagger and went out on deck.

"Hide," Liz said and ran after Black Patch to face Captain Barnet.

$$$

Bright sunlight blinded Elizabeth as she pounded her way onto the deck. Wang was on the quarterdeck and Daniel went below to greet Barnet. Black Patch stood beside Daniel with his dagger at the ready. Ten marines and Barnet stood on the main deck. Mary Read was among them.

Mary Read was one of the fiercest fencers in pirate history. She and Anne Bonny stood alone defending their ship while the men of their company drank themselves to oblivion. But that was another story. Liz needed Mary Read on her side to win Barnet over.

"The captain is not aboard," Liz said, brushing Daniel aside. "He's ashore drinking himself silly."

Captain Barnet stared at Liz. She had stopped to put on the ball gown that was stashed in Daniel's cabin before showing herself to the men of the Royal Navy. Barnet gave her a slight bow.

"And who might you be?" he asked, puzzled.

"I am Elizabeth Latimer. Our ship was robbed and scuttled by pirates, and I was taken prisoner by those swine to be used in unspeakable ways. Alas, for your fortunate arrival, I am saved."

"How many aboard this sloop?" Barnet asked.

"Only what you see," Elizabeth said.

"How is it that you speak for these men?"

"Perhaps I was not clear," Liz answered. "I am Lady Elizabeth Latimer, cousin to the governor's wife. And this is Daniel, my brother."

Daniel's eyes popped wide with amusement. Liz could hardly keep a straight face. She swallowed and pointed to Black Patch and Wang. "These men are my domestics."

Liz intercepted a gleam in Wang's eye, and even Black Patch caught on.

Why Mary Read didn't expose them was something Liz couldn't quite wrap her brain around. Surely Mary recognized her despite the fancy dress.

Barnet looked at Mary. Mary shrugged.

"Where is the crew? They left you unguarded?" Barnet asked.

Liz looked around her and flounced her hands helplessly like two flowers fluttering in the wind. "Where could we go? My brother here is a gentleman of letters, not to mention mute. He knows nothing of sailing ships, though they forced him to wear their costume. And my servants, they cook and attend to my needs. What do they know of ships and such? There is sea all around us and none of us swim. We are stranded as they have taken the dory."

Liz hoped they hadn't noticed the dory fastened to the other side of the ship. She also hoped that Daniel hadn't spoken before her appearance on deck as she had just called him mute.

"Then have no fear, Lady," Barnet said. "You and yours are now under the protection of his Majesty's Navy."

Elizabeth curtsied. "I thank you, sir."

"Come aboard the *Tyger* and I shall escort your company to town."

Liz had to think fast. If they boarded the *Tyger* . . . Well, that was one way to get to town.

Perhaps Captain Barnet would be so kind as to escort her to the governor's ball? Only problem was: did the gov's wife have a cousin? Oh, dear. This was a pretty pickle. But she'd worry about that later.

"If you give me a moment, sir, to collect my things? And if you would lend me this young boy," she pointed to Mary Read.

"He is nothing but a young scoundrel, up to no good I suspect," Barnet said. "I do not trust him."

Liz smiled sweetly. "Your men must make the ship ready. You are attending the governor's ball, are you not?"

Barnet nodded.

"Then I mustn't impose upon any of them. This young sir can help me with my things."

For some reason, Mary Read followed Liz into the captain's cabin. For an even stranger reason, Captain Barnet did not question her wish to take the pirate boy with her when she had two perfectly good menservants.

"Captain Rackham?" Liz whispered as she entered his quarters. There was no answer. She swung around and drew Mary Read inside. CJ fluttered down onto Liz's shoulder.

Mary stared at the parrot, then at Liz. Maybe it was because Liz had stuck to her word and not betrayed Mary's gender that Mary was going along with Liz's charade.

"I need your help," Liz said.

Mary narrowed her eyes. "Why should I help you?"

"Because if you don't, Captain Barnet will clap you in irons. He thinks you're a pirate."

Liz was free with her threats because she could see that Mary had been relieved of any weapons.

"I am not a pirate," Mary retorted.

Liz nodded. "Do you know the pirate woman, Anne Bonny?"

Liz waited for the answer. One thing that Mary Read didn't

know was that Liz would know if she was lying.

"Aye," she said. "I know of her."

"Then you know her predicament."

Mary scowled.

"She wishes to return to her captain, Jack Rackham."

"And why should I wish to help a pirate?" Mary asked.

Because one day you will be one, too, Liz thought. And you and Anne Bonny will be the best of friends.

"Because she is a fellow seafarer and a woman who lives the life of a man, as do you. And because you are one of the fiercest fighters in the Caribbean."

Mary's eyes flashed. "How do you know that?"

"Your reputation precedes you, Noah Harwood," Elizabeth said.

"And if I agree?"

"If you agree, you will get your freedom. The freedom to choose your own master."

"And you, Elizabeth Latimer, who is *your* master?"

Liz hesitated. "Not Jack Rackham."

"Yet you fight for him," Mary said.

"I fight for myself," Liz said. "As will you."

CHAPTER TWENTY-THREE
If You Really Think You're In Danger, Then How The Crap Do You Think I Can Leave You?

Captain Barnet allowed Liz to take her domestics and the mare to his vessel. Barnet didn't know about CJ, so Liz left CJ in Rackham's cabin. Liz gave the cabin a quick once-over before she left it, but she couldn't find Rackham. The important thing was to get Barnet and his men off the *Curlew*. Barnet's men scoured the sloop and found it empty. They decided not to leave a sentry to guard it. They intended to capture Calico Jack Rackham before he returned to his ship from his alleged bout of drinking.

What Liz proposed to do with Fancy right now, she wasn't sure. But whatever happened, in the end, Fancy would have to be freed. Barnet's men took Fancy below the hatches. Liz refrained from objecting even though it would seem like prison to the skittish mare. Once they docked, Liz would get her out.

Aboard the *Tyger*, Daniel was invited to tour the ship with the captain. Could Daniel remain mute? She giggled at the predicament she'd landed him in.

The *Tyger*'s first lieutenant showed her to the captain's quarters where she could freshen up. Liz curtsied in her bone lace gown. The lieutenant bowed. His face was completely deadpan. Did she look that bad? Liz requested that Mary accompany her and sent her men away. Liz stared into a gilded mirror that hung on the wall opposite the captain's bunk. Yeah, okay, she looked pretty bad. She looked like a cat had wrestled a bird in her hair. The contrast between the messy hair and the ostentatious gown made her look like one of Madam Molly's prostitutes. Liz sat down at a small table beneath the mirror and combed her fingers through the tangles.

"I need help," Liz said. She swung to face Mary, scraping the chair on the floor. "Help me do my hair."

She needed a chroma-shine fix and only Pantene Pro-V shampoo would do that. Too bad she hadn't thought to bring any with her. But who was thinking of silky, shiny hair when time travel was involved? Liz sighed. When on shipboard, improvise. But how?

Mary waited, jeeringly, for orders. Failing to get any, she shook her head impatiently. She stepped out of the cabin and returned fifteen minutes later with Wang and a bucket of water.

"No shampoo?" Liz asked.

"I beg yer pardon?" Mary said.

"You know, soap?"

"Soap will dry yer hair and make it sticky," Mary said.

We couldn't have that.

Liz washed her hair in plain water and dried it with a cotton cloth. Then she sat in the sun, where it shone through the captain's window at the stern of the ship. She fluffed her hair up with her fingers. Wang waited at the door grinning at her in her girly-girl costume, doing girly-girl things to her hair. Shut up, Liz informed him with a perfectly razor sharp glare. Wang pinched his lips together and tried not to smile. Mary watched Liz return to the mirror, braid her hair into a single long rope, then wind it into a pretzel-like figure eight behind her head. Mary brought Liz some hairpins and helped Liz to fasten her do.

"What is this?" Mary asked, touching the flying dagger earring on Liz's left lobe.

Only my lifeline, Liz thought. Or was it her deathline?

"An ear bobble," Elizabeth said.

"I have never seen anything the likes of that. It looks to be a pirate's token."

And so it was, Liz thought.

"It is pierced through your ear."

"Yes." Was there a problem with that? Didn't eighteenth century women have pierced ears?

Mary stepped back from her as though she had cooties. After not washing her hair for several days, she wouldn't be surprised if things were growing in there.

"You don't like it?" Liz asked. "I'll remove it." She unhooked the earring and slipped it into the bikini top she wore under her gown. Oh-oh. Now, Mary was ogling her red thumbnail with the chipped, black skull and crossbones. Liz tucked her thumb into her fist.

Mary continued to rudely ogle, but Liz ignored the sailor woman's dropped jaw and monkey-wide eyes. Liz felt her chest where the earring was buried in the cup of her orange bikini top. Would Daniel disappear because she'd removed the earring? She bit her lip. Probably not. He had appeared before she ever possessed the earring.

"How do I look?" Liz asked, standing up, patting her coif, and twirling for Wang.

"Goofy," Wang said. "Like Madam Pompadour."

Liz punched him in the arm. Mary stared at them both. Her eyes narrowed suspiciously. "What language is that you speak?"

"As you can see," Wang said, pointing to his Asian features, "I am not from around these parts. We don't speak the same as you."

Liz punched him again. That was lame.

"Why do you let your domestics speak to you that way?" Mary asked Liz. She narrowed her eyes, totally checking Wang out. He was too smooth-skinned and pretty, and his muscles were not that of a servant. "He is not your domestic, is he?" she said.

Liz exhaled. "You know he's not. You've seen him in action. He is part of my crew."

"I do not understand what manner of woman you are. One minute you are as a pirate and the next you are a parading, fine lady."

"I have to get into the governor's ball," Liz said. "Your stint as a merchant sailor is over, Noah Harwood. Captain Barnet thinks you're a pirate." In fact, Mary had chosen the name of a pirate to impersonate. "Will you trust him or will you trust me?"

"I cannot trust you," Mary said. "You stole my captain's ship and gave it to that pestilent hellion of a rogue, Captain Vane."

"Then stay here and rot," Liz said, frustrated.

Liz turned to Wang and nudged him toward the window. She stared outside to locate the vortex.

"That was a bit harsh, don't you think?" Wang asked. "Mary Read has every reason not to trust us."

"Don't call her that," Liz said. "She might hear you."

Wang glanced at Mary who was deep in thought. She was probably still wondering about the pirate symbols. "What are you planning, Liz?" Wang asked. "I know that look."

The window was steamy with sea spray. From this side of the ship, Liz couldn't see the vortex, the opening to the time chute. But she knew it was out there, somewhere. And if they didn't use it soon . . . Liz swung back to Wang. "I want you to go home, Wang."

Wang was silent.

"I can't let you get trapped here."

Wang swallowed.

Liz dropped her voice. "I can finish the rest of this escapade with Daniel and Black Patch and Mary—if she'll help me."

Wang still didn't say a word.

"I have to know that someone I trust will be there for Lulu."

"What about your cousin, Stevie?" Wang asked.

"Stevie's head is messed up. She has a thing for Cal. And I

absolutely do not trust Cal Sorensen. He can't be allowed to steal my mother's salvage operation while she's gone."

"And I can't leave you alone here."

Liz raised her hands impatiently. "I won't be alone. There's Daniel."

"That slippery eel is up to something. Why doesn't he tell us the truth about himself?"

"I don't know," Liz said.

"Well, I know this," Wang replied. "If he isn't going to be upfront with his own background, how do we know he's telling the truth about anything?"

Elizabeth inhaled. Wang didn't know that she had seen her mother, that Tess had refused to give up the bottled letter. Liz grabbed Wang's shoulders. He looked down at her hands, then up. "Everything Daniel told me about the letter, about Tess, is true," she said, releasing her death grip on him. "I spoke to her while you were floating around the Atlantic with a knife wound in your chest. She won't return to our time and fix everything because she thinks my father is trapped somewhere in the past."

Wang threw his arms up in stupefaction. "Then she really *has* lost it."

Liz bent her head, whispered. "I don't know. All I know is that the time chute is real." She raised her hands to take in Captain Barnet's cabin. "The *Tyger* is real." She shot a sideways glance at Mary Read. "And Mary is real. Everything Daniel told me is true."

Liz looked out the window again, but she knew she wouldn't see the vortex this time either. She turned back. "Please, Wang. Go home. I managed to sneak your scuba gear in a sea chest that I pretended held my personal things." She pointed to the wooden chest that sat on the floor. "Get your gear on and go home."

"No," Wang said.

"Why not?" Elizabeth wailed. "I don't want to be responsible for—" Liz clapped a hand over her mouth.

"For what?" Wang demanded. "For if we don't get out of this caper alive? If that's what you think, if you really think you're in danger, then how the crap do you think I can leave you?"

"Wang!" Liz said, her voice choking in surprise. "Oh, my God, Lu was right! You like me."

Wang lowered his eyes, then shot her a direct look. "Of course, Lu was right."

Liz swallowed. She rustled around in her bone lace-trimmed gown. "She was right about me, too," she said.

Wang smiled. "I know." He exhaled, pulled in her eyes with a serious look. "What about Daniel? How do you feel about him?"

Elizabeth fidgeted with the lace at her elbows. Could wearing girly clothes really make you act like a girly-girl? Remind me never to wear lace again, she thought. She looked up. Wang was studying her. She shrugged. "I think this is all kind of irrelevant, if we don't get home."

"Where does Daniel come from?" Wang asked.

"I don't know. I think he comes from the future."

"So he won't be going home with us?"

Liz smiled. "No. I'm pretty sure not."

All this time, Mary was staring at them while they whispered by the window. Her eyes were huge like coconuts, and she was shaking her head like they were both loopy as bats.

"But you like him," Wang said. "I can tell."

Liz was reminded of her annoying little sister asking her, Who do you like better? Kung Fu Boy or the Pirate Fencer? Oh crap, Liz thought. She looked into Wang's eyes. He gazed back at her, his black lashes unblinking. It was strange how being in a sticky situation made people say things they wouldn't otherwise say.

"Go home, Wang," Liz insisted. "We have a chance to try out this dating thing—if you go home." He shook his head. She exhaled. Who knew he could be so stubborn? Liz tried again, this time foregoing the emotional route and appealing to his reason. "The vortex is closing, Wang. And with it, your ticket home. You saw Stevie's message. I don't want you to miss it."

Wang glared at her. "I won't leave you alone with a bunch of sadistic pirates and soldiers. You saw what they did to Cal. And if Barnet finds out you're a fake, he won't just string you from the yardarm."

Liz smiled through eyes that wanted to cry really big tears. "I won't sacrifice you again. I don't know if I'll wrap up this escapade in time. But I'll catch the next time chute home if I don't."

If Wang didn't say something soon, Liz was going to grab him and kiss him.

"What about Daniel?" Wang asked.

"What about him? I don't know why he's helping me and I don't know where he comes from, but I do know this. When this whole fantasy nightmare adventure is over, I'll never see him again." Liz stared Wang down with serious eyes. "I also know when all of this is over, I want to see *you* again . . . Promise me, Wang, you'll be there. Go home and make sure Lu's not alone. Make sure that Stevie is safe from that skank, Cal."

"How can I go, Liz?"

"Because it's the right thing to do."

Liz's bone lace gown rustled as she went to the chest and raised the lid. The smell of the sea and aged wood rose with it. She removed Wang's purple wetsuit, his flippers, mask and oxygen tank, and then dug further to fetch Rackham's sealed letter to his lover.

"I have to go to the governor's ball and get this letter to Anne Bonny."

Wang scrutinized her, then shot a glance at Mary Read, who

was gawking at the scuba gear like she had seen a witch's hat and broomstick. Oh, crap, Liz thought. She'd forgotten all about Mary.

Wang was horrified at the look on Mary's face. "It's okay," Liz whispered, trying to sound reassuring. "She thinks I'm a witch."

"And that's okay?"

Liz heaved a sigh. "I don't know what's okay anymore, Wang. But nothing will be okay if you don't go home. There's nothing more you can do here. You're done playing bodyguard. I can't get you into the governor's ball even if I wanted to. I don't think servants are invited. And I don't want you coming as a servant anyway."

Wang clenched his jaw, but Liz knew she had won him over. He crouched to gather his scuba gear. Somehow, he would have to slip overboard without being seen. She would have to create a diversion, do the runaway servant scenario. Then convince Captain Barnet to give her Noah Harwood, AKA Mary Read, as Wang's replacement.

Liz called out to Mary. "What will it be, Mr. Harwood?" Liz asked. "Will you help me or do you want to return to Captain Barnet's brig?"

"I will help you," Mary said.

CHAPTER TWENTY-FOUR
Aren't You Anne Bonny, Cutthroat Female Pirate?

The *Tyger* docked at the wharf in Nassau harbour. Liz was escorted to a carriage with Daniel and Captain Barnet. As the captain's men made horse and carriage ready, Liz glanced to the horizon. She was looking for Wang to make sure he'd escaped unnoticed, but instead she saw the silhouette of a twelve-ton sloop.

She quickly turned away so as not to draw attention to the harbour. She entered the carriage, trying hard not to trip on her skirts. Barnet had found Daniel some gentleman's clothes, and the captain himself was in dress blues. Both men smelled spicy like cologne and wore white wigs. Daniel sat to her left, continuing the sham of being mute, while Barnet sat to her right. Mary rode Fancy. Because Barnet didn't know what to do with the hapless lad, he agreed that Noah Harwood, AKA Mary Read, would make a fine substitute for the runaway servant Wang.

Liz glanced at Daniel, who scowled. He couldn't make a sound lest he gave himself away. As the horses clopped into town, Liz lowered her eyes demurely to her gloved hands. It was a good thing Molly had included a pair of matching lace gloves with this dress. Mary had noticed the pirate symbol on her thumbnail, and Elizabeth did not want Barnet or the governor, Woodes Rogers, to see it.

When they arrived at the governor's mansion, Mary and Fancy went to the stables with the horses and carriage. Liz really had rendered herself totally alone by telling Barnet that Daniel was mute. Liz swallowed hard. This would be the performance of her life. It was show time.

There were soldiers all around the perimeter of the governor's mansion. Liz entered the house on the arm of Jonathan Barnet. A delicious aroma of fresh baked bread and cakes, roast goose and rum punch greeted her. To her complete and utter horror, the footman announced her as Lady Elizabeth Latimer, Mrs. Woodes Rogers's cousin. Fortuitously for Liz, the lady of the mansion was not in the ballroom when they arrived. Near a table loaded with savoury food and sweet drinks, Liz instantly noticed a woman who looked remarkably like herself. Daniel watched the said woman's every move. He nodded at Liz. Yeah, that was Anne Bonny. With a flicker of his eyes, he told Liz that she should follow her. Without tasting the glass of punch that Liz had just been handed by a servant, she set the glass down. She sent a sidelong glance at the roast goose and tore herself away. She gave Barnet the slip before he could think to tail her.

Anne floated into the foyer in a bone lace gown very similar to Liz's. Beneath a crystal chandelier, fully lit with white candles, Anne glided past a winding staircase. Liz followed, careful to avoid the dripping candle wax overhead. Now, where had the wily pirate woman gone? Liz caught a glimpse of bone lace and a whiff of French perfume as the lady drifted through a set of French doors. Aha! Rackham was going to owe her big time—starting with a goose dinner.

Liz stepped outside into the garden. It was quiet and dark except for some torches lighting the courtyard. Voices caught her attention and she shrank back behind an orange poinciana tree in full bloom.

"It's me, love," she heard someone whisper.

Liz froze dead still. At first, she thought the voice was talking to her. Then, she realized there were two people beside a tall trellis of climbing, purple morning glory. The man tilted his hat enough for Liz to catch a glimpse of Rackham's face beneath a pathetically flimsy disguise.

Liz grinned as Anne stepped back, astonished, when she recognized her lover. "How did you get in here? I thought you were Captain Barnet!"

"Naturally, you did. That was the intent."

"Has the governor seen you? Or my nasty Jemmy? He will have yer throat if he finds you here." Anne laughed.

"Let's not talk about throats and such, my precious ewe in shark's clothing. I bin too near to dancin' the hempen jig these last few days. Come, I have something for you."

"What could you possibly have that I would want?"

"Meself?"

"Ha," she said. "And where have you bin keepin' yourself this past fortnight?"

"I bin makin' to carry you off from this cockerel's mansion."

"And why should I be goin' anyplace with you?" Anne demanded.

Rackham waved to the windows of the house where the crowds were milling about in the north wing of the ballroom. "You want to stay here?"

"You spineless cur! You knows I don't and yet you left me to rot. And now, you thinks you kin just take me back. The devil take you! I am not chattel to be bought and sold for a handful of guineas. I once beat a man senseless fer tryin' to rape me. I'll get out of this myself."

She shoved him in the chest as Captain Jonathan Barnet appeared in the French doors. Rackham ducked behind the tree where Liz was hiding. Anne Bonny glared in their direction, shook her head in disgust, and stormed past Barnet into the house. Barnet turned, followed.

"He didn't see you," Liz said to Rackham.

"Aye, that he didn't."

Liz crept out of her hiding place and floated in her fancy bone lace gown to the French doors. The foyer was empty. Barnet's back disappeared into the ballroom's south entrance. "Anne must have gone to her room," she said to Rackham, whom she knew, by the smell of rum, was right behind her.

"I told you that this attempt at rescue be fer naught," Rackham said. "The house is surrounded by bluecoats, but if Anne wished her freedom, she could easily slip those blue-coated clam brains as easily as I slipped in here."

"And how *did* you do that?" Liz asked.

"I had yer parrot make sounds like a fracas, and the feathered sea lawyer drew them away. Then I climbed the wall."

Liz looked up and saw CJ perched on the poinciana tree. She squeezed her eyes shut and sent him a mental message. Stay put.

Arrgh, CJ said.

Liz looked back at Rackham who clung to the doorjamb peering into the foyer. "P'raps it be best if I wait for her to settle her petticoats down. She will only scratch my eyes out like the claw-cat she is."

"We don't have time for her to cool down," Liz argued. She stared through the foyer to either entrance of the L-shaped ballroom. She nudged Rackham in the arm. "The coast is clear. Go, now."

Rackham grabbed Liz's wrist and jerked her back into the shadows. "Look there. At the north door. Tis James Bonny, good old Jemmy, a-coming our way."

Liz craned her neck, trying not to knock her hairdo askew on the edge of the door. "That puny guy is Anne's hubby? You're afraid of that little worm?"

Rackham stepped away from the door. He tugged on his collar and tapped the plumed hat that sat cockily on his head. Rackham was only partly disguised, and Liz could hardly keep herself from rolling over backwards and laughing out loud. One part pompous gentleman, two parts verminous pirate.

"Tis one thing to deceive the governor with this costume," Rackham said, thumping his chest. "That whey-faced dog of a king's puppet don't know one sea wolf from another. To him, a man of the coat looks no different from an adventurer's captain. But it's entirely a different thing with Jemmy there. A gentleman of fortune knows his own, and that rascal was a scourge o' the seas long before he became the governor's man. He knows me. So I ask you. What good will it do Anne or yerself to have that wood-headed prick of a barnacle land me in the gallows?"

Liz ignored the tongue-tripping diatribe. Her sight was fixed on Bonny. "He's turned away," she said. "He's looking for someone. Slip upstairs while he's not looking."

"Very likely he be lookin' for his wife. As fer Anne, her bedchamber is under surveillance day and night. Only tonight has she leave to wander the house."

"Oh, for crying out loud," Liz said, sick of his excuses and his blathering pirate talk. "*I'll* go."

Rackham raised his brow, then ducked as James Bonny looked their way.

"Be forewarned, Elizabeth Latimer. Anne Bonny's chamber is guarded."

"Yeah, you said that."

Liz peered into the foyer and waited while Bonny hesitated at the bottom of the stairs. She muffled a laugh. It was true. Scourge o' the seas he may be, but when it came to his own wife, ole Jemmy was a scaredy-cat.

Bonny followed a servant into the ballroom and hijacked a glass of brandy. While he was busy dumping liquor down his throat, Liz passed through the French doors to the winding stairway. Her gown rustled as she hiked up her skirt to take the steps two at a time.

She reached the landing and paused. Where was Anne's room? No sentry stood at any of the doors. Was Rackham wrong? Or were Bonny and the governor so full of it as to think that Anne wouldn't try a valiant exodus during the crowded ball?

It was dark up here, and the only light came from the multiple candles in the crystal chandelier downstairs.

Liz paused at the first door she came to. She smoothed down her dress, adjusted her lopsided hair, and pinched her lips together. This was the ultimate test. Would the pirate woman accept the letter or not?

Liz knocked and listened. The murmur of women's voices drifted through the door. Who was she with?

"What is it?" a female voice asked through the closed door.

"I have a letter for Anne Bonny," Liz said in her most affected ladylike voice.

The latch lifted and a maid opened the door.

She was holding a candlestick, using her hand to shade the flame from the drafty hallway.

In the shadows of the bedroom, Anne's voice said, "Come in quickly."

The maid ushered Liz in and shut the door behind them. Liz felt the darkness close in as the maid set her candlestick on a small table. The only other light came from two candles in burnished pewter holders that were sitting on a mahogany armoire. A draft from an open window made the shadows bounce eerily. Liz quickly glanced around her at the fine Georgian furniture, the heavy draperies and thick carpeted floor.

Anne squinted, glared at her. "Well? You claim to have a letter for me?"

Liz turned back from checking out her surroundings and stared at Anne Bonny. The resemblance between herself and the notorious pirate woman was creepy.

Liz was careful to keep her face in shadow and hidden from Anne and the maid. Anne motioned to her servant to leave them alone. The maid curtsied, retrieved her candle and went out, but not before catching a glimpse of Liz's face with her passing flame.

"Well?" Anne repeated. "Where is the letter?"

Liz couldn't tear her eyes away from the woman who was her ancestor. How to start? How to tell someone that you were her descendant? She had done it once with Jack Rackham. But Anne was no fool.

Liz decided to go for the jugular. "Captain Rackham wants you back."

Anne stared at her, lips ready to split into laughter. "Aye, does he now?"

"He wanted me to give you this." Liz plucked the sealed letter from the ruffled lace at the top of her dress and passed it to Anne.

Anne karate chopped it to the floor before Liz could get a juggling act together and save it from landing near the low-burning hearth. "That devil's spawn left me here to rot," Anne spat. "Why should I read any jabber of his?"

Liz glared at her. This woman was really beginning to piss her off. "Aren't you Anne Bonny, cutthroat female pirate?"

When Anne was silent, Liz ripped into her. "The security in this mansion is pretty crappy. You're not surrounded by a moat. Your room's not on the edge of a cliff that plunges into the sea. The Tower of London, this is not. You can stroll down the stairs and out the door. I saw you in the garden. So what in the name of all that's holy and unholy is stopping you?"

Anne whirled to her armoire, pulled a metal nail file from a drawer, and flashed it like a dagger. "Who are you, impudent witch? What unholy gibberish is it that tumbles out of your mouth? Speak before I splits yer throat from ear to ear."

"My name is Elizabeth Latimer," Liz said, holding her ground.

"And if you and Jack Rackham don't get back together, I won't be Elizabeth Latimer much longer."

Liz realized that what she'd said had made no sense. Anne dropped the makeshift dagger onto the armoire and plucked the letter from the hearth before the flames could eat it. She handed it to Liz and went to a small table by the wall where a silver plate of tiny, stale cakes lay next to a china teapot and a hand-painted teacup.

Anne lifted the teacup and smashed it against the wall. "The governor's hospitality is unimpeachable," she announced. "The food, it be excellent, and the bed soft." She kicked over the table, and the cakes went flying. She tugged the sheets off the mattress and left them twisted rope-like on the floor. "And look at this finery they dress me in," she said flouncing her skirt like a prissy girl and flapping the lace at her wrists.

"Ye wants to know why the lily-livered coward left me here? I has a bounty on me head, that's why! He knows if I was to be seen on the streets, I'd be nabbed and thrown before a justice. The governor has a mind to ship me to England. I'll be tried for piracy and adultery because I won't return to that maggot of a horse's arse, James Bonny. Then it will be Newgate Prison for me!"

"Isn't that better than hanging?" Liz asked mildly.

"I'll be hanged in London town. And Jack, if he tries to rescue me, will be hanged, too."

Liz shoved the slightly browned letter into Anne's face. "That doesn't have to happen. He has a plan."

Anne pinched her lips together the same way Liz did herself when she was frustrated.

Anne took the letter and split the seal. Unfolding the slightly crispy parchment, she read it in full view of Elizabeth.

Liz watched Anne's face. No expression broke through whatsoever. Liz spoke. "If you don't want to return to your husband, then listen to me. Leave this place and go back to Jack Rackham."

"And why, might I inquire, should I listen to you?" Anne refolded the letter and placed her hands on her hips, the letter in her right fist. "You ain't yet explained to me who you are."

At first, Liz had been grateful for the darkened room to mask her identity, but now she wished for more light. If Anne saw her face, would she believe her story?

"If you and Jack don't get back together, I will never be born," Liz said.

Anne laughed. "That explains nothing."

"I'm a descendant of yours and Jack Rackham. I come from the future."

Anne sneered. "Well, and *now* that explains everything."

Liz widened her eyes like a monkey. "Don't you believe me?"

"What do you take me for? A mindless clod of a dawcock? Naturally, I don't believe you."

Liz sighed. "Jack Rackham believes me."

Liz turned from Anne. What could she do to convince her? She walked out of the shadows and went to the armoire where a small mirror hung on the wall.

A knock came on the door.

Great timing, Liz thought.

"It is I, your lawful husband," James Bonny called from the hallway.

Now what? If Bonny saw Liz . . . if Bonny saw two Annes, how would she explain that?

The door was unlocked. Anne had neglected to bolt it. Quick as the slash of a cutlass, Anne drew the satin drapes, shoving Liz behind them, just as Bonny opened the door.

Anne tucked the letter into a large silk bow on the back of her gown and palmed the metal nail file from the armoire.

"The governor wishes the presence of my wife in the ballroom," he said.

From where Liz was hiding, she could see everything through a slight gap in the curtains. The tension between husband and wife burned like an unanswered text. Anne was a pirate as ruthless as any, and if she murdered James Bonny, they would hang her before Liz could scream 'plead your belly!'

"It's a slight to the governor not to attend his party," Bonny said. "He could have you hanged or flogged. You best come to your senses and agree to return to me."

Anne's hand clenched. One sudden jab in the right place and James Bonny would be dead.

The mirror over the armoire behind Bonny reflected Anne's face. Liz had never seen such a look of cultured hatred. Anne's hand moved behind her back, and the blade lowered into the bow of her dress. Liz exhaled as Anne told her bully of a husband that she must powder her face first. He accepted her excuse to delay her appearance downstairs and left. Anne glanced at the drapes where Liz was hiding, then went to her armoire and removed an empty rum bottle from the top drawer. She retrieved the letter from her silk bow, reread it, rolled it up, and then dropped the letter into the rum bottle. After corking the bottle, she lifted the lid of a small, wooden box and placed it inside.

Liz came out from behind the curtain and stood beside Anne in front of the armoire. They stared at each other in the mirror. Elizabeth looked almost identical to Anne Bonny.

CHAPTER TWENTY-FIVE
What You Do Next Will Affect Everything
I Do In The Future

Liz had done what she could. Now it was up to Anne. Liz stepped out of Anne Bonny's room only to bump into the maid. The maid stared at her face. She was holding a candlestick, and Liz had no light to show her the maid's face. Dressed in a long linen dress and apron with a lace cap to cover her hair, all Liz could see was the maid's mouth open in a silent gasp.

Liz walked swiftly away. The maid stared after her, then went inside Anne Bonny's room. Before Liz was halfway down the stairs, she heard a door shut and she caught a glimpse of candlelight from above. Was Anne coming? Quickly, Liz looked up.

No, it was just the maid again. Had the maid recognized her, thought she was seeing double? If Liz had known that Barnet was going to escort her to this party, she wouldn't have insisted on wearing a dress so similar to Anne's. The idea of doing double duty had seemed a good one when she didn't know how she was going to get into the mansion without an invite. But Barnet had saved her the trouble and made it easy.

Liz hurried, but it was hard to outrun the maid in this stupid flouncy dress. Before she could reach the bottom of the stairs, the maid grabbed her shoulder from behind. When Liz turned, she almost screamed.

The maid put a finger to her lips and gestured her back upstairs. Liz followed, stupefied.

It was dark at the top of the landing except for the chandelier light from the foyer and the candlestick in the maid's hands.

Liz stared at the maid, then at Anne Bonny's door. The maid was slightly shorter than Liz, but almost exactly the same build. The maid put a hand to her head, and Liz yanked off the bonnet for her. With the flame of the candle flickering under her chin, even the distortions of light and shadow couldn't hide the maid's face. This woman was no maid. She was Tess.

Liz grabbed her mother, but Tess pushed her away with her free hand. Okay, so she didn't want any public displays of affection. But who was watching?

"The candle," Tess said. "You almost set yourself on fire."

Liz backed into the shadows and her mother followed, shielding the candle flame. "What are you doing here?" Liz demanded. "I thought you'd left me for good."

"I will never leave you, Elizabeth," Tess said. "I will always know where you are. It's a mother's intuition, or call it what you will, but I sensed you were in danger."

Tess thought she was in danger, *now*? Where was she when Rackham threw her in the brig? When Vane nearly made meatloaf out of her? When those cutthroats tossed her into the Spanish Town jail to await hanging? Where the heck was she then?

"You came with Captain Barnet," Tess said.

A twitch started near the corner of Liz's mouth. She was trying hard not to react, but her nerves and muscles were reacting all on their own. "Are you stalking me?" she asked.

Tess smiled. Liz tended to be a drama queen and Tess knew it. "I wouldn't have come, Liz, if it hadn't been for your unlucky meeting with Captain Barnet."

"Barnet's a pussycat. I took care of him. He thinks I'm the governor's cousin, Lady Elizabeth Latimer." Liz spread her petticoats and curtsied in mock emphasis.

"Yes, who has an uncanny resemblance to Anne Bonny, James Bonny's wife," Tess said.

"The slimy coward didn't see me," Liz argued. She pulled at her chin to make the twitching at the corner of her mouth stop.

"Has Barnet seen Anne yet?"

Liz shrugged. "I don't think so. But wouldn't you know better than me? You're Mrs. James Bonny's lady-in-waiting."

"Not lady-in-waiting," Tess said, shaking her head. She always hated it when Elizabeth was sloppy about historical facts. "I'm temporarily her chambermaid."

"Well, if you were going to be here anyway, couldn't you have saved me the trouble of almost getting killed and convince Anne Bonny, yourself, to go back to Jack Rackham?"

"I wasn't supposed to be here at all," Tess said. "But I heard from the servants' gossip that the captain was escorting a beautiful young lady to the governor's ball and that she bore a remarkable likeness to Mrs. James Bonny."

Liz grinned. "The servants called me beautiful?"

"Elizabeth, don't be vain." Tess smiled.

Liz nodded. "Okay. So, does that mean you're here to help me?"

Tess licked her lips. She clutched the candlestick, and Liz knew she was nervous because the candle flame trembled. "I can't stay. I came here to find you, to tell you something important. I have a lead on your father, and I have to follow it before the trail goes cold."

Liz inhaled. She clenched her fists to keep from shaking. "I want to come with you," Liz said.

Tess shook her head. She tried to hold the candlestick steady, but it wavered with her emotion. "You have to save yourself and me and Lulu and Stevie. But you also have to save your father."

"That's what I said. I want to come with you."

"No. You have to get Jack Rackham and Anne Bonny back together. But in the process, you mustn't kill Jonathan Barnet. And you mustn't let anyone else kill him either."

Well, that was a pretty tall order. Liz planted her hands on her hips and shook her head in disbelief. "That's what you came to tell me?"

Tess nodded her head firmly. "No one must kill Captain Barnet. It's not his time to go yet."

Liz was getting really frustrated. Save everybody. Don't kill anyone. Cry me great big cartoon tears. This was getting too complicated.

"Why?" Liz asked.

Tess stared at Liz in the semi-dark. "Surely, you know?"

"No, Tess. I don't know," Liz said. "It seems like everybody's my enemy and everybody's my friend. Hell's bells, Tess. Speak English or French, Spanish or Chinese if you have to. But give me a language I can understand. This pirate stuff makes no sense at all."

Tess hesitated. "Captain Barnet is your—"

Oh, no, Liz thought. It can't be. Pirate and pirate hunter. Did she have the blood of both in her veins?

Tess touched Liz's arm, causing the candle to tremor. "If Captain Barnet dies before his time— "

"Yeah, yeah, I know," Liz said, irritated. "If we interfere and Captain Barnet is killed, then John will never have been born. Is that it?"

Tess nodded. She leaned forward, avoiding the candle flame, and squeezed Elizabeth's hand. She kissed her on the cheek. "Be careful," she said. "What you do next will affect everything I do in the future. I am going to find your father now. Goodbye, Liz."

"Mom!" Liz shouted for the second time in her life. But Tess had snuffed out the candle and vanished behind one of the closed doors.

Liz stared dumbfounded at the dark. She could bang on every

door until she found her mother. But what good would that do? She would bring the governor's men running and spoil her own chances of getting Rackham and Anne out of here, with Barnet nary the wiser.

Talk about a double whammy, Liz thought brutally. Her father, John Latimer, was the descendent of a pirate hunter. It figured.

Liz started back down the stairs. She had to find Daniel and Rackham. If Anne didn't act on her own, they would have to take her by force.

After talking to Anne, Liz was pretty sure Anne still had the hots for Rackham. They only had to see each other again to set off the fireworks.

Liz glanced up the stairs. It was perfectly quiet. Anne wasn't coming down. Maybe Rackham should try the Romeo and Juliet thing. When Liz had left Anne in her bedroom, her window was wide open.

How many minutes had passed since James Bonny left his wife? He'd be expecting her downstairs any second. They had to work fast.

Liz walked into the ballroom to look for Daniel. At the far corner, dressed in the official colours of the Royal Navy and a powdered white wig, James Bonny was speaking to the governor. Daniel was dancing with some courtesan, an overly dressed, overly made-up female. She probably wasn't a courtesan, just looked like one. They waltzed like born dancers.

Daniel caught her eye. He danced a few seconds longer before deserting his partner. Elizabeth felt someone approaching her. She turned and saw it was James Bonny. Oh crap. He probably thought she was Anne. If he got any closer, he'd know she wasn't.

Liz glanced frantically for an out. Daniel suddenly swept her into his arms and whirled her away to the other side of the ballroom. "Rackham's here," Liz whispered into his ear. "We have to find him."

Daniel nodded toward the window. Someone in a ridiculous plumed hat was peeking through the windows. Well, at least he hadn't abandoned her.

"I think James Bonny saw me," Liz whispered.

"It's okay," Daniel said. "At this distance, he'll think you're Anne. That gives us time to fetch her. Did she read Rackham's letter?"

"Yeah," Liz said, whisking her feet in time to Daniel's. "But I don't know if she's convinced."

"You just left her?"

"What could I do? I couldn't drag her by the hair. I'd have every soldier up in arms if I'd done that. She's a screamer."

"Runs in the family," Daniel said mockingly, and stepped on her dress.

Liz elbowed him, hard. He grinned. "That was for telling Barnet I was mute."

Liz giggled into his ear as his arm tightened around her waist. "How did that work out?"

"Do you have any idea how hard it is not to talk?"

Not really. Talking was one of her best things.

They were waltzing to the north entrance where Rackham was waiting in the shadows outside. Liz looked over Daniel's shoulder to see if Bonny still wanted to nab her. Apparently, Captain Barnet wished a word with the governor's latest recruit. They were huddled in a corner.

"Now's our chance," Liz said.

In unison, they whirled out of the ballroom's arched doors, past some fancy dressed ladies and gents in the foyer, and into the garden. It was dead still outside. Rackham was nowhere in sight. Had the coward changed his mind and taken off like the worthless rat he was?

"I'm going to look around," Daniel said. "Stay here in case he comes back."

Liz almost grabbed Daniel's arm to make him stay but stopped herself. It was too late anyway. Daniel's back disappeared behind the stone wall in the direction of the stables.

Liz looked up. CJ? He was no longer in the poinciana tree.

She noticed, now, that the tree rose up near the side of the house. It was not a thick tree, but it could be climbed. Anne's window was just above the topmost branches. The curtain fluttered, so the window was still open.

A rustle came from behind her. Liz searched again for CJ. She heard the flutter of wings, then a voice in her head. Pirate at six o'clock, CJ said.

Rackham sprang from behind a bush, grabbed her around the waist and cupped her mouth before she could object. He dragged her away from the windows, deeper under the poinciana tree.

"Barnet and our weaselly friend are searching for you," Rackham whispered into her ear. "That was none too bright to allow ole Jemmy to see you. He thinks yer Anne. And if Anne does decide to show her face at the ball, the hue and cry will be up. The servants is talkin'. Already, the governor's help thinks they's seein' double."

Rackham released Liz's mouth, but before she could reply, a voice shouted from a high window of the mansion. "Jack Rackham!"

Liz grinned. It was Anne. "Get me the devil out of here before that serpent Bonny comes back to take me," the feisty pirate woman demanded.

Rackham grinned. He bowed theatrically. "Immediately, love."

He climbed the poinciana tree to the branches spreading alongside the mansion wall. When he reached her window, he perched on the strongest of the top branches, swaying like a comical parrot. The branches would not hold much more weight. If Rackham didn't get off that tree in a minute, the branches would break.

"Strip to yer petticoats and climb out onto the sill," he ordered.

Rackham removed his jacket, swung it toward her.

"A moment!" Anne said. She vanished back inside her bedchamber. When she returned, she tossed him a wooden box which he dropped down to Liz. Liz recognized it for the box that held the letter. "Come inside for just one minute!" Anne ordered.

Rackham looked down, shrugged at Liz, and did as he was commanded. Liz smiled, placed the box at the foot of the tree, and waited.

One minute turned into ten, then fifteen. Liz tapped her foot on the ground, impatient. How long did it take to make a baby?

"Captain Rackham!" Liz shouted. Her voice came out in a hoarse whisper. "We have to go." She seized a lower branch of the blossoming tree and started to shake it like a maniac, perfuming the air with poinciana blooms and making the orange petals shower down like confetti.

A scurry of footsteps approached from the house. Someone pointed at her with a lighted torch. "There she is!"

It was Mary Read. Crap. The blasted sea woman, soon-to-turn pirate, had double-crossed her. Liz was accosted by two soldiers and forced to turn to face her escort, Captain Barnet.

"This woman is no relation of the governor," Mary accused. "She's a pirate!"

Mary grabbed Liz's left hand and stripped off her glove. Her red thumbnail with the chipped black skull and crossbones glared rudely at the governor and his men.

"Imp o' Satan," Mary said, flashing the torchlight onto the emblem. "Did I not say so? She bears the mark of the devil!"

Barnet took Liz's hand. He looked into her eyes. "Is this true?"

Elizabeth swallowed. She stared at the governor and his lady who had joined them. Husband and wife were dressed in frilled finery with stiff white wigs on their heads.

"I do not know this woman," Mrs. Rogers said, worrying the lace at her elbows. "She is no relation of mine. But I swear she is the identical of Mrs. Bonny."

Dammit, why was the eighteenth century so primitive? Liz wondered. If they'd had nail polish remover, she wouldn't be in this pickle. How to get out of this. And where the heck was Daniel? He seemed to have a fine way of vanishing when she needed him most.

"Well?" Captain Barnet asked. He didn't seem to be fully convinced. "What mischief are you up to Miss Latimer, if that is your name?"

"That is my name, sir," Liz said, curtsying. It never hurt to be polite, right? "And I must apologize to his worship, the honourable governor and his lady for the deception. But yes, it's true, I am not her cousin. I only wished to come to the ball. I am a lady of France." She threw in a couple of *oui*'s and *n'est-ce pas*'s for good measure. "I truly was captured by pirates as Captain Barnet will attest as he found me on board a pirate's ship. And this— " She pointed to the red painted thumbnail with the Jolly Roger, "—is simply the latest Paris fashion."

Mrs. Woodes Rogers moved forward to see the pirate symbol more clearly, sending a gust of hair powder into Liz's nose. Thank goodness for Daniel Defoe, who had set all of eighteenth century Britain's imagination afire with his writings about the thrilling but dastardly deeds of pirates.

"Oh my," her ladyship said, staring at Liz's painted thumbnail. "Paris? What a delight. The French are so inventive, so inspired. I simply love it. How is it done, my dear? You must show me."

The governor went to guide his wife away, but she placed a

firm hand on his arm. "Don't be silly, Mr. Rogers, my dear. This young lady is not a pirate. Good heavens, look at her. As pretty and dainty a thing, on these islands, I haven't seen in many a long year."

Elizabeth tried not to sneeze. She thanked the gracious lady and curtsied again.

Mary scowled. "She is a witch. She has piercings in her ears and the mark of the devil on her thumb. Her accomplice, the Oriental, has a suit of some inexplicable cloth that sheds the water like a whale's skin, and he wears a giant flask upon his back. Now I ask you. What is the meaning of such things? She told me herself. She is a witch."

Liz frowned at Mary. Why can't you just put a lid on it? If Liz exposed Mary Read as a woman, would that shut her up? Mary seemed to know what Liz was thinking. She stepped back, as though Liz could jinx her, and snapped her jaw closed.

"Throw that lying, calumnious boy into the brig, Captain Barnet," Mrs. Rogers ordered.

"No, please," Liz said, fluttering her hands in exaggerated distress. "The lad is confused. He's had a rough time of it. The pirates killed his father and tossed him into the sea for shark's meat. That was where the good captain found him, wasn't it, Captain Barnet?"

Liz batted her eyes. Too bad she had no mascara. It would have improved the effect. No matter. It worked. Captain Barnet nodded. "The sea was, indeed, where I found him." He turned to Liz and gallantly returned her lace glove. "I apologize for this son of a sea hag's indefensible behaviour. Do you truly wish to retain him in your service despite the malicious accusations? Else I shall have him flogged for his wicked, slanderous tales."

"I wish to retain him in my service," Elizabeth said. "And please, no flogging." Liz drew on her glove to cover the betraying thumb.

Captain Barnet smiled. He extended his elbow to lead her back into the ballroom. Liz glanced nervously up at Anne Bonny's room. The curtain flapped.

"If you don't mind, sir," Liz said, "I think I would like to take the air. All this excitement, you know. I feel rather faint."

"Of course," Captain Barnet said. "I shall accompany you."

Daniel appeared in the courtyard gates. He opened his mouth, then remembered he was supposed to be mute. Liz stifled a giggle despite the tension she was feeling. Why couldn't she get rid of the bombastic skipper?

"There is my brother," Liz said. "Hello, Daniel." She smiled at Captain Barnet. "My brother will stay with me. But thank you, sir. You are most kind." Liz curtsied again.

The governor and his wife smiled and returned to the ball. Captain Barnet glanced briefly at Anne's window and signalled his men to follow.

Whew, Liz thought. That was a pretty pickle.

Mary Read glared at her. Liz glared back. "Look," she said. "I didn't give you away. To me and to all of these people, you are the ship's boy, Noah Harwood. For the last time, will you trust me? Because you *can't* trust them." Liz jabbed her thumb at the windows to the ballroom.

A scraping sound and an *oof* came from above. Rackham leaped from the window into the tree. Branches cracked and a few twigs came raining down amidst a confetti of orange petals. Anne Bonny, in nothing but a chemise and bloomers, leaped to the tree in his wake. She grabbed onto the jacket Rackham held out to her and, like a true swashbuckler, swung from a high branch to the ground. Rackham followed.

"What happened here?" Rackham whispered. "I saw the governor's men and thought you was finished."

"Finished, I?" Liz said cavalierly. She smoothed down her full ivory skirt and looked at him, squinty-eyed. "Elizabeth Latimer is never finished until she's done. Let's get you and Anne back to the ship before anything else happens."

Liz tucked a strand of hair behind her ear and glanced over her shoulder. Too late.

In the foyer of the mansion, James Bonny was running toward the French doors. Liz slammed the glass doors shut and told everyone to scram, but not before Bonny recognized his half-naked wife, linked arm in arm, with fellow sea dog, Jack Rackham.

"The swine!" Bonny hollered. "The limey of a cockroach had the cheek to attend the ball! Musketeers to the garden. Calico Jack has got my wife!"

Rackham, Anne, Daniel and Liz raced through the courtyard gates with Mary at their heels.

CHAPTER TWENTY-SIX
Musketeers, To Your Horses!
They're Headed For Sea!

Fancy! Liz glanced around. CJ!

A nearby whinny told Liz that Fancy was answering her silent call. The hue and cry was up. Liz, Daniel and Mary were safe as long as Bonny didn't add three and three together and figure out that they were in cahoots with Calico Jack Rackham and his abduction of James Bonny's wife. Fancy reared up and Liz threw the reins to Rackham. He and Anne would have to make it to the ship first. The *Curlew*, Rackham said, was in the harbour. The dory was on the beach. They would meet there.

The pirate and his petticoated lover leaped onto the back of the spotted mare and galloped in the direction of the pier. Liz and Daniel slipped off toward the stables to steal another horse. Mary was free to do whatever she damn well pleased.

Liz gathered her flouncy skirts and leaped behind Daniel as he one-handed her onto the big black stallion he had mounted. CJ fluttered down onto her shoulder. Liz glared at the soon-to-be pirate woman who was watching them from the roadside.

"Noah Harwood," Liz said. "Should we meet again—and I hope to God we don't—remember this. I *always* keep my word. Good luck to you!"

Mary bowed. "And to you, Elizabeth Latimer."

Daniel dug in his heels, flicked the reins, and the horse was off. CJ shot into the air ahead of them. Close behind, they could hear the sounds of James Bonny rallying the governor's men. Liz turned to look. Captain Barnet burst through the courtyard gates onto the road.

"Go!" she shouted to Daniel, and he spurred the horse on.

Barnet stood with Bonny, stupefied, coughing in the dust.

"Musketeers, to your horses!" Barnet bellowed. "The blasted pirates are headed for sea!"

$$\$\$\$$$

Liz and Daniel fled into the night. Black Patch better have the ship ready to sail. One advantage they had over Barnet and his men was that their ship was anchored in the bay, not docked in the wharf. They could make a fast getaway, provided five hands were enough to sail the bloody ship. Liz clung to Daniel's back, knowing her life depended on him. Had Rackham and Anne made it to the beach? Would they wait for her and Daniel? In a few minutes, she would know.

The pungent stink of the sea reached Liz's nose. The reassuring odour of horses followed. She searched the beach. She saw nothing but blackness, then something charged out of the night and whinnied. It was Fancy. She was riderless. So Rackham and Anne must be somewhere nearby. Liz slipped off the back of the stallion, followed by Daniel. Cautiously, they walked toward the water. Where had Rackham beached the dory? Liz squinted to the shoreline and saw the shadows of two figures shoving a boat into the tide.

She could care less if Rackham and Anne wanted to leave her behind—except for one thing. Jack Rackham had her scuba gear on board the *Curlew*, and she needed the gear if she was to ever get home. Liz was just about to shout to Rackham, when out of the night came the thunder of guns. The stallion bolted. Fancy whinnied. Liz ducked and Daniel threw himself on top of her. CJ squawked.

Musketeers! How?

Liz raised her head from the ground, spitting out the taste of seaweed and grit. She dodged as a musket ball nearly hit her skull.

To protect her, Daniel forced her face down, and she held her breath to keep from inhaling sand. Seconds passed and the guns stopped. Rough sand grains rained off her cheeks as Liz twisted her neck to look for the snipers.

"Where did those soldiers come from?" Liz whispered.

"Barnet's men," Daniel answered from over her shoulders.

Liz thrust herself up on her elbows, forcing Daniel to shift his body overtop hers. "How could it be? We were way ahead of them. They weren't even mounted yet when we left them in the dust!"

"Different men," Daniel said. "Not marines. Land soldiers." He slid off her back and flattened himself on the cool sand. "Crawl to those rocks there."

Liz followed him. Of course. Barnet had said he would set a trap for Rackham when he returned from his alleged drink fest. These were the men Barnet had left for the ambush. But how had Rackham slipped past Barnet's men to get to the governor's ball? Evidently, Jack Rackham was smarter than he looked.

The shooting began again in earnest. A barrage of musket fire pelted the beach from the west. Liz flattened herself to the sand, behind a cluster of boulders, before inching her head up to see what was happening. From the dory, a volley of gunshots could be heard. Since Rackham was returning fire, he must have a pistol. Two guns were active behind the dory, so Rackham had thought to bring a flintlock for his lover. That helped Anne and himself, but it didn't help Liz and Daniel. CJ was nowhere in sight. A cool wind blew back the wispy hair around Liz's face, bringing with it the stench of seagull dung. Liz pinched her lips together and wondered if Anne Bonny was doing the same. How many men were there? Liz strained to see. She could count six. Barnet had left six men to ambush one drunken pirate.

A musket ball whizzed past her head.

"Get down," Daniel ordered. He stuck his dagger between his

teeth and inched away, muttering, "Stay here. I'm going to see if I can't catch a couple of them shooters by surprise."

Liz rose to her elbows. "No way am I staying here. I'm coming with you."

She crawled on her hands and knees past the safety of the boulders. It seemed the musketeers, though clearly marksmen, didn't know she and Daniel were there. They were fixed on bringing Calico Jack Rackham to justice.

Rackham's pistol hit its target. A man went down groaning. Anne Bonny fired a shot immediately following Rackham's, and a second man went down. Now, there were only four. Daniel crept up behind a man, who was crouched on one knee, aiming his musket at the dory. Daniel plunged his dagger into the sharpshooter's shoulder, forcing the man to release the gun. Using a torn strip of fabric from his shirt, Daniel hogtied the marksman to keep him out of trouble.

Now, there were three.

Liz snagged the injured sniper's musket by its cold, steel barrel. Daniel raised his hand, threatening to confiscate the weapon. "Do you know how to use one of those?" he asked.

Liz didn't answer. She lay on her stomach and rested the polished wooden butt on her shoulder and aimed the long barrel at a shadow that was creeping in the sand toward the dory. She closed one eye, mumbled to herself, "Hit his hand, hit his hand, hit his hand."

She hit his foot, but it did the job. His foot shattered and he dropped his musket, howling in pain. Liz had never injured anyone before. It was an ugly feeling. But the man would live.

Two left. Liz did a quick scan for Daniel. He had his eye on one more sniper. Before either of them could take him out, Rackham's pistol finished the job.

It was silent now. Liz's heart continued to beat rapidly. Daniel crept down the beach to retrieve the wailing sharpshooter's musket, and to bind his hands and feet. Not so sharp after all, Liz thought. There was one more musketeer. She knew there was. Where was he?

She could smell the gunpowder in the air, feel the gusts of wind battering her dress, taste the sea spray that was near and yet too far, hear the silence of the sniper that watched her but that she couldn't see. The shore was black, and she had no idea which direction he would come at her.

It was too quiet. "Daniel, there's one more—"

Liz turned her head to stare down the steel barrel of the sixth musketeer.

Five paces along the beach, Daniel froze. If he moved to take the marksman with his dagger, the man would fire and blast Liz's brains to Kingdom Come.

"Rise, whore," the musketeer said.

Liz severely objected. "I am not a whore." What made him think she was a whore? Her dress was tattered and her hair was falling down, but she hardly qualified as a whore. She rose to her knees.

"Why else would a woman be out with pirates in the dead of night?"

Maybe because I'm trying to rescue them? Save their lives and my life and the universe?

"I should blast a ball between yer eyes," the musketeer warned. "Now, to your feet."

A flush of indignation cut through Liz's fear. Just for being a whore?

"I saw yer shoot me mate, there. What kind of a woman can handle a musket like that except for a pirate's whore?"

Again with the whore thing. Did nobody shoot guns here except pirates and whores?

The musketeer braced his gun against her forehead. Liz realized that the man meant business and that Daniel couldn't do a thing to save her. Liz squeezed her eyes shut. She was on her knees, begging for her life. Did Tess sense Liz's danger now? Her heart was hammering. She could hardly breathe. Was this it? Was this what it all came to? At the bottom of the beach, Liz could hear Rackham and Anne shoving the dory into the sea. The ingrates. You get them back together, save them, and this is the thanks you get? Liz swallowed, hard. Her lips were dry. Her throat ached. The jokes weren't working. CJ, where are you? She opened her eyes.

"Calico Jack," the musketeer shouted. "Do you want your whore? Because if you leave this beach and head out to sea, I will blast her to smithereens."

Jack Rackham raised his head. Anne Bonny raised hers. Were they going to escape only to let her die? Liz stifled a gasp. What would happen in the future if she died here in the past?

Rackham hoisted his pistol. "Let her be," he said. "Else I will blast ye to Jamaica afore ye can blink an eye."

"She be dead long before that," the musketeer answered.

"But not afore *you* are," a voice said behind the musketeer.

Liz looked up to see Mary Read holding a flintlock pistol to the marksman's head. "Let her go. And I won't put a hole through your skull and blow your brains clear out to sea."

Liz had never been so glad to see Mary Read. She looked beautiful in her black britches, white shirt and man's hiplength jacket. She wore a small tricorn hat similar to Calico Jack's, with her hair wildly flying out from under it. It took less than three minutes for Mary to relieve the offending sharpshooter of his musket, and for the two of them to hogtie him with some strips of fabric cut from Liz's dress.

CJ fluttered down from wherever he'd been hiding and perched on the musketeer's head.

"No, CJ," Liz said. "Bad man." She was beginning to worry that CJ would join the ranks of the Royal Navy.

"If you's coming, you best be gettin' aboard," Rackham yelled from the dory. He and Anne were already inside the boat, which was drifting out to sea.

"Wait," Liz said. She called the spotted mare to her. The black stallion had bolted the minute the shooting began, but the faithful mare had returned. Liz stroked Fancy's long mane.

"No time for that!" Rackham hollered. "As yer captain, I orders ye to get on board."

Liz slapped Fancy on the rump and sent her to freedom. Daniel waved Liz toward the shore, but she turned to look for Mary.

Mary Read was still standing by the musketeer where Liz had left her, her blouse and britches flapping in the wind. "Are you coming?" Liz asked.

Mary grinned and nodded.

They raced down the beach together. Liz hiked up her skirts and splashed into the water. She and Mary climbed into the dory behind Daniel. The dory was weighted down by too many passengers. Rackham rowed, then Daniel rowed until they reached the *Curlew*'s portside. They clamoured up the rope ladders.

"Fetch up yer hook!" Rackham bellowed to Black Patch. "Hands to halyards. Crowd that canvas. I want every inch of sail beatin' to the wind!"

Black Patch and Daniel ran to the capstan and cranked like beasts. Where had they got the new anchor? No time for questions. Liz hoisted her skirts and raced to the bow to man the jib. Like the pro Mary was, she climbed the rigging and hauled on the braces. Anne, in bloomers and Rackham's jacket, followed suit. The sails swelled.

"Haul away, sheet home," Daniel hollered.

Before Liz could act on the quartermaster's command, Anne

shouted from the mainmast. "Ship ahoy!"

Oh no, how had Barnet's men set sail so fast? Liz fastened the sheet, and the sloop shot forward. She leaped from the bowsprit to the forecastle deck, catching her already ripped skirt on a hook, and peered across the waist of the ship to the stern. The view was black except for the stars and a crescent moon. Against the sky, Barnet's ship was barrelling down on them.

"Can we outrun her?" Liz yelled, unhooking herself.

"We can try!" Rackham hollered.

Liz stared at the billowing sails and saw that they were tight to the wind. The wind gusted with them and sent the *Curlew* flying out of the bay. Liz bunched up her tattered skirt and jumped from the forecastle to join Daniel on the main deck. "What now?" she asked.

"If they board us, we fight," Daniel said.

Liz tossed up her hands. "They'll have an entire squadron. How can we beat that?" She went to the rail, dug her nails into the wood, and stared at the fast approaching ship.

Daniel joined her. "It's no longer your fight."

Liz swung on him. "What do you mean, it's no longer my fight?"

"Your job is done. You got Rackham and Anne back together. The pair of them stayed together a very long time in her bedchamber. I happened to notice that when I joined you and Barnet in the courtyard. I believe the deed is done. It's time for you to go home."

Daniel searched the sea for the vortex. "Go below, get your gear on. As soon as we spot the vortex, I want you to dive in."

"What about you?" Liz demanded. "You don't belong here."

Daniel's eyes twinkled. Though it was dark, Liz knew his eyes were the colour of sapphires. "Don't worry about me, Elizabeth Latimer. I'll be okay."

Liz grabbed Daniel by the arms. His biceps were hard and strong and rippled under her touch. "I'm not worried about you, you arrogant cockerel." Okay, she was spending too much time with pirates and couldn't think of a better word. "I want to know who you are. I am not leaving until you tell me."

Daniel gently released Liz's death grip from his arms. "Nice to know you can't keep your hands off of me," he said with a grin.

He stroked her hair with his right hand and bent to kiss her on the forehead. "Stop trying to distract me," she warned. "It's not going to work. You are not getting away without telling me who you are."

"You have the earring?" Daniel asked.

Liz fumbled inside the top of her ragged lace gown to the orange bikini top underneath. The earring was there.

Daniel took it from her and hooked it into her left earlobe. He looked to the sea. A flotilla of ships was streaming toward them.

"Go, get your gear on," he ordered. When she hesitated, he shouted, "Now!"

Liz wasn't use to taking orders, but those ships meant business and she wasn't about to take on the Royal Navy in this girly-girl dress.

Liz went to the quartermaster's cabin and found her equipment under Daniel's bunk. She changed clothes fast and looped Lulu's iPocket around her neck. Her hair had fallen out from its pretzel shape and now hung down her back in a single braid. She tucked it into the back of her wetsuit. There was a window to the rear of the cabin and Liz looked out. The Navy was amassing.

Liz grabbed Daniel's cutlass from where it hung on the wall. This was the final showdown and she wasn't going to miss it. She left her flippers under the bunk and pulled on her boots. She tucked the oxygen tank beneath her discarded gown. For the last time, she sashed her borrowed white pirate shirt over her neon blue wetsuit.

She was pretty sure the pirates wouldn't ask any questions about her fashion sense; they'd be too busy defending their lives.

Liz went to the door.

On deck, Rackham was frantically pacing in front of the helm. Captain Barnet's snow, the *Tyger*, was within firing range. A cannon blasted from the snow, striking them aft starboard, spilling seawater onto the *Curlew*'s decks.

"A miss!" Daniel shouted.

"Thank the stars for that!" Rackham yelled back. "Crowd sail! We need more speed!"

Liz knew more sail was not going to do it. The *Tyger* was almost on them now. They were within hailing distance.

"I will blast you a broadside," Captain Barnet shouted from the helm of the *Tyger*. "Is that how you want to die? Surrender now, and none shall be hurt."

Rackham stared frantically at the rapidly approaching flotilla. His shoulders sank. "Arrgh," he said, more to himself than to anybody else.

CJ fluttered down to land on the helm. "Arrgh," he mimed. "We's done for."

Rackham waved the parrot away. "Fer once ye's right, me jolly fella. I be shot or I be hanged. 'Tis the same thing. Death is death." He called down to Daniel. "Quartermaster, strike sail. We's done for. Hoist the white flag!"

"Not on yer life!" Anne shouted from the mainmast. "I will fight with cutlass and dagger before I go back to that cockroach, James Bonny!"

"Fire!" Barnet bellowed from the *Tyger*.

The shot that burst from the gun was not a cannonball. It was langrage, a concoction of nails, bolts and twisted pieces of scrap iron.

The shot hit the rigging and disabled it, shredding the sails and snapping the lines.

So much for more sail, Liz thought. The ship wavered and heeled to the left.

"Surrender if you don't want more of that!" Barnet warned.

Over the rail, Liz could see Barnet and his men dropping boats into the water. As far as Barnet was concerned, Rackham and his crew were going to surrender whether they liked it or not.

"To arms!" Anne shouted. "Get yer lazy good-fer-nothing stumps moving and look lively!"

Black Patch and Mary hoisted their weapons. Anne dropped from the mainmast, raced to the captain's cabin, and returned with a pistol and cutlass. Daniel raced along the main deck. He drew his dagger as grappling irons hooked the rails, and his Majesty's Navy spilled over the starboard side.

Liz stared at Rackham, who was frozen at the helm. Was he just going to stand there and do nothing? Jack Rackham reared his head. He whipped his cutlass from his baldric and raised his blade.

"Charge!" Liz shouted, and the ship's company met Barnet's Navy head-on.

Barnet went straight for her. He was pissing mad because she had duped him twice. He glared at her half-pirate half-scuba costume and, for a second, was struck dumb. Liz slammed her cutlass into his, jolting him back to reality. She had never killed anyone in her life. And she wasn't allowed to kill Barnet.

Barnet reciprocated. His cutlass came for her throat and she ducked, almost missing her footing. Crap, she thought. Too much playing girly-girl lately. She was losing her touch.

He slashed at her again. He meant business. His party wig had flown off, and the scent of cologne was replaced by the stink of sweat. Liz could feel his rage in the sting of his steel. He hammered her up against the cabin bulkhead and snarled. "So, my lady, you are nothing but a vile minx of a pirate after all. A serpent in ewe's clothing."

"I am not a pirate," Liz retorted, sounding pathetically like Mary Read.

"Then why do you run with pirates?"

"I am not running with them."

He swung low, then high and slammed his cutlass against hers until she could feel the bite of his blade near her throat. "Then how did you learn to fight like a pirate?"

Liz ducked, limber in her wetsuit and pirate shirt. She slipped out from under his sword and fenced into open space.

"Speak, pirate woman. Or speak no more."

Oh, great, Liz thought. Now her other ancestor wanted to kill her, and she couldn't lift a finger to kill him. Grumbling, she ducked again and ran. Footwork was the most important part of fencing. It could make or break a fencer. Daniel sprang over a marine's body to replace her and took the force of Barnet's steel, swing for swing.

Rackham leaped from the helm and planted his body in front of Liz, shielding her from the battle and edging her back to the quartermaster's cabin. Anne Bonny and Mary Read, Daniel and Black Patch took the impact of the remaining soldiers.

"You must flee, gal," Rackham said over his shoulder as he knifed a marine in the chest. "Go back to where you came from if you don't want to be gutted like a shark."

"What about you?"

He whirled on her. "Me? I have a monkey up my sleeve."

Liz laughed. That was something *she* would have said. "You have a plan?"

"I do. But I don't need you in order to implement it. Into the quartermaster's berth with ye now, and through the window. Go safely!"

He shoved her toward the stern. She turned to check out the sea and saw, beyond her, a swirl of water rise, a gaping vortex. The time chute!

"Daniel!" she yelped. She wanted to say good-bye. He waved her on, tripped his opponent with his sword, and stopped for a breath, pausing just long enough to flash her his two-fingered salute. Then he turned and was back to fending the Royal Navy from Rackham's sloop.

"Wait!" Rackham said as Liz took a step into the cabin. "Before ye go, girl. Tell me how I die."

If he knew, he could save himself. Elizabeth desperately wanted to tell Rackham how he died so that he *could* save himself. She didn't want him to die—anymore than she wanted Barnet to die.

"I can't tell you."

"Tell me, girl!" Rackham insisted. "Tell me how I die. When, where do I die?"

Liz hesitated. If he knew, he would save himself and change the future.

Liz opened her mouth to answer him just as a soldier grabbed her from behind. She swung to stab him with her cutlass and almost choked with stupefaction. This was no soldier, nor marine. The boy who was pulling her into the quartermaster's berth was Wang. Fully dressed in his scuba gear, he was ready to dive. Rackham recognized him and touched a finger to his brow. Must be a guy thing, she decided. The pirate captain returned to the deck to clash steel with a real brother of the Royal Service, while Wang hauled her scuba tank out from its hiding place where the air valve was partially visible.

"Where the blazes did you come from?" Liz asked.

"I was waiting for you in the captain's cabin. When you didn't come and I heard all the commotion on deck, I decided to keep low. Never know when the element of surprise will come in handy. I snuck in here when the troops started to board. By the way, was that Anne Bonny that raced into Rackham's cabin to grab weapons?"

"I told you to go home!" Liz chastised him.

"And I told you, I couldn't leave you."

Liz grabbed Wang by the forearm. She didn't know whether to slug him or to hug him. Taking the time to debate the trifle was a mistake. Captain Barnet stormed into the cabin with his dagger swinging and a pistol in his hand. When he saw the two of them dressed in their colourful scuba gear and Wang with a tank on his back, Barnet's mouth dropped open.

"Can't kill him," Liz whispered to Wang. "I'll explain later."

"Don't need to," Wang answered. "I can guess . . . Another ancestor?"

Liz nodded. Wang grabbed the scuba tank that Liz hadn't yet put on and hurled it through the window. The glass shattered. They leaped, hand in hand, through the opening and tumbled into the sea.

The ship was keeling. The last thing Liz remembered was saltwater shooting through her nose, Barnet sending an iron shot in their wake, and a boat on the horizon that looked suspiciously like Captain Charlie Vane's hijacked sloop, the *William*.

CHAPTER TWENTY-SEVEN
I Can't Stand Not Knowing . . .

Elizabeth burst through the surface of the sea into starlight. She gasped, spitting out seawater, and searched for Wang. They had shared his air tank until the vortex had sucked them into the time chute. All was silent as Liz steadied her breathing. Wang suddenly broke through the water beside her and spat out the mouthpiece that was linked by a hose to his tank.

"You okay?" he asked. "I was going to pass you some air when everything went white."

Elizabeth nodded. It was strangely quiet. Surreally still. And nothing was white anymore. The seascape was dark. A multitude of lights twinkled from the city on shore. They were back in Nassau harbour, but no longer in the past. To their left, Liz could see the pier where *Tess's Revenge* was berthed alongside several million-dollar yachts. There were lights on in the windows. She turned her head, and it occurred to her, oh my God, where was CJ!

Avast! CJ said, as he circled the moored boats, then came swooping at her.

Avast yourself, Liz responded, half-annoyed, mostly relieved. Come here!

CJ dived down to claw her head, then rose again into the night sky.

"I wonder what time it is?" Wang asked. He glanced at his waterproof watch. "I think it stopped working." He tapped the crystal.

Liz treaded water with one hand as she felt for the iPocket PC that should have been around her neck. It was there. The electronic clock on the corner of the screen said it was midnight.

Liz shot another glance at the salvage boat. Why were all the lights on? Shouldn't Cal, Stevie and Lulu be asleep? Or was Cal up to something?

Liz texted Rebel Goddess.

I'm back!

She got a response almost immediately.

TGYB! Where exactly?

Lk out the window.

Liz sent Lulu some excited electronic hugs (((H))), logged off, and waved Wang toward the pier. They swam several metres until the water got shallow, then they forged through the breakers by foot onto the beach.

Wang glanced backward over his shoulder. Liz knew what he was thinking. What had happened after they left? Why had Vane's ship been on the horizon? Liz sighed. Would they ever know? Liz and Wang approached the pier and hurried up the wood planks until they reached the end slip, which was occupied by Liz's mother's salvage boat.

"Lizabeth!" Lulu screamed from the rear deck of *Tess's Revenge*.

Liz could see that Lu was not alone. The skank, Cal, was there, and he had his arm around Liz's cousin, Stevie.

"So you made it," Cal said as Liz and Wang stopped at the base of the ship.

"Did you ever doubt it?" Liz asked.

"*I* didn't," Lulu said.

Stevie broke free of Cal's embrace and reached down to help Liz climb up the stern ladder of the ship onto the deck. Wang followed.

Stevie gave her a big, whopping bear hug. "Thank goodness, you two got back in one piece. We were chewing our nails off. Where's Tess?"

Liz glanced at Stevie's immaculate French manicure to confirm her suspicion that Stevie was exaggerating. Lulu was burning a hole through her with majorly serious eyes.

"She's not coming," Liz said.

"Then she's alive?" Stevie asked.

Liz nodded. "She's very much alive."

"Next time, I'm coming with you," Lulu said.

"If you know what's good for you," Cal answered from behind her, "there will be *no* next time."

"There has to be a next time," Lu argued. "We have to get Tess back."

But how? Liz wondered. The last time she spoke to her mom, it was clear that unless Tess found John Latimer, she was not coming back.

Lu demanded confirmation. "Right, Lizabeth? We have to get Tess back." When Liz didn't answer her, she persisted. "You saw her, didn't you? You talked to her, didn't you? What did she say?"

"I'll tell you everything tomorrow, Lu. Right now, I'm really beat. I need to crash."

Stevie agreed. The explanations could wait. It was time for all of them to hit the sack. Stevie got all maternal, which ordinarily Liz would have found annoying, but tonight she welcomed her cousin's inappropriate mothering. With Stevie here, Cal didn't dare deny Liz, Lu and Wang access to the boat's interior. Stevie unlocked the door to Tess's cabin and told Liz and Lu they could sleep in there. Wang could sleep in the galley on a bed that folded out from the table.

Where was Stevie going to sleep? Liz wondered. She had to clench her fist to keep from putting a finger down her throat and gagging. *Yuck.* Stevie was following Cal to his cabin. Well, I guess that answered *that* question.

When Cal had shut the door behind him and Stevie, Lulu

insisted that Liz tell her everything that had happened since they last saw each other in front of the vortex. Liz tried to put her off by making a big show of changing into sweatpants and T-shirt. Lu wouldn't let her alone—she understood Liz not wanting to talk in front of Cal and Stevie—so Liz cut to the chase and told her sister the most critical parts of her exploits in the past.

"Tess stayed to look for John?" Lu asked incredulous. "Tess thinks our father is still alive?"

Liz nodded. "But not to worry. Tess had everything in control when I left her."

"And what about Daniel?" Lu asked. "What happened to him?"

Liz shook her head. "I don't know."

Liz lovingly lifted the iPocket from around her neck and draped it over Lu's head. "Thanks," she said, kissing her sister on the cheek. "Giving me this gizmo was a lifesaver."

Lu made a face over the kissy episode and hugged the device to her chest like a teddy bear. "I can't believe it worked."

"I can't either, but boy, am I glad it did, or I might be dancing the hempen jig right now."

Lulu made gigantic monkey eyes at her, then grinned. "You don't mean it."

Several unsavoury images flashed in Liz's mind, including Rackham swinging from a noose before Daniel had cut him down. Liz groaned and decided to spare her sister the gory details.

"Was Wang a hero?" Lu asked.

Liz smiled. "None of your beez."

Lu smirked. "Well, you just answered *that* question. What about Captain Rackham and Captain Barnet? Do you think they killed each other after you and Wang jumped ship?"

Liz clapped a hand to her mouth. Oh crap. The box containing the letter. Rackham had dropped it down to her just before they escaped, and Liz had forgotten about it and left it under the poinciana tree. Did it matter that they hadn't brought the letter back with them? Apparently not. She, Lu and Stevie were still here, weren't they? So Rackham and Barnet couldn't have possibly killed each other. But what *had* happened? The thunder of guns and the clash of steel still rang in Liz's ears; the sight of Vane's boat in the dusk was firmly impressed on her memory.

Liz told Lu she'd be back in a second and went to the galley to fetch Wang, who had changed into summer T-shirt and sweats like her, and was getting ready to catch some Zs. She dragged him into Tess's room and closed the door.

"Hey, what's up?" he asked. "I thought you wanted to crash."

"I do. But I can't stand not knowing what happened to Rackham and Barnet." She paced around the small room and lifted her hands into the air. CJ, who had followed from the galley where he had intended to keep Wang company, landed on her arm. "I need ideas. Give me anything you've got."

"Well, we're not going back there," Wang said adamantly.

"Can't anyways," Lu piped in. She was perched on the edge of the bunk in her PJs with the iPocket that Liz had returned to her. She fidgeted with some keys. "Look at this."

Liz and Wang crowded onto the bunk on either side of her. The whirling, digitized mass, representing the subaquatic time chute's vortex, funnelled, then shrank and vanished.

"Holy crap," CJ said.

"I'll say," Wang punctuated, his eyes locked onto the motionless screen. "That could have been us."

Liz rose and went to the porthole and looked out. The vortex, the time chute, was gone. It had spit them out, returned them to the twenty-first century and exited, stage left.

"Where do you suppose the time chute went to?" Liz asked.

Wang shrugged. Lulu clicked her iPocket closed. "We can find it again," Lu said. "Stevie's working on it. She has some ideas."

Liz hoped she wouldn't have to wait for Stevie's ideas to germinate. She wanted her mother to come to her senses and return of her own free will.

"I wonder where she is?" Wang said, reading Liz's mind.

"You wonder where who is?" Lu asked.

"Your mother, Tess."

Lu pressed her lips together. She inhaled and jumped off the bed. "I have an idea," she said. She went to Tess's computer and logged on.

"What are you doing?" Wang asked.

Liz shushed him. Liz didn't call Lulu a brainiac for nothing.

Lu clicked down to some files until she found what she was looking for. It was a downloaded, complete, and unabridged, digital edition of Daniel Defoe's *A General History of The Pyrates*.

"I don't get," Wang whispered to Elizabeth.

Liz nudged Wang to silence. She watched Lulu access the chapter on John Rackham, AKA Calico Jack Rackham. Lu enlarged the print on the screen so that all three of them could read it at the same time. The small-time pirate was sentenced to hang on November 16, 1720, by a British Court Admiralty.

So the date of his death and the way he died hadn't changed. Rackham and Barnet did not kill each other. But she already knew that. What *did* change, and what had not formerly been in the book, was the episode where Rackham rescued his lover from the clutches of the governor of the Bahamas. Vane's ship had appeared in the nick of time. Charlie Vane had come to the aid of fellow pirate Calico Jack. Barnet had double-crossed him and threatened him with the gallows for letting Rackham slip the noose in Port Royal. It was all the incentive Captain Vane needed to return to his pirating ways. The Navy retreated under Vane's unexpected attack in the dark, sinking several strategic ships, and Captain Jonathan Barnet survived the ambush to fight another day.

"Well, now we know," Liz said.

"And now we know how to find out if Tess changes anything in the past," Lulu added.

That was right. Tess no longer had an iPocket and would remain out of touch. But that didn't mean they couldn't track her. They had this book, the electronic version that rewrote itself with every change that she made in the past.

"You mean, because we were there, all of the books' histories have changed now?" Wang asked.

"I don't know," Liz said. "But this one has. Luckily, our presence there didn't change the major course of events."

Lulu rubbed her eyebrow. "Where do you think Tess went?"

Liz shrugged. "Where do *you* think she went? Where do you think John would go?" Because wherever Tess thought her husband was . . . that was where she would go.

"I think she would go somewhere where there are pirates," Lulu answered.

"That goes without saying," Liz said. But where?

Wang broke into her thoughts by grabbing her hand. He laced his fingers between hers and gave them a squeeze. Lulu grinned. Stud muffin, she mouthed.

Liz made a face at her sister. Wang caught the look between them and buried a smile.

Liz dropped Wang's hand. "Go back to bed and get some sleep, Wang. You too, Lulu. We'll work on it tomorrow."

CHAPTER TWENTY-EIGHT
I Will Never Give Up Until I Bring My Mother Home

They thought about it. All four of them—Elizabeth, Lulu, Stevie and Wang—thought long and hard about where Tess might go next, and where John Latimer, if he was still alive and living in the piratical past, would lead her. They thought about it all the way home, on their flight from Nassau to Vancouver and on to Victoria.

None of them could agree.

Liz sat down at her dresser in her bedroom back in their refurbished farmhouse at Gordon Head, in the Greater Victoria municipality of Saanich. She had to trust Tess like Tess had trusted her.

Liz pinched her lips together, then opened the top lefthand drawer of her dresser. Inside, Daniel's earring, with its delicate flying dagger, lay in a gauzy pouch by itself. She and Wang still couldn't figure out what metal alloy it was made from, and she didn't dare take it to a jeweller's in case they wanted to keep it for testing. Liz lifted the pouch and dumped the earring into the palm of her left hand.

How did the time chute work? This earring had got her to the past and it had returned her to the present. Did that mean the earring was an artifact of eighteenth century piracy days or was this some kind of voodoo? Liz shook her head. She drew the line at voodoo. Everything, cousin Stevie said, had a scientific explanation. Well explain this, Stephanie Rackham. How do I go back into the past to find Tess? She wanted to know what the earring could do, not how it did it.

Did she dare try it? Daniel had said he would come if she put it on.

Elizabeth hooked the flying dagger into her left ear. She waited, stared at the empty space in front of her, wondering if Daniel would miraculously appear out of blank air.

Nothing.

She shook her head to swing the earring from side to side. She looked into the mirror over the dresser, hoping to see the quartermaster's surly smile behind her.

Maybe the earring was broken. He *did* say to put it into her left earlobe, didn't he? Liz sighed. Maybe she had dreamt the whole thing. Maybe there was no such thing as a Daniel Corker, and maybe this earring was just a piece of junk jewellery that some co-ed had dropped on the gym floor. Maybe this whole episode was like the *Wizard of Oz* and she was back in Kansas. And mama Tess—no Professor Tess Rackham, the instructor for the Archaeology of Piracy course at UVic—would come waltzing through Liz's bedroom door to tell her she was late for school. And maybe John Latimer would be there, too, in the garage, working on one of his miniature model pirate ships.

The earring dangled lightly on her ear.

Elizabeth stared at her naked thumbnail. She had stripped off all of the chipped polish and she felt oddly shaky. She needed to feel that power again. The surge of the pirate—no, the surge of the pirate hunter—in her blood. She shook the bottle of red nail colour and took out a black ink pen from the opened dresser drawer.

CJ sat on her bedpost and ruffled his feathers. "Crap," he said.

Liz looked up from doing her nail. She sent him a telepathic question. Do you mean that literally?

Aye, he said.

"Bad bird," Liz said out loud, waving her painted thumb in the air.

"Screw you," CJ said, louder, and crapped on her bedpost

again.

Liz blew dry the fourth coat of clear varnish on her thumbnail. The black skull and crossbones on the blood-red nail polish gleamed as a reminder of what her ancestry had bequeathed her. She looked up.

"Nuts," she said, as she saw the black and white bird poop dripping down the bedpost toward her pillow. She capped the nail varnish and got up from her dresser, planting her hands on her hips, glaring at her parrot. "How many times do I have to tell you not to do that?"

She grabbed a Kleenex from her nightstand, mopped up the mess, and threw the soiled tissue into a garbage can under her dresser.

"Avast," CJ said. CJ lifted his wing to his head and if he'd had fingers instead of feathers, he might have flipped her off. Instead, Liz could swear that the parrot had just given her a two-feathered salute.

"Yeah, I kinda miss him, too," Elizabeth said.

"That's nice," Daniel's voice answered from the doorway. He sauntered in.

"Daniel!" Liz squealed, whirling to face him. "You came!"

"You put on the earring, didn't you?"

Liz nodded vigorously.

Daniel was dressed in his pirate clothes. A clean, white, blousy shirt, black britches and leather boots on his feet. He wore a red kerchief around his ponytailed scalp. His sea blue eyes twinkled.

"Will you always come?" Liz asked.

Daniel shook his head. "Not for no reason."

"But you came now."

Daniel smiled. "I believe you have a reason."

Elizabeth narrowed her eyes at him. She walked over to where he stood inside her bedroom and touched his arm.

"Still can't keep your hands off me, I see," he said, grinning.

Liz scowled. "I was just checking to see if you're real."

"And am I?" Daniel asked.

Liz exhaled. "You seem to be. How do you do that? How do you come and go like that?"

Daniel shrugged. "I don't know what you mean."

He was frustrating her on purpose. "Of course, you know what I mean. You aren't even wet. You didn't come from the aquatic time chute. You didn't use the vortex unless it appears in thin air, as well as in the sea."

"Well, that's a thought," Daniel said.

"Stop it," Liz said. "I want to know how you do that, how you travel through time."

"I told you this once before, Elizabeth Latimer. You ask too many questions."

"Well, if you didn't come to give me the answers, why are you here?"

"You called me. I came."

Liz blasted him with a gust of exasperation. "I almost wish I hadn't."

Daniel shrugged. There was a commotion on the steps as Lulu's voice floated upstairs. "Lizabeth's in her room. Come on."

The pounding of feet came up the stairs, and Lulu and Wang burst into her doorway. Daniel swung around and greeted them with a big smile.

"Daniel!" Lu squeaked. "When did you get here?"

"Just now," Daniel said. "The backdoor was open. I didn't think anyone would mind."

"Of course, we don't mind," Lu said. She grabbed Daniel's arm. "Can you stay?"

Daniel glanced at Liz. Liz looked at Wang. Wang tried really hard not to frown. Liz suddenly felt like she was trapped between a rock and a hard place—or rather, between two gorgeous guys and a hard place.

Wang composed himself first and went straight to the point. "Where's Tess?" he asked. "Do you know?"

Daniel shook his head. "Tess Rackham is no longer my problem."

What did he mean by that? Liz frowned. How was Tess *ever* his problem?

Daniel let his glance bounce off the three faces staring him down.

"Well, was there anything else?" he asked. "I guess you know everything worked out between Captain Rackham and Captain Barnet the way it was supposed to, since you and Lulu are both standing here. So, if there isn't anything else you need me for, I've got to go."

This time, Liz grabbed his arm. "Where? Where are you going?"

Daniel's eyes went soft. Liz felt her knees cave slightly. Two gorgeous guys and a hard place. Wang didn't like the look Daniel was giving Liz, but Liz ignored Wang's feelings. She locked her knees and stood tall. She had to know. Where was Daniel from?

Daniel glanced from Wang to Lulu. What? Liz thought. He couldn't talk in front of them? Okay, then she'd give him some privacy. She asked Wang and Lu to wait downstairs. The hurt look on both of their faces crushed her, but if that's what it took to get him to talk, then their feelings would have to be sacrificed. They left reluctantly, and when Liz and Daniel were alone, Liz shut the bedroom door.

"Okay, now talk. Where are you going? To the future? Is that where you come from? And if so, is it *my* future? Do you play some important part in it? Tell me, Daniel, because I swear if you don't, I will fetch my foil down from its hook and shove six inches of blade into your belly."

"Spoken like a true pirate hunter," Daniel said.

Liz wailed on him, pummelled his chest with her fists. He laughed, caught her wrists, and yanked her face up to his with a grin that hid really serious eyes. Liz suddenly felt scared. This feeling she had, as he held her wrists and stared into her face, sent goose bumps all over her flesh. She didn't like it one bit.

Daniel glanced at the window, in the direction of the sea. He looked at her, at the closed door, and smiled. "Don't you think Wang will get jealous?" he asked, knowing he was yanking all of her strings.

"Screw you," she said, flinging him off. "At least Wang and I have no secrets."

"That's good," Daniel said. "For now."

What did he mean by that? Wang was the best thing that had happened to her in ages. Daniel, on the other hand, was the most frustrating, annoying, frightening thing that had *ever* happened to her in her life. Okay, so she was being a drama queen again. Who cared? There was no one here but her and Daniel.

Daniel went to the window and opened it wide. He breathed in the fresh air. Liz could smell the pickly stench of low tide drifting in with the breeze. Beneath her window was a grove of oak trees. They were so thick with leaves that you couldn't see the grass below their heavy branches.

Liz stayed where she was at the opposite end of the room. "Why did you come if you aren't going to answer any of my questions?"

Daniel swung around from the window and came to her. He grabbed her fist. He raised her left hand and stared at the painted thumbnail. He smiled and dropped her hand.

"I came to see if you could answer *my* question."

"What question?" she asked.

"The one that you just answered by painting that skull and crossbones on your thumbnail."

Elizabeth planted her hands on her hips and scowled at him "I will never give up figuring out how *you* and this whole time travel thing work. And if Tess doesn't come home soon, I fully intend to go back to the past and bring her home. And I won't quit searching until I find out what really happened to my father."

Daniel nodded and smiled his surly smile. Before she could stop him, he climbed over the window sill and dropped into an oak tree outside.

Elizabeth rushed to the window. She looked down. Daniel was standing in a small clearing, the only visible space between the foliage, at the edge of the front yard.

"Daniel!" she shouted. "I *know* you're from the future!"

Daniel smiled. He gave her his two-fingered salute and promptly vanished.

About the Author:

Deborah Cannon was born in Vancouver, British Columbia. She is the author of five short stories and four novels and she has contributed articles on writing to the Canadian Writer's Guide and the professional writer's web sites, absolutewrite.com and suite101.com. She is author of the archaeological manual, *Marine Fish Osteology: A Manual for Archaeologists.* Most recently, her anthropological thriller *The Raven's Pool* was cited in a scholarly study, *Archaeology is a Brand! The Meaning of Archaeology in Contemporary Popular Culture* (Holtorf 2007) alongside treasure hunters Indiana Jones and Lara Croft. Her second novel, *White Raven* was a 2007 Adult Summer Reading Club pick at the Hamilton Public Library. Applauded by award-winning authors T.J. MacGregor and Barbara Kyle, *Ravenstone* is the third book in the series. *Elizabeth Latimer: Pirate Hunter* marks the beginning of a new series for teens or anyone who can imagine themselves encountering a pirate.

Acknowledgements

Creating Elizabeth and her world was the most fun I have ever had writing a novel. Thanks go to Jackie Leventhal for giving me permission to use her screen name in the book and for her infectious enthusiasm for my idea of a smart and feisty pirate-hunting, teen fencer. Many thanks also to historical novelist Barbara Kyle for her superb insights on the original story idea, my nephew Alex who never tires of what I write and to my wonderful proofreader, Catherine Starr and my fantastic husband, Aubrey Cannon, for creating my awesome book cover.

Coming next:

Elizabeth Latimer, Pirate Hunter: EMPRESS OF DEATH
by Deborah Cannon

Everyone agrees that Elizabeth Latimer's dad drowned in a vicious squall while out sailing. But Liz's mom knows he was sucked into the pirate past, and that's where she's looking for him. When he turns up alive in modern day China, Liz leaps into the past of Chinese pirates to locate her mom, only to lose her boyfriend, and a 21st century remote sensing device, to the pirate witch Mrs Cheng.

Buy now:

Elizabeth Latimer, Pirate Hunter: THE PIRATE VORTEX
by Deborah Cannon

Teen fencing champ, Elizabeth Latimer, is a girl of her times. Armed with the latest palm computer, she leaps into an oceanic vortex in pursuit of Daniel, an oh-so-awesome pirate. He knows the whereabouts of her missing marine archaeologist mom, but instead of reuniting them, he leads her into an impossible mission—to help the pirate Calico Jack Rackham rescue his girlfriend Anne Bonny.

Ask for this title at your local bookstore or order online:
The Pirate Vortex: www.trafford.com